A Timely Revolution

By Tempie W. Wade

A Timely Revolution

This is a work of historical fiction. While some of the names in this book are the same as real-life historical figures, the actions and words of the characters are strictly figments of the author's imagination and any resemblance to actual events, places, and persons, living or dead are entirely coincidental.

UPDTD

 For more information, the author may be reached by email at TempieWade @cox.net

Printed in the United States of America.

Print Edition - ISBN: 978-0-9600257-0-1

Digital Edition - ISBN: 978-0-9600257-1-8

For more Information, please visit

www.TempieWade.com

A Timely Revolution

By Tempie W. Wade

ACKNOWLEDGMENTS

To Jen... thank you for being my biggest fan. Without your motivation, wonderful enthusiasm, and regular kicks in the ass, this book would have never seen the light of day. I am so thankful for all your help and support on this journey.

To Travis... I am beyond grateful for all the guidance that you were kind enough to freely offer someone who had never written anything before. Your advice, encouragement, and reassurance have been invaluable to me.

To Tara... bless you for indulging the 'newbie' and not throwing up your hands and walking away.

To David, Alex, and Daniel, I offer my undying gratitude for putting up with my long days and extremely late nights while I was getting this book off the ground. Thank you for having my back and always being there when I need you.

And to the reader... thank you for buying my book. I hope you enjoy the ride and will continue to allow me to bring you along on many more adventures in the future.

Blessings to you all!

Fate is a fickle creature.

From the time you are old enough to know what you want out of this life, you plan— career, home, family, and some even, their own funeral. You depend on that carefully laid road map to get you where you want to be in this world. Sometimes, despite all your best efforts and good intentions, things simply go awry. It may not be your, or anyone else's fault, but you still must stop, clean up the mess, and attempt to do your best to get back on the right path. Other times, however, it will be impossible, especially if the fates decide to have a say in the matter. Your journey will become so disrupted that there is no possible way to get back to where you were before. That is when you are forced to make a decision. You can either wallow in self- pity, cursing the fates for the new circumstances you find yourself in, or you can take what is left and commit yourself to building something new and glorious from the pieces you have been given. If you happen to be an exceptionally rare, fortunate soul, the fates may just see fit to use you for their own intents and purposes— and just might reward you with a few special surprises along the way.

Preface:

In December of 1777, after a series of setbacks to the Continental Army during the American Revolution, George Washington moved his army to Valley Forge, Pennsylvania for winter quarters. During that time, General Washington appointed a very bright, young man by the name of Major Benjamin Tallmadge as his Chief of Intelligence. Major Tallmadge would go on to establish a small network of trusted spies that would come to be known as 'The Culper Spy Ring'. The valuable knowledge gathered by this team would provide vital information to Washington, eventually leading to the victory by the Americans. Their tireless efforts would also lead to the discovery of a traitor in Washington's inner circle, a man by the name of Benedict Arnold. Arnold's path to defection was laid by his wife, Peggy Shippen, a young lady from a wealthy Philadelphia family, who had developed a friendship with the future head of the British Secret Service, Major John André — a man whom she first met as a captain during the British occupation of Philadelphia in 1777.

John André, by all accounts, was a charming young man, well-liked by all, fluent in several languages, an accomplished artist, and an author. Major André was eventually captured by the Americans during a series of unfortunate events. He was held for trial, convicted, and hanged to death on October 2, 1780 in Tappan, New York. Major André held the respect of his captors and fellow countrymen alike, many of them on both sides, greatly saddened by his death. He was known to be a gentleman to the very end, choosing to leave this life with dignity and grace. Major Tallmadge became very fond of Major André during his imprisonment and was greatly aggrieved by the punishment that he received.

Major Benjamin Tallmadge would remain in Washington's army until the very end, doing everything in his power to protect the people in his spy network and to ensure their safety even after the war ended. He would marry Mary Floyd in 1784 and go on to have seven children. These children would serve their country in many ways over the years. Major Tallmadge passed away in March of 1835 at the age of 81.

1

CHAPTER ONE

Outer Banks, NC - July 2018

Maggie lay on the hotel bed staring at the ceiling. She lifted her arm, admiring how the moonlight caught the sparkle of the newly placed diamond ring on her left hand. It was at least three carats surrounded by eight smaller stones. Brad had really outdone himself – becoming a partner in the family law firm had its advantages.

She looked over at him, fast asleep and snoring so loud it was a wonder the curtains were still on the windows.

Maggie's chest tightened at the sight of him.

"I need some air," she whispered.

Slipping on her jeans, bra, and t-shirt, she stuck her phone and key card in her back pocket as she grabbed a flashlight. A long walk on the beach would clear her head.

The beach was unusually empty for that time of the evening —no kids out looking for crabs and no couples snuggling on the beach— just Maggie and a big, bright gorgeous full moon. She inhaled the salty ocean air while listening to the peaceful sound of the crashing waves and smiled; she loved this place. Her parents brought her here every year on vacation. Her father, being a history professor, would always tell her the legend of the Lost Colony, the first colonists that came to Roanoke Island in 1585, only to disappear, and to never be heard from again. They would take turns making up stories about what might have happened to them.

"Maybe they built a raft and sailed to the Caribbean," her dad would say.

"Perhaps they were taken by fairies," her mom had suggested.

Maggie's theory was that they all had found their true loves and sailed off into the sunset to live happily ever after — the musings of an eight-year-old girl with her head in the clouds.

She had always felt there was something intriguing and mystical about the barrier islands. Whenever she closed her eyes, she could almost make out a faint voice whispering softly on the warm breezes.

Maggie had jumped at the chance to go when Brad suggested they head down for the weekend, having no inkling that he planned to propose. She never turned down a trip to the beach, even though lately she had begun to wonder if they were drifting apart.

They rarely saw each other because Brad was always working. Every time they made plans, he was either very apologetically late, or he canceled altogether, promising to make it up to her when things at the office slowed down; she had only seen him once a week for the past month.

Maggie had been so astounded when he dropped to one knee and asked for her hand, that she said ‘yes’ before really considering it.

Well, now she was considering it, and she just wasn't so sure that she had given the correct response. She and Brad had never looked at each other the way her parents did, and she was certain that they never would. But, then again, not many married couples she knew did either. Her mom and dad shared a special love; one that you did not see every day, or ever, for that matter. Maggie found herself wishing for that kind of fairytale ending for herself.

She also wondered if she was overreacting. The reality was that most of the people she knew who had married, ended up living more like roommates than they did lovers. Sure, the fire and intensity were there in the beginning, but always seemed to fade with time and the drudgery of living everyday life.

Do I really want to settle for a roommate who happens to share my bed?

Maggie plopped down on the sand and wrapped her arms around her knees, staring out at the water hoping for some clear answer to magically come to her.

“Hey universe,” she called out, “how about a little help for a girl over here?”

All she heard in response was the roar of the ocean.

“You're a HUGE help,” she mumbled sarcastically back to the ocean.

Maggie picked up a shell from the beach and stood up. She walked towards the water line, and as she took a step into the water to throw it, something rolled beneath her foot. She slipped, falling flat on her back, and cursed as the waves crashed over her.

Maggie came up sputtering.

"Fuck! Fuck! FUCK!" she screamed, smacking the water with her hands and feet.

She was completely drenched from head to toe in sand and water.

The wave receded, and she slapped at the sand one more time for good measure. This time, her hand made contact with something hard. Jerking back, Maggie held her arm to her chest, yelping in pain, and screamed, "Seriously universe? What the actual hell? You just had to add a little insult to injury, didn't you? Well, thanks for nothing!"

Maggie looked around to see what she had hit with her hand. Something glinted in the moonlight, and she could make out an outline in the water. She reached over and brushed the sand off as the wave receded.

It looked like a bottle —a strange one. She picked it up and walked back to the dry part of the beach.

Some couple probably enjoyed a little wine while they were taking a romantic stroll.

"Well, at least someone is having a good night," she said aloud, rolling her eyes.

She plopped back down on the shoreline, rolled to one side and pulled the flashlight from her back pocket. She flicked the button; thank God it was waterproof. She aimed the beam at the bottle.

It was a peculiar little thing —very ornate, an emerald green with lots of little details in the glass and, as she turned it, the color seemed to change to a bluish hue, appearing to give off a slight, mesmerizing glow.

Looking closer, Maggie could make out some shapes in the glass. There were several little etchings that looked slightly familiar, but what were they?

Maggie searched her mind, and it dawned on her that they looked like some of the symbols in a book her father had about Scottish folklore. He was fascinated with Scottish history, mainly because his beloved bride was from there, and he always had several books lying around on the subject. Maggie loved to read and had since she was a child. Her father often found her picking through his piles of books. She had seen those symbols in one of them, she was sure of it.

"Well, at least dad hit the jackpot tonight. You will make a perfect gift for him," she said to the bottle.

But where had it come from? She looked back at the water. It was not uncommon for items to wash up on shore here, and not all that unusual for them to be old. The area was littered with sunken boats from hundreds of years back, hurricanes always uncovering new little treasures, but there hadn't been any storms recently. She looked back down at the bottle to see some small red and black stones were attached along the top. There also appeared to be something inside.

Maggie tugged at the cork until it popped loose. She shined the flashlight into the bottle to see there was a piece of paper rolled up in it.

Message in a bottle?

She flipped it over and shook it until the rolled-up page inched out of the neck, pulling it the rest of the way out before setting the container to the side. Holding the flashlight between her teeth, she unrolled the page. It appeared to be incredibly old, thick, and stiff —almost like papyrus— but surely it couldn't be that. Maggie smoothed out the paper and saw legible, clear writing which would have been very unusual for something as old as she started to suspect this bottle might be. She took the flashlight in her hand, aimed it down, and read the words out loud.

"A step in time one must make, to correct a wrong in human fate.

A revolution will guide your way until the fates will have their say.

A warrior's love will heal a heart and restore mankind's missing part.

When your mind fills with fear, trust your true destiny has always been here."

Maggie scrunched up her nose and read it aloud again.

"What the heck? Are people putting bad poetry in old bottles now?" she asked herself.

A slow realization washed over her.

"Okay, you got me," she called out, "Ha-ha, very funny. You can bring out the cameras now, so we can all have a good laugh."

It occurred to her that this had to be some kind of practical joke, and she had fallen hook, line, and sinker. Most likely some college kids were down for the weekend and having a little fun at her expense. They had probably been waiting hours for some sucker to come along. She looked around and called out again.

"Hello? Come on out. The jig is up. It was a good one, I'll give you that."

Silence.

Maggie laughed, low, uncertain, and looked around again.

Nothing but the roar of the ocean.

She was alone; there was no one else around. She decided that they had probably gotten tired of waiting for someone to come along and left, forgetting to take their bottle with them.

"Okay, this day has been crazy enough. This is just the icing on the cake. Time to head back." Maggie stood up, her head spinning, and fell back onto the sand.

"Whoa! That was crazy," she muttered. "I must have inhaled something when I opened that bottle."

A terrifying thought entered her mind. What if someone was hiding close by and had somehow managed to drug her? A wave of panic kicked in.

"I have to get out of here," she mumbled, scrambling on the sand.

Maggie tried to stand again, only to be hit with a bout of nausea that forced her back down. She attempted to crawl but fell over to her side. She lay on her back, looking at the stars, all of which had started moving of their own accord, only they were going in the opposite direction, moving backward.

Dizziness slammed into Maggie again. She looked up at the full moon, it too moving in reverse. The roar of the ocean became deafening; Maggie felt her eardrums were going to explode. She tried to move, but her body refused to obey.

She started to feel even more bizarre, almost weightless, like she was floating upwards and out of control. There was only blackness —no sound, no weight, just Maggie and her thoughts. Out of nowhere, she heard a voice, but she could not understand what it was saying. She saw a face—distorted—but she couldn't make out any of its features. Maggie was sure that whatever was in that bottle had ended her life before it had a chance to begin.

This must be what it feels like to die.

She was not ready. Maggie had so much more she wanted to do with her life. She thought of her parents; they needed her and she them. Her mind was flooded with so many things at once, until the dizziness hit so hard and fast that it was instantly wiped of everything. She could not focus on anything but the disorientation that overwhelmed her. It lasted for what seemed like an eternity before she felt the sensation of falling at an extraordinarily high rate of speed. She had to be dead —no one could possibly survive anything like this.

All at once, an unbearable pain slammed into her body —an excruciating agony that spread throughout every fiber of her being. Maggie could do nothing more than scream before everything went black.

2

CHAPTER TWO

The sounds of seagulls and crashing waves greeted Maggie as she came to, lying face down on the sand, her back warm from the heat of the morning sun. She pushed herself up slowly, checking for aches and broken bones, before rolling onto her backside and shielding her eyes from the bright rays. A soreness permeated her body, a headache raged, and her stomach churned. Up on her elbows, she was more than a little surprised to see a horse grazing in the seagrass a few feet away. The shiny, black steed raised his head, let out a loud huff, and returned to his meal.

"Well, 'good morning' to you too," Maggie mumbled, getting her first look at her surroundings.

She was astonished to see nothing —no people, no houses, no hotels— nothing except ocean, beach, seagrass —and a horse.

"Must be one of the wild horses that roam around Corolla," Maggie said to herself, "I must have walked further up the shoreline than I realized last night."

Last night! She had been gone all night. Brad must be worried to death. She stood up to get a better look around, but she had no clue where she was. While the shoreline looked familiar, the rest of the landscape did not. Maggie was unaware of any place on the Outer Banks that was still completely untouched by modern times, as this appeared to be.

The bottle was still there, so she must be close to where she was before she blacked out— but there had been houses around last night. She reached over and picked up the container, looking down at it, then back up at her surroundings again.

Weird!

She reached around to feel her back pocket.

Yes!

Her phone was still there. She pulled it out to call Brad. No bars, no service.

Seriously?

Maggie climbed to her feet and stumbled around, holding her phone above her head, even jumping as high as she could to try and get some service. Nothing.

Crap.

The horse raised his head again, cast a judgmental look in her direction, and went right back to his breakfast.

"Don't look at me like that!" she scolded. "Haven't you ever seen a person trying to get cell reception before?"

She realized all she could do was walk until she had service or reached the hotel, whichever came first.

Maggie turned back to the way she was sure she came the night before. With the bottle in one hand and her phone in the other, she started off.

It was a beautiful morning, albeit a little brighter than she preferred. Maggie had a terrible case of 'cotton mouth', feeling as if she had a bad hangover. She tried to recall exactly what happened the night before, remembering everything until the moment she had fallen back dizzy on the sand. She was convinced she had somehow been drugged but couldn't for the life of her figure out how —unless the bottle had something in it — but wouldn't that have hit her immediately? And if someone were trying to kidnap her, why wouldn't they have taken her while she was passed out. Who would want to kidnap her anyway? Maggie's brain started to go into overload, so she took in a deep breath to calm herself down.

Geez, how long have I been walking?

Maggie looked around again. Still no signs of any kind of civilization. How was this possible? The entirety of the Outer Banks was settled, and this place was always crawling with tourists in the summer.

What gives?

Where were the houses, the hotels, the streets, and the people? The whole place was eerily quiet; she was completely lost now.

Maggie decided to try a new tactic. She turned and started walking away from the shoreline instead of parallel to it. Surely, the road had to be close by. Reaching the top of a dune and looking out, she stood flabbergasted.

There was no road, no buildings, no cars—nothing at all.

Maggie plopped down on the sand, tears streaming down her face. She wrapped her hands around her knees, laid her head down, and bawled, never feeling more helpless or lost in her entire life. She had no idea what she was going to do.

Something warm and wet touched the back of her neck. Maggie jumped and screamed. Spinning around, she was stunned to find the horse from earlier and he had just licked her — he must have followed her. He moved closer to Maggie and nudged her shoulder. She reached up, rubbing his muzzle, which the horse seemed to find quite nice because he butted against her for more.

"Okay, okay, I get it." Maggie stood up, brushed the sand off, and pulled her fingers through his mane as she rubbed his ears.

The horse whinnied and pawed at the sand. Maggie laughed, which seemed to please the horse even more. She reached over, hugging him and began to feel better.

"I needed that, my new friend. I'm a strong, independent woman, and I don't need no man, but apparently, I REALLY need a good horse." Maggie giggled.

She took a good look at him for the first time. He was not a large horse, but he was a beauty —stout, muscular, and as black as the night was dark, with a beautiful, flowing mane and the kindest eyes in an animal she had ever seen. Maggie knew the descendants of the horses from ships that wrecked in earlier years lived on the Banks, but they were endangered and tended to stay away from people. It was against the law to be even close to one, but this guy seemed a little different —friendly and a real 'people person'. He probably belonged to someone who was looking for him.

"Well, I can't walk around calling you 'horse', so let's figure out a name for you." She looked at him thoughtfully. "How does 'Midnight' sound?"

Maggie could have sworn that he shook his head. She laughed.

"Okay, how about... 'Shadow'?"

The horse shook his head again.

"I MUST be losing my mind. I'm talking to a horse AND getting answers," she mumbled.

"Okay, let me think... hmm.... how about...'Onyx'?"

The horse seemed to like that a great deal.

"Okay! 'Onyx' it is. Where to now, Onyx? I'm a little lost, and you seem to be a local, so please lead the way," she said and swished her hand dramatically.

Onyx started out across the sand— head raised confidently, set on a clear and definitive path. Maggie blew out a long breath, picked up her stuff, and followed her new guide.

Well, I managed to get lost, find a strange bottle, and name a horse, one who is apparently now in charge. This day could not possibly get any weirder.

After what seemed like an eternity, Maggie was just about to stop and rest when she looked up. There, in front of her, stood a small beach cottage. The house was simply built with a picket fence surrounding it, and she could see a woman working in the garden. A great deal of smoke rolled from the chimney, which Maggie thought odd for the middle of summer.

Maggie came around in front of Onyx, raised her hand, and shouted 'hello' to the lady. The woman stood up from her place in the garden, wiped her hands on her apron and then waved back.

"God bless you, Onyx!" Maggie rubbed his muzzle and gave him a hug.

Onyx whinnied in return, happy for the praise.

Walking towards the small house, Maggie noticed the lady was dressed unusually. She had on a long gray dress to her ankles, a white apron over it, and a kerchief around her head, which seemed like a great deal of clothing for summertime at the beach.

The woman greeted Maggie at the gate. "Hello! Can I help you with something?"

"I sure hope so," said Maggie, "I seem to be lost and dying of thirst."

"Well, I can probably lend a hand with both of those if you want to come with me," she said.

The lady smiled and led the way inside. "My name is Mary Cooke and you are?"

"Maggie Bishop," she replied. "It's nice to meet you and thank you so much for helping me out."

The lady nodded, poured Maggie a cup of water, and invited her to sit down.

The house was a little rough around the edges, more like a rustic cabin on the inside, with unfinished walls and floors. A rather large fireplace took up one side of the room and in the far corner, there were slabs of meat and drying herbs hanging from the ceiling. Maggie's attention immediately went to some of the unusual shelves on one wall that appeared to have been constructed from driftwood. Those ledges were covered with everything from seashells to glass bottles, along with a wide array of other miscellaneous items. The only furniture that room contained were two rocking chairs in front of the fireplace and a long, primitive table with four chairs. Maggie set her things on the floor, gratefully accepted the cup, and gulped the water down.

“Thank you so much,” she said and watched Mary pour her another cup,” I’m not sure how much longer I would've lasted out there. I seem to have lost my way on the beach last night.”

Mary gave Maggie a good look over. The poor girl must have been through quite an ordeal. She wore a pair of torn, very strange-looking men's trousers, a shirt that was completely worn bare, and no shoes whatsoever. Bless her heart! Mary could only imagine what she must have been through. Some of those horrible pirates that sometimes came ashore at night wreaking havoc must have been holding her captive, doing God only knows what to her. Those beasts! Thank goodness she had somehow managed to get away from them. Mary looked at her with concern and a great deal of pity in her eyes.

“You look starved, my dear. Can I get you something to eat?”

“Oh no, thank you. I'm really not hungry,” Maggie lied.

“Can you just point me in the direction of the hotels on the beach in Nags Head? I can't seem to figure out which way I need to go.”

Mary seemed confused. “Hotel? I'm not sure what you mean, dear. What's a ho-tel?” she asked.

“You know, the hotels? The places people stay when they come to visit?” Maggie blinked.

How can someone not know what a hotel is?

“Oh! You mean the boardinghouse,” said Mary, “but, I've never heard it referred to as a ‘nags head’.”

“No,” Maggie chuckled, “the hotel is IN Nags Head.”

It had been a really long day and she couldn't wait to get back to her room.

“I'm sorry, my dear, I've never heard of such a place, and I have lived here all my life, but there is a boarding house a little ways up, near ‘Chickahawk’ if you need a place to stay. You are also welcome to remain here for a bit if you need to rest.”

Maggie started to think that she had stumbled upon the home of a mentally ill woman. This poor lady's mind must be going. She didn't even know where she was herself, much less the right way to point Maggie. Maybe, it was best if she just continued on, until she found someone who could help her. Just as she was about to thank her and leave, the lady grabbed Maggie's hand.

“Are you alright, my dear?” she inquired, “I only ask because you're barely wearing any clothes, and you have no shoes. Did something truly awful happen to you?”

“My clothes?” Maggie pulled at the restraining hand, her heartbeat speeding up. “What's wrong with my clothes?”

"I know something dreadful must have happened, and I understand that you may not want to talk about it…" Mary's words trailed off.

"Really," Maggie said, "I am perfectly fine...just a little lost. I really should be on my way."

Mary jumped up and headed into the other room. "Before you go, let me give you something," she called back, "I can't in good conscience let you leave looking like that."

Maggie looked down at her jeans and shirt. "What's wrong with the way I'm dressed?" she mumbled, "Sure, my hair is a mess, I'm sure all my makeup is gone, and I don't have any shoes on because it IS the beach, but do I look THAT bad?"

Mary returned with an armload of clothing. She took the whole pile and hoisted it over Maggie's shoulder. "My dear, you can't go into town looking like that. What would people think?"

"I really don't give a damn what people think," Maggie muttered. She had to remember she was dealing with someone who wasn't all there.

Just be cool and go with it.

Maggie smiled at Mary. "I can't take all of these clothes."

Mary shushed her. "Of course, you can. None of these fit me anymore, and they are just taking up space. Please, I would not be able to sleep tonight if I knew you left here without them."

Just go with the flow Maggie.

"Um…thank you so much, Mary. This is very generous of you, but I should be on my way."

Mary turned around, took down a piece of cloth off the shelf and rapidly started wrapping some things in it, before tying the corners together. She shoved the parcel on top of the pile of clothing.

"Just a little food for the trip, in case you get hungry." Mary smiled and gave Maggie a little hug. "I wish you well, my dear. Take care of yourself and if you need ole Mary, you are welcome back here anytime."

Maggie smiled. Mary's mind might be going, but her heart was pure gold. Kindness was in short supply these days, and Maggie was warmed by the generosity the old woman showed her. She thanked Mary again, gathered her stuff and walked out the door. Mary pointed her in the way of 'Chickahawk' and Maggie started off, Onyx close at her heels.

Mary waved to Maggie. "God be with you, Maggie. I hope things turn out well for you," she said before turning and heading back into the house.

Once Maggie was a good distance away from the house, she stopped and plopped down on the ground. She wasn't sure what kind of Twilight Zone episode she had stumbled into, but boy, it was a doozy. Her head throbbed, and nothing made any kind of sense. There was no reason she should not have found the hotel strip by now or ANY signs of the Banks she loved so much for that matter. She knew this place like the back of her hand and, where she stood, simply did not exist. Maybe this was all a bad dream. She reached down and pinched her leg as hard as she could.

"Ouch!"

Okay, not a dream.

She looked around; there were too many trees. Where did they all come from? This type of growth simply didn't happen overnight.

What the hell was going on?

Maggie decided to pick through the pile of clothes. She found an old-timey shirt that resembled a peasant top. There was also a long skirt like the one Mary had on, stockings for her feet, and even a pair of old leather shoes. There was also something that looked like a long white nightgown.

Not exactly the height of fashion.

Maggie put the clothes down and rubbed her temples. Her stomach growled, reminding her that she had not eaten since the day before. She picked up the cloth package Mary had given her and untied it. In it was a half a loaf of bread, a couple of apples, and some strange coins. Maggie pulled off a chunk of the bread and stuffed it in her mouth before handing an apple to Onyx, who had been nudging her in the back.

It was delicious— freshly baked, still warm, and the best she had ever tasted. Maggie picked up one of the coins and looked closer while she enjoyed her meal. It was a very strange piece, with a cross on the back and the image of someone on the front.

"Is that a man or a woman?" She squinted her eyes as she looked harder.

The coin looked strangely familiar, but where had she seen it? It did not look like any amusement park or subway token— it looked more like an old piece of currency, only much newer. Maggie wracked her brain until it finally hit her.

"No way!"

She looked again, rubbing the coin and flipping it over. It was a shilling, from the 1700s, like those she had seen in one of the museums her dad had taken her to. Maggie picked up some of the others and took a better look at them — more of the same — a whole bunch of them. They had to be replicas, right?

Something told Maggie that they were not.

How did a bunch of rare coins from the 18th century end up in the beach cottage of an old woman with dementia? The shelves in her home came to mind — ledges covered with shells, bottles and all sorts of knick-knacks. Perhaps, Mary had found them washed up on the beach and picked them up. Strange things like that washed up all the time. Wreckage littered the coast, 'The Graveyard of the Atlantic' not being a term earned lightly. Early Outer Bankers made their livings from scavenging what washed up from shipwrecks, so it wasn't totally out of the realm of possibility. Good ole Mary might have a small fortune sitting in that ramshackle cabin of hers.

Something else nagged at Maggie — the name Mary kept calling the closest town.

'Chickahawk'.

That name seemed strangely familiar as well. Nags Head, Kill Devil Hills, and Kitty Hawk were all fairly recent names—those places had been called something else, usually taken from the Native American language.

Chickahawk? Kitty Hawk?

Was that an early name for the town? It certainly sounded like that one could have morphed into the other. Diverse people and dialects came through that particular area a great deal and spellings and pronunciations changed all the time.

Maggie's headache was getting worse. She broke off another piece of bread and started chewing on it while looking back over the landscape, trying to make sense of things.

The ring on her finger glittered in the sun. She thought about Brad and how worried he must be. By now, he had probably called the police. Surely, someone was looking for her. Maybe someone in 'Chickahawk' could get her back to her nice, comfy hotel room.

I am definitely hitting the day spa tomorrow.

Onyx whinnied behind her. "I haven't forgotten about you back there." She smiled and reached around to rub his muzzle. "I am just trying to figure out how we are going to fit you in the car so we can take you back home with us."

3

CHAPTER THREE

Maggie gathered all her things together and tried to figure out what to do with the rather bulky pile of clothing. Onyx pawed at the ground and huffed. Turning, she heard what he was reacting to — voices, coming from actual people. She must be close to civilization after all. Maggie looked around to see where the noise was coming from.

The landscape sloped down a little ways from where they had stopped. She peered over and was shocked to see two men leading a horse pulling a full cart. Maggie scrunched up her nose and made a face as the smell of fish wafted up the hill. The odor was strong, as if the fish had been in that cart for a good little while. She opened her mouth to call out but hesitated. The two men were traveling on a dirt path that was just wide enough for the two-wheeled wagon being pulled by a rather old and tired looking pony. Why were they using this poor animal to haul fish when there were so many more other, easier ways to transport things like that?

"Where's PETA when you need them?" she wondered out loud.

She was debating on whether to call out or not when the shorter and older of the two men shouted at the nag about being too slow, raised the staff in his hand, and hit the poor creature.

Fury rose inside of Maggie! She had no tolerance for animal abusers and was convinced that there was a special place in Hell for those kinds of people. No reason he shouldn't be punished before that time came. She was about to slide down the hillside, take that stick out of his hand and beat the hell out of HIM with it when Onyx stepped in front of her.

"Move Onyx! I need to see a man about a horse… pony!" She tried to shove him away, but to no avail. "LET...ME...BY!" She pushed even harder, throwing her weight into it, but ended up sliding back a little bit instead.

Onyx stood firm, solid as a statue. When she went to move to the left of him, her eyes shifted in the direction that the men were headed.

There was the town! Thank goodness!

She was finally back to civilization; her first order of business would be to get that God-awful man arrested for beating that poor animal. Her happiness was short lived, however, when she shifted closer to get a better look.

Maggie couldn't believe what she saw. She closed her eyes, opened them again, rubbed them and focused downward. It was a town alright, but not the town she was expecting. There were no hotels, restaurants, cars, or scantily clad tourists.

What she saw shook her straight to her core.

The 'town' consisted of dilapidated structures that looked like they had been thrown together over a couple of days. Most were covered by wooden boards and a few had thatched roofs. She could see an open-air market, filled with various types of produce and plenty of fish. But what shocked Maggie more than anything, was the appearance of the people. All the women wore long skirts and dresses like Mary did, with their hair up and tied back with kerchiefs, and all the men had on trousers or breeches, with long sleeve shirts, tall boots, and hats. There was not a modern dressed person among them.

Maggie saw what Mary meant about not fitting in.

There were no cars, bicycles, or any modern means of transportation, only saddled horses, bareback ponies, and several different types of carts. No new reenactment villages had been added in years — if there had been to such an extent as this, her father would have brought Maggie and her mom out to see it.

These people weren't actors, and if there WERE a group of people living in a village like this on the Outer Banks of North Carolina, she had no doubt in her mind that she would know about it. A slow, sinking, horrifying feeling settled into her bones. She turned around, took two steps to the side and emptied her stomach.

Maggie had a strange feeling that her name was Dorothy, Toto was a big black horse, and that she was not in Kansas anymore.

She staggered backwards until she fell onto a large boulder. Maybe sitting down was a good idea right about now.

How is any of this possible?

The annoying little headache that had been bothering her all day increased tenfold. She tried to make sense of everything. Perhaps, she had been out in the sun too long and had a sunstroke. Hallucinations were a common sign of heat exhaustion or maybe, she HAD been drugged and all of this was just in her mind. The renewed stench of old fish and a gentle nudge in the back from Onyx laid those two theories to rest. None of this made any sense and Maggie needed some answers.

Only one thing to do— make a game plan. She needed answers and they were somewhere in that town.

However, she could not just waltz in there in her current state, with a wild horse trailing behind her and start demanding answers. She would stick out like a sore thumb, or worse yet, seem like a crazy person. No telling what they did with people they thought were unwell in the head. Then again, maybe, she WAS insane. THAT would happen to explain a lot.

The heaviness of the ring on her hand reminded her that she was not out of her mind. She had been at the beach and she had gotten engaged; she did not imagine that. She looked over at the pile of clothes that Mary had given her. Her best bet was to slip into town, attracting as little attention as possible, and try to gather as much information as she could.

Maggie started to strip down and change into the clothes.

“Don't look!” she said, shooing Onyx away.

She got all the bulky pieces on and sat down to put on the stockings and shoes. They were actually a surprisingly good fit. She then eyed Onyx up and down.

"Well, it's going to look pretty strange if I walk into town with a wild horse just following behind me. Guess you have to get dressed up too." Onyx eyed Maggie and huffed. "Oh, don't be a baby. If I have to do it, then so do you." Maggie looked around on the ground and up in the trees; she saw some vines and had an idea.

She pulled as many of them down as she could, sat down on the rock and braided them like hair. She finished two sets and tied them together on the ends to make a loop big enough to slip over Onyx's head. Then she made another set that looked like a piece of rope that she tied to the circle. Holding up the loop to slip it around Onyx's neck, he shied away.

"Now look, I know, and, you know, that this will not actually hold you, so you must pretend, or this isn't going to work. Please Onyx, I am begging you here. I have to figure out what's going on."

A small tear slipped out of the corner of Maggie's eye.

Onyx seemed to feel her despair and begrudgingly surrendered to his fate.

Maggie smiled and hugged him. "Thank you, my friend."

Looking into his eyes, she had the feeling that this horse was special and understood every word that she said, and, for that, she was extremely grateful.

4

CHAPTER FOUR

After finding and following another worn path down the hillside, Maggie and Onyx stood on the edge of town. Maggie sucked in a deep breath, looked back at Onyx, nodded, and started towards the village.

"Here goes nothing."

Maggie had tied her own clothes and the bottle back up in the cloth and slung them over Onyx's back to make it look like he was a pack horse. The skirt Mary had given her had a roughly sewn inner pocket, so she slipped the coins inside just in case she was able to use them. Now that she was closer to the buildings, she got a better look at what stood before her.

They seemed to be put together with a wide array of materials. One looked like the outside of an old ship, another looked like the cottage Mary lived in with open timbers, and a third even looked like one of the huts from Gilligan's Island. In addition to the open-air market, there were a couple of rudimentary tents made of sticks and ship sails.

The entire village was constructed out of items that would have washed up from a shipwreck. The sight was incredible, but the smells were a whole other story.

Merchants in the town square had different kinds of fish laid out in the sun with no ice, and those were rapidly becoming covered by flies. The pungent smell made Maggie's stomach churn. Mixed in with the fishmongers were several people selling produce. Cabbages, radishes, corn, apples, and potatoes seemed to be the specials for the day. There was only one person selling freshly baked bread.

Maggie walked through the square cautiously, trying to take it all in without seeming like too much of an outsider. On the other side of the market stood a two-story building made of brick, and adjoining it was a stable holding several horses. Lots of people moved throughout the town, all with their own important errands to carry out. Merchants were calling out trying to sell their wares and buyers were haggling back and forth with them for the best deals.

Fish odors were not the only strong aromas in the air. The stables smelled of fresh manure and the people reeked of horrendous body odor. Bathing did not seem to be a priority. Maggie looked towards the outer part of town and saw several small houses spaced out about a hundred yards from the edge.

"Those houses must be where most of these people live," she thought.

People moved around her, and Maggie realized she was standing and staring like a moonstruck tourist. She tugged on the vine around Onyx's neck and made a little clicking sound with her mouth.

Onyx kindly obliged, and they moved to a corner on the far side of town in order to observe a little better.

Maggie's mom had taught her, from the time she was little, to pay attention to the details, especially the smallest ones.

"It is one of the best skills to have in life, especially for a woman," her mom had said on multiple occasions. They would make a game of 'people watching' when they would go out for ice cream, picking out the tiniest details that no one else noticed.

Maggie observed the citizens standing in the town square. These people were not actors; this was their life and they were at home. Women negotiated over items as if they were spending their last dime, the exchanges even getting heated to a certain extent. Maggie was watching the big picture when she noticed him. A boy, about eleven or twelve, looking nervously at the people around him to see who was paying attention. When he thought no one noticed, he slipped an apple in each pocket from one of the vendors before slipping quietly into the crowd.

"You little thief," Maggie muttered.

She watched him squeeze between two buildings and then emerge behind her. Smiling to himself, like the cat who had gotten the cream, he proceeded on his way, until Maggie slipped around the other side of Onyx and grabbed him by the arm.

"Hey, let go of me, lady!" he cried out.

"I will, after, we have a little chat," Maggie snapped. "I saw what you did back there and, unless you want me to tell the apple seller, you need to do a little something for me."

His eyes widened, and he made an audible gulp. "Like what?"

Maggie loosened her grip. "Just answer a few questions for me and I'll let you be on your way."

"What kind of questions?" he asked, plucking at a tear in his shirt.

"Nothing too complicated," she said and pulled him behind the building where no one else was, using Onyx to block them from being seen. "What's your name?"

The boy looked her up and down, trying to decide whether to answer or not.

"Apple vendor?" Maggie threatened.

"Alright lady, no… need… for… that," he stuttered out. "Jack, my name is Jack."

"Hello Jack, I'm Maggie, and I need to know exactly where I am. What town, I mean village, is this?"

"You don't know where you are?"

"No, I'm lost," Maggie said, "so, where am I?"

After a little hesitation, Jack answered, "You are in Chickahawk."

"Okay," replied Maggie, "what other towns are around here?"

Jack put his finger to the side of his head as if he were thinking hard. "Well, there's Cape Hatteras that way," he pointed, "and there's Curratuck that way," he pointed the other direction, "and there's the island of Roanoke," pointing in the third direction.

"Any others?"

"Nope, that's about all of them."

That is what Maggie was afraid of. She looked around. It would be dark soon. “Where's the hotel...I mean, the boardinghouse here?”

Jack pointed towards the two-story brick building next to the stables.

“Anything else you want to know?” Jack took a bite of one of the apples.

“Just one, Jack. What's the date?”

“Oh, that's an easy one. Today is June 6th in the year of our Lord 1765. Anything else?”

“No, that's all. You can go. Thank you, Jack.”

He tipped his hat and scurried off, ducking through the crowd.

Maggie felt like she had been punched in the gut. She had suspected but had not really believed it. Her entire body went numb, she felt sick to the stomach and thought she might pass out.

There was no way this was true; it just was not possible. People did not just go to sleep in one century and wake up in another, it just did not happen —it couldn’t happen. Yet, here she was, with all the proof staring her in the face. Facts were facts, and the fact of this matter was that she was in the year 1765, not 2018.

Maggie had no clue how she ended up here and no idea how, or if it was even possible, to go back. She had a bizarre inner feeling that this was a one-way trip.

Tightness formed in her chest and she found it hard to breathe. She reached for the building next to her to steady herself. Maggie pressed her back to the building, slid down it, and onto the ground. She pushed her hair back from her face, trying to focus on forcing herself to take in a breath as she started to see spots.

Just as everything started to go black, she felt a gentle, familiar nudge.

Onyx rubbed his muzzle against her to calm her down.

Slowly, the spots went away, and Maggie was able to breathe normally again. She reached up, rubbing Onyx's muzzle, grateful for the comfort this wonderful creature brought her.

The sun was sinking low in the sky. It would be dark soon. How much time had passed there behind that building? She could not spend the night on the street.

Maggie rose and peeked around the corner. Most of the people in the market had cleared out, and things were settling down.

"Now what?"

The adrenaline from the initial shock of the understanding of her current situation had worn off, and a deep, penetrating fatigue had set in. She had to figure out something fast.

"Okay, Onyx, one crisis at a time. Let's get through the night before we worry about tomorrow."

A slight jingle in her pocket reminded her that she was not totally up a creek without a paddle, at least not for the moment. Young Jack had told her where the place was with rooms for rent, and it had a stable.

After making her way to it, Maggie stood before the boarding house, looked back at Onyx, took in a deep breath and opened the door. That is when she realized that this wasn't JUST a boarding house, but a tavern. The entire first floor was basically a bar straight out of your worst nightmare. The place had several, well-worn sets of tables and chairs, about half of them occupied by nothing but men. A few looked like fishermen, ones she recognized as sellers from the market, and the rest appeared to be pirates.

“Great,” Maggie grumbled, “this looks super safe!” She raised her shoulders, straightened her back and headed straight for the bar.

A woman with her back turned was filling a pitcher with ale. She spun around and looked up, a little startled to see Maggie as she did. She sighed and rolled her eyes. “I have no need for a barmaid, and I don't allow women to offer their OWN services here either. I run a respectable establishment, and I don't need YOUR kind hanging around and ruining my business, so move along, missy,” she said gruffly.

Maggie started to answer before she figured out what the woman meant. She waved her hands in the air. “Oh no, I need a .... hey, I am NOT a prostitute! Why would you think... oh, never mind... look...I am just looking for a room for the night for me and my horse. Well, a room for me, and a stable for my horse... well...you know what I mean. We need somewhere to stay tonight and maybe tomorrow night as well, I'm not really sure yet.”

The lady looked Maggie up and down. “Begging your pardon, miss,” she said, in a little kinder voice, “I did not mean to insult you. It is just that I have been getting more than my fair share of drifter women through here lately, and well, I just wrongly assumed. Please, forgive my mistake.”

“Can you just tell me how much your rooms are, please?” Maggie sighed, too weary from the day to care that she had been mistaken for a ‘lady of the night’.

"Will your husband or father be coming along soon?" asked the tavern owner.

"No, it's just me and my horse," Maggie pointed with her thumb to the front door.

She caught Onyx out of the corner of her eye staring through the window of the tavern. Maggie shook her head; a man near the window who had obviously had way too much ale, took note of Onyx staring back at him. He looked at Onyx, down at his ale, back at Onyx and pushed his tankard away.

There really was something a little strange about that horse.

The tavern lady shifted uncomfortably, "You're traveling alone? That is not very safe these days."

"I don't have any choice," Maggie replied. "I have no one else."

"Surely a girl your age is married?" the lady continued to inquire.

It was annoying, but Maggie was too tired to argue and knew how it was looked upon at the time, so she lied.

"I'm widowed."

"Oh, I'm so sorry, my dear."

This conversation was taking way too long for Maggie's liking. "Please, how much?"

The lady gave her a compassionate look and replied, "I have a small room in the back, here on the first floor. It's nothing fancy, but there is only one bed, so you won't have to share with the likes of any of these ruffians," looking around the room. "For three shillings, it's yours for two nights. It comes with two meals a day and a stable, with hay, for your horse. My son will get your horse, take care of him for you, and I can bring tonight's supper to your room, so you can eat in peace. The good Lord knows you look like you need a bed sooner rather than later."

"SOLD!" Maggie exclaimed. She paid the lady, got Onyx settled, and found her way to the room directly next to the kitchen.

'Nothing fancy' was putting it nicely. The room was the size of her walk-in closet at home. There was a tiny window, so she could not accurately tell how late it was. There was a small bed covered with a threadbare, handmade quilt, a tiny table next to it that held a half-burned candle that, thankfully, had been lit so she was not in complete darkness.

She was startled by a knock at the door; it was the tavernkeeper. The lady set a bowl of stew, a spoon and a tankard of ale on the table.

Maggie thanked her.

On her way out, the lady turned and said, "Make sure you bar this door. These drunkards are always losing their way and ending up in the wrong places. Sleep well, and I'll see you in the morning."

A little shiver went down Maggie's spine and she bolted the door, jerking the handle to make sure it held. It was best to remember that she was not in 2018; women in this time were treated very differently and were constantly in danger on many levels. She looked at the table, her stomach growling. Sitting down on the bed, she was surprised to hear it crunch. Standing, she peeled the cover back to find that it was stuffed with dried seagrass and God only knows what else.

Again, she was too exhausted to care. She pulled her feet up and folded her legs underneath her before she took a bite of the stew. It was surprisingly good. She wasn't sure what was in it, deciding it was probably best if she didn't know. She took a sip of the ale. It was strong, unlike any beer she had ever had, and not half bad. She finished the food and alcohol, that had started to go to her head a little, lay back on the bed, fully clothed, and closed her eyes.

"Good night Onyx," she whispered to the air.

She raised her head; she could have sworn she heard a response.

Sleep came as soon as she closed her eyes. She slept soundly the entire night, not waking up once.

The smell of food and the sounds of the kitchen woke her the next morning. The first thing that came to mind was an urgent need to pee. She went to the door to inquire about where to do her business when she looked back under the bed and noticed something underneath. She peered under the bed and had the answer to her question.

"You have got to be kidding me."

It was a chamber pot, the way 'business' was done in colonial times. Well, she could not say she didn't have a pot to piss in—so she did —and she felt much better.

Maggie unbolted the door and peeked out. The tavern lady walked by toting a bowl of something to the main tavern area.

"Good morning. I hope you slept well," she said in passing. "By the way, my name is Sarah. This tavern belongs to me and my husband, Edgar. He's a fisherman, and I run things while he's gone."

"I'm Maggie," she replied, following closely on Sarah's heels.

In the tavern, Sarah spooned out a bowl of something and handed it to her, along with a slice of bread. "There's plenty more here if you like. Help yourself," she said and scurried back to the kitchen.

The large room was empty except for two men, who didn't bother to lift their heads, too absorbed in eating their breakfast.

Maggie took her bowl to the table closest to the window. It was a beautiful morning, and her head was much clearer with some food and rest. She had woken up, resigning herself to her fate. She had no idea how she ended up here, and by the same token, she had no idea how to get back. Maggie wanted answers but had no clue where to look for them.

Survival was the main thing. She was here, she couldn't change that, but she couldn't sit around and do nothing. That would be suicide and becoming a victim wasn't in her nature. Her parents had always instilled in her the need to be self-sufficient and productive. It was a necessity, not an option, that creed being more important than ever.

She needed to figure out her next move. She needed food, clothing, and shelter and for that, she needed money. Did women in the 1700's get paying jobs? Or just husbands? She didn't want one of those. No way.

Sticking to the widow story might be best, and it could possibly keep people from asking her questions that she didn't have the answers to. Lost in thought, she never noticed the old man in the corner opposite her staring at her.

"Beautiful morning isn't it, lass?"

Maggie was torn away from her thoughts. She looked up and that's when she saw him—the old man, sitting in a chair with his back against the wall in the corner, smiling at her. Maggie was surprised she hadn't seen him when she came in. He was the kind of man that was hard to miss.

He was a large fellow who had to be in his late 40s or early 50s, very tall and muscular, extremely well groomed and quite striking. His hair was jet black, as was his beard, but it was streaked with just that right amount of gray that made older men look more dignified and handsome. His voice was smooth as silk, and the slight Scottish accent just added to the package.

For an instant, Maggie thought that the 'most interesting man on Earth' from those alcohol commercials had sailed back in time with her. The comical thought caused her to smile to herself. His face was very pleasant, and his personality seemed warm and inviting, the type of person that made everyone feel good just by being in the same room.

But his striking eyes were what she noticed the most. They were a warm amber, a color unlike anyone else's she had seen before —stunning, magical, the kind of eyes that you could stare into for hours, making you oblivious to anyone and anything around you. The confidence and sexiness he exuded rolled off like the fog from a lake. He was the type of man who people would follow through the gates of Hell only to thank him for the trip.

"Yes, it is!" Maggie looked down at the table and tucked her hair behind her ear.

He stood up and made his way over to where she sat. "Mind if I join ye, lass?"

Maggie couldn't have said 'no' if her very life depended on it. "Please," and she motioned to the chair.

Gracefully and in one swift move, he seated himself across from her. "If ye don't mind me saying so lass, ye seem to have a great deal on your mind."

"I do," Maggie replied, "it's been an interesting and complicated couple of days, to say the least."

"Well, I just happen to be a good listener if ye need to talk. By the way, my name is Finn, and ye are?" he said with a twinkle in his eye.

"I'm Maggie Bishop."

"Well, Maggie Bishop, I am very pleased to make your acquaintance." He took her hand and planted a small kiss on it.

Maggie giggled like a schoolgirl. This guy was a charming devil, for sure.

"Now, tell ole Finn what's troubling ye so much. I do hate to see a damsel in distress."

"I just have a lot of things to figure out and I am not quite sure where to start," she said and smiled up at him. "I ...uh...arrived here yesterday by accident, without any money or a place to live and I am just trying to decide what I should do next."

"What about your family, lass, or your husband? Won't they help ye?" Finn asked.

"I don't have any family here, I'm afraid it's just me." A small tear escaped her eye, an empty loneliness for her mom and dad welling. How would she ever make it without them?

"Ah, I'm very sorry lass. Sometimes, this world can be a very uninviting place, but I am a firm believer that everything happens for a reason. I have no doubt that ye are exactly where ye need to be." Finn laid his hand on top of Maggie's.

She immediately felt better— tremendously better— like everything WAS going to turn out just fine. This man had a special, reassuring energy, no doubt about that.

Finn noticed the ring on Maggie's left finger. He picked up her hand to get a better look. "A gift from your sweetheart?" he asked.

"Um...yes. But... well...I am...um... widowed." Maggie lied—again.

Finn raised his eyebrow and gave her a look as if he could see right through her deception. "Ah, well lass, that's probably for the best."

"Excuse me?" Maggie thought that was a harsh thing to say to a widow.

"Well, being as you're widowed," Finn said with his eyebrow raised again, fully knowing she was lying, and letting her know that he knew, "ye will be able to own property and such, whereas if ye were unmarried, ye would NEVER be able to. Probably best to mention that ye are, indeed, a widow, wherever you go, so there's no question, you ken? And being that ye ARE a widow, no one would question if you needed to sell that rather lovely ring on your hand, from your husband's estate, ye know, to take care of yourself, since ye have no husband here to take care of ye." He was obviously repeating himself for emphasis.

Well, that was an idea and a pretty darn good one at that. It wasn't like Brad would be searching for her in 1765.

"You think I could find a buyer, and that I could get a good price for it?" she inquired.

What would be a good price for this ring in this time?

"Oh, aye! I know for a fact that ye could. Ye see, diamonds that big are very uncommon around here. There's a man up in Norfolk that buys stones like that for a special clientele he has, and I know for certain, he would be willing to pay a great deal for that ring, especially since it is set in gold, that is, if you are willing to part with it. I'm sure it would give ye plenty of money to start a new life."

Maggie could have kissed the old man. This was the answer she had been looking for. "That's wonderful! But how do I get all the way up there? I don't know anyone, and I have little money," she deflated from the instant exuberance.

"Oh, I can handle that for ye, lass. There's a boat headed up to Norfolk tomorrow. I can make arrangements for ye and your horse to be on it. The captain owes me a favor," he winked, "and once ye sell your ring there, I hear that land up around Williamsburg is going for a fair price. It's quite an exciting little town from what I understand, if that would be of interest to ye."

Williamsburg? Home!

Maggie and her parents had lived in Williamsburg for the past ten years after her dad took a job at the College of William and Mary. She knew the colonial area like the back of her hand. She would at least have some knowledge about things there, and maybe, just maybe, she could find a way home.

"Finn, you are an angel!"

"Not quite," he said with a little wink and a mischievous look in his eye.

"Well, you're an angel to me. I don't know how to thank you."

"No thanks needed, lass. I should thank YE for keeping an old man company this morning," he smiled warmly, "But can I ask ye one question?"

"Anything," Maggie said, excited again.

"Where did ye get that lovely necklace ye are wearing?"

Maggie reached up and touched the pendant. She had completely forgotten about it. She never took it off, not even in the shower, and it had become as much a part of her as her own skin. It was a large, exotic stone. She had never actually been able to find out what kind of gem it was. It was multiple colors, changing with the light, never the same color twice. Her mother gave it to her when she turned eighteen.

Up until then, her mother had never taken it off, either.

'A Faerie stone' was the only answer she ever received from her mother when she asked what kind it was. It had been a gift from her own father a very long time ago, and her mother had always treasured it.

"My mother gave it to me," she said, stroking it lightly, thinking about her mom. "Her father, my grandfather, gave it to her and she passed it on to me."

"He must have loved her very much," Finn said, a faraway, almost sad look in his eye, "Daughters hold a special place in their father's hearts."

"I suppose they do," Maggie thought about her own dad, "I never got the chance to meet him, my grandfather, although I would have liked to."

"Well, that necklace is as lovely as ye are, lass. Now, I am going to make plans for ye to get on that ship. Ye be at the dock at noon tomorrow. The tavern owner can tell ye how to get there. Just tell the captain who ye are, and he will see ye safely to Norfolk."

A sudden thought hit Maggie. "Can I hug you, Finn?" Maggie asked.

Finn's smile was bright. "I would be very happy if you did."

They embraced.

"Thank you. I will never forget you, Finn."

"Take care, lass. I won't forget ye either."

Maggie watched him leave the tavern. She was over the moon because she had a plan.

Finn stopped outside the tavern and smiled. "That lass is something else," he thought to himself.

He walked next door to the stable. Onyx looked up and walked over to him as soon as he saw him.

"Hello, my old friend," Finn said to Onyx, rubbing the horse's muzzle and mane.

Onyx was happy to see him and let him know it, butting his nose into the man's hand.

“You are doing a fine job. Make sure ye take care of young Maggie. She needs ye something fierce.”

Onyx whinnied in response.

Finn bid his friend ‘goodbye’ and disappeared into the crowd of people on the street as quickly, and as quietly, as he had slipped in.

5

CHAPTER FIVE

Maggie stood on the edge of Williamsburg with a rather hefty bag of gold in her pocket. The past few days had been a blur. After a—surprisingly—smooth and enjoyable sail up the coast —for her anyway Onyx was not a big fan —she found the buyer for the ring. Finn had been right; the man had been very eager to buy the piece, not to mention, very generous, and he had paid in gold, no less. She was able to purchase some better clothes, a couple of restful nights in a good tavern, safe passage to Williamsburg, and even a new blanket, bridle and saddle for Onyx.

She looked back at him and smiled.

Onyx looked regal in his new attire. He had protested profusely at first, but after explaining to him that it just wasn't normal for a person to have a horse follow them everywhere of their own accord, and a whole lot of telling him how wonderfully handsome he looked, the horse gave in, and seemed to wear his new gear with pride.

Maggie could swear that horse understood every word she said. She didn't know how, but, what the hell, there were a bunch of things that she didn't understand, and that one just happened to work in her favor. She was just going with it.

Williamsburg in 1765 was a much different place than it was in 2018. In 2018, the streets were normally filled with tourists in shorts, tank tops, and flip-flops, fanning themselves from the heat, snapping pictures of the restored buildings, the horses, and of their kids in the stockades to post on Facebook and Instagram. Only some of the buildings were open to the public, and they tended to alternate, depending on the day and the time of the year.

Maggie preferred the mornings before everyone came out for the day. Every chance she got, she would take long strolls on the paved street down the middle of the town, taking in the peace and quiet, before the day became busy.

Williamsburg in 1765 was also a bustling, busy town, full of hundreds of people dressed in full colonial attire, moving to and fro, greeting friends, and conducting business. Men on horses trotted up and down the street, and Maggie had to step out of the way to keep from getting trampled. Gone were the black-paved roads of Duke of Gloucester street —replaced with dirt and mud.

There were an extensive number of buildings open and new construction was going on all around. The lawns were well maintained, and there were gardens everywhere, both flowers and vegetables, obviously the pride of their owners.

People from all walks of life mingled here. Gentlemen, noble ladies, store owners, peddlers, farmers, and slaves all engaged together in this vibrant, magnificent little town.

The smell was also a little different —a complete unwarranted assault on the senses. In 2018, all you smelled were the faint smells of wood fires, and the drifting aroma of lavender soap collections from the stores.

Here, in 1765, you smelled everything. Fireplaces, human excrement, body odors, cooking smells and, yes, horse shit. No employees walked up and down the street to ‘scoop the poop’ behind THESE horses.

Maggie stood there, taking in the atmosphere of this glorious little town in its heyday. “Welcome to the 18th century! Ain’t it grand? Come on Onyx, let’s see what this town has to offer.”

It was hard to take it all in. Everything seemed familiar, yet unfamiliar at the same time, and she was having trouble getting her bearings. She knew she was in front of the Capital and was trying to figure out exactly where the Raleigh Tavern was, when she noticed a large crowd standing around a short, rather funny looking man on some steps. She stopped and listened.

“Alright folks, who here wants to buy some property? A lovely house with five hundred acres, the whole lock, stock and barrel going for one low, low price.”

Maggie’s ears perked up.

Property? For sale?

A man in the crowd called out to the man on the steps, “Giving it another go, are you Silas?”

The crowd laughed; the man tried to ignore him.

"Who will give me an opening bid on the vast estate of one Mr. Hubert Rawlings?"

Another man shouted at him, "No one is ever going to buy that place, Shipman. You might as well save your breath."

A third man laughed and yelled too, "Haven't you gotten tired of coming out here every week to try and unload that place, Silas? You'd have an easier time selling that horse shite on the steps next to you."

The crowd roared with laughter.

The little man looked down.

Damn, he WAS standing next to horse shite.

"All right! All right!" Silas Shipman said with exasperation and desperation in his voice, "Do I have ANY offers on this property, any at all?" He looked around the whole crowd wishing for just one person to speak up when his silent prayers were answered.

"I'll give you ten pieces of gold for it," Maggie shouted out boldly and without thinking it through.

The entire crowd went silent and turned to see where the offer had come from, and thirty pairs of eyes now stared at Maggie.

Maggie turned around and looked behind her to see if, possibly, they were looking at someone else.

Nope! No such luck!

They were most certainly all gawking at her. She turned her head back to face them.

The stunned little man made eye contact with her, and, after picking his mouth up off the ground, he shouted, "SOLD!"

No one moved.

Maggie suddenly started to feel nervous.

The house agent hopped off the step and made his way towards her, the silent, dumbfounded crowd parting for him. The man grabbed her arm and started pulling her towards a small building that looked like an office.

"Come right this way, young lady, so we can take care of your paperwork."

The crowd parted again as they headed that way.

Maggie realized that she still had Onyx by the reins. "My horse…" she started to say.

"Don't you worry about him, miss," he gestured to a young boy and handed the reins over, "your horse will be just fine. Come inside."

"I am Silas Shipman, attorney for the final estate of one Mr. Hubert Rawlings. What is your name?" he asked, showing her a seat and taking his own.

"Maggie Bishop."

"Ah. Miss Bishop or is it Mrs.?"

"Um no, it's...uh... I am a widow."

Silas started writing, not bothering to look up. "My condolences. You DO have the money, correct?"

"Yes," Maggie replied.

"Good, good. Remember, you made the offer and I accepted it on the steps. That is a binding contract. You cannot back out of it."

Maggie looked at him askew, "And why would I want to? I DID get it for a fair price, didn't I?"

"No reason, no reason at all to want to back out, and yes, you got this estate for quite a bargain, my dear. You are a shrewd businesswoman indeed. Please sign here and here," he handed her the pen and ink, pointing at the form.

Maggie took the pen, gave him a strange look, and signed the paperwork.

He took the page and waved it so the ink would dry.

"And the money?"

"Oh, of course!" Maggie took the bag of gold out of her pocket. She handed him ten pieces and put the still mostly full bag away.

"Lovely! Now here is a copy of your deed. Everything in the house and on the property now belongs to you. And this is yours," he said as he slipped the heavy, iron key across the desk to her, "I have to go. I have a ship to London to catch."

He started packing up his things in a most timely hurry. The whole deal took less than ten minutes.

"Um, Mr. Shipman, one question."

Maggie tapped the table to make sure he paid attention.

He looked at her with wide eyes, frozen with fear, and unable to breathe, as if the next words out of her mouth might be the death of him.

"Can you tell me where the property IS?"

He exhaled, looking rather relieved. "Certainly! Head out of town west along the road for nine miles and look for the sign that reads 'Beechcroft'. It is all yours now! Everything!"

Silas rushed to the door with all his things but seemed to have a momentary thought. He stopped, and gave her a look of concern, as if a pang of guilt had hit him. "Mistress, take care of yourself." He gave her a small smile, went out the door and left Maggie sitting alone in the office with the key to her new home.

Maggie wasn't sure if she should be ecstatically happy or completely terrified.

She was anxious to see her new purchase. 'Sight unseen' could go either way, but it was probably best to see it on a full stomach. Maggie wasn't sure what kind of shape the house was in, and what, if anything, would be there in the way of furnishings. Honestly, she was not expecting a great deal from her new abode judging by how quickly Mr. Shipman unloaded it. She would probably be lucky if it had four walls and a roof.

She did not know much about how much things cost in 1765, but ten pieces of gold seemed unbelievably cheap for a house with five hundred acres. Well, whatever the case, she would not be throwing money away renting boarding house rooms. The land alone would be worth something, and besides, with everything that had happened, Maggie desperately needed a place to call her own right now, something she could physically hold on to, a place to be alone, to clear her mind and collect herself.

She decided to grab a bite to eat before seeing exactly what kind of fine mess she had gotten herself into. Outside of the small office, the crowd had dispersed. Bringing attention to herself was probably not the best of ideas. As she looked, Maggie realized that the sale had been conducted on the steps of the Raleigh Tavern.

Turning to search for Onyx, she saw him tied to a post, happily munching away on some hay. He would be just fine for a little while.

The aroma of food lured her to the front door of the tavern. Opening the door, she heard the sounds of people talking, laughing and enjoying themselves, but when she walked in, everyone went silent and turned to stare at her.

Maggie was the unwelcome center of attention. After what seemed like an eternity, a kindly, middle-aged barmaid started towards her, scolding the patrons, and even smacking a few on the back of the head.

"All of you go on about your business, nothing to see here." The noise level picked back up. She approached Maggie with a welcoming smile and asked, "What can I help you with this fine day?"

Maggie was beyond grateful for the warm welcome. "I just wanted to get something to eat."

"Well, we might have something edible back here. Come with me." She led Maggie to a small corner table out of sight.

"My name is Gracie. I don't think I have seen you around here before."

"My name is Maggie Bishop, and I am new here."

Gracie smiled. "Well, welcome to you. How about we get you a hot meal?"

The tavern was packed. Some people were eating, some were drinking, and some were doing both. One table of gentlemen played cards, while another table played dice. In one corner, near the fireplace, a fiddler strummed out a lively tune while patrons laughed and danced. The whole atmosphere was jovial.

Whenever Maggie had toured the colonial area, she had always felt that it must have been an exceedingly difficult and depressing time to live compared to modern day times, but it really wasn't. These people seemed to enjoy life a great deal, at least for the moment.

Occasionally, someone would give her a strange look, then quickly dart their gaze away and go back to what they were doing. Maggie attributed that to being the new person in town, but it did seem very strange, and a little unnerving.

Gracie returned with a large plate of food and a glass of spiced rum.

The food was delicious, even though Maggie wasn't sure exactly what was in Shepherd's Pie and the rum was, well, absolutely delightful. Yes, the rum had so far been the high point of the 18th century.

With her belly full, not to mention being a little tipsy from two glasses of rum, Maggie stepped back onto the street and tried to focus her foggy mind on what to do next, when she noticed a general store.

"Well, that looks like a good place to start." She stumbled slightly inside the small establishment, noticing a few other people shopping and a rather large, balding shopkeeper, with his elbow propped up on the counter, his face in his hand, fast asleep. She watched him for a moment, just to make sure he was indeed alive until the man started to snore rather loudly, causing her to chuckle to herself. An older lady, shopping next to her, looked at Maggie and let out a little snicker behind her hand.

"Oh, let him sleep. The poor man's wife just gave birth to three babes not two weeks ago. I expect that's the longest Mr. Holt has slept since then."

Maggie whispered as not to wake him, "Three? That doesn't happen often, does it?"

"Oh no!" said the woman, whispering as well, "In twenty-nine years of bringing babies into this world, it's the only time I have delivered that many, at once anyway. I don't believe we have met."

"No," replied Maggie, "I am new here. I just bought a place a few miles outside of town. My name is Maggie Bishop."

"Oh, well, welcome to Williamsburg, Mistress Bishop. I am Catherine Blaikley, the town midwife. It is very nice to meet you."

Maggie smiled. "It's nice to meet you too." She nodded toward the shopkeeper. "I need to get some supplies, but I hate to wake him."

"Oh, I wouldn't worry about that, I expect he needs the money more than he needs the sleep."

Mr. Holt's hand slipped, smacking himself in the face, and his eyes flew wide open as he looked around, seemingly confused as to where he was. When he noticed the pair, he coughed and said, "Oh, good afternoon, ladies."

Maggie and Catherine looked at each other and laughed.

"Good afternoon, Mr. Holt, and how are the babies?" Catherine nodded at him.

"Oh, very well, Mrs. Blaikley, thank you for asking, though they don't seem to sleep very well at night. O'course, they sleep perfectly fine during the day."

"That's not unusual. Babies keep their own schedules. Mr. Holt allow me to introduce our newest resident, Mistress Bishop. Mistress, this is Mr. William Holt, proprietor of this general store."

Maggie smiled at Mr. Holt and him back at her.

"Well now, welcome to our little town." Mr. Holt stood and nodded.

Catherine put her items on the counter, paid for them, bid them both 'good day' and left.

Mr. Holt turned his attention to Maggie and asked, "Mistress or is it Mrs.?"

"Mistress is fine; I am widowed."

Maybe I should just tattoo it on my forehead.

"Oh well, I'm sorry for your loss. What can I help you with?"

"I need supplies, but I don't know what, how much, or anything really. I just purchased a place, and I have not seen it yet. The selling attorney was not much help. As a matter of fact, I am not even sure how many things I can take with me. I only have my horse." Maggie realized how ridiculous the whole thing sounded when she said it aloud.

Mr. Holt looked at her compassionately. "Well, I can have anything you buy delivered to you, so that solves one of your issues. Maybe if you tell me what place you bought, I might have some knowledge of it. I know just about everyone and every place around here."

"Yes!" Maggie replied, still feeling the effects of the rum. "The place is about nine miles outside of town and the attorney said it was called 'Beechcroft'. It belonged to...oh what was his name?"

Mr. Holt cut her off to finish her sentence, "Hubert Rawlings," in a grim voice. He looked at her with a furrowed brow and a frown. "Why in the world, would you ever buy a place like that?"

Maggie was a little taken aback. "It seemed like a fair price for a house and land, and I needed a place to live..."

Mr. Holt finished her sentence again, "And that slimy English lawyer Silas Shipman saw a young widowed woman he could take advantage of to unload that God-forsaken place on." He smacked the counter with his hand. "You should march right over there and demand your money back!"

With her rum buzz wearing off, Maggie became a great deal more concerned about her 'sight unseen' purchase. "But, he's gone," Maggie stuttered out, looking back towards the street, "he was headed for London, and in a big hurry. Besides, he said there was no going back on the contract anyway."

"I guess he WAS in a hurry, that miserable, sorry excuse for a human being. Someone should have given him what he had coming a long time ago." Mr. Holt seemed genuinely upset.

"At any rate," said Maggie hoping to calm him down a bit, "it IS mine now, and since there is no changing that, I will do everything I can to make the best of it. DO you, by any chance, know what I might need?"

Mr. Holt sighed. "Oh yes, Mistress! I am afraid to say you will need a great deal for that place."

That's what she was afraid of. Maggie smiled, her nerves making her lips stiff in their curve. "How about we start with the basics that can get me through the next few days?"

Mr. Holt started calling off items and making a list. By the time they were done, she had everything on it she needed to get her house up and running.

"Is there anything else, Mistress?"

Maggie looked around and saw a bottle of rum on the shelf.

"How much of that rum do you have?" she asked.

Mr. Holt turned around and smiled. "I have a whole case in the back if you are interested."

"Then, I will take the whole case."

Mr. Holt nodded and added it to the list.

"Yes, I suppose you will be needing it."

Maggie paid her bill; Mr. Holt promising to have everything delivered in the morning by his employee. He was kind enough to pack up a few food stores to get her through the night.

"Thank you, Mr. Holt."

"Oh, you're welcome Mistress Bishop... and Mistress... please take care of yourself, especially out at that place of yours."

Maggie forced another smile, going back out on the street.

"What have you gotten yourself into, Maggie?" she muttered to herself. "This place must be a real shithole judging by the reactions of the good citizens of Williamsburg, and it must be in a fairly bad neighborhood to boot if the amount of advice to 'take care of yourself' is any indication." She sighed. Nothing to do but make the most of it.

Maggie retrieved Onyx, who seemed pleasantly full of hay, and loaded her saddlebag with the few provisions she was taking with her. She led him by the reins, meandering through the rest of town, Maggie soaking all of it in. They passed by the Market Square, that no longer carried trinkets for the tourists, but actual produce, meats, and loaves of bread for sale by vendors. In addition to that, there were puppet shows, music, dancing, and a place where children and adults were playing games.

Maggie grinned. It was good to see Williamsburg this way, here and now, because she had knowledge of what was to come. She knew that when the Capital was moved to Richmond, all of this would go away. In a few short years, this place would be deserted, and the deterioration would only continue to worsen until W. A. R. Goodwin and the Rockefeller family came along to restore it to its former glory.

So much could, and would, happen in a span of a few short years. Eastern State Hospital and the courthouse on Duke of Gloucester street hadn't even been built yet, but their demise was already on the horizon. Seeing the town springing to life from the beginning was nothing short of astounding, and Maggie decided to appreciate it while she could.

After all, this was her home now, and if, by some miracle, she did manage to make it back to 2018, the knowledge she gained from her time here would be monumental.

Approaching the end of town, where the crowds had started to thin, she was still lost in thought, marveling at the sights of the Governor's Palace, Bruton Parish Church and all the other buildings around her. She didn't notice the two men coming towards her until it was too late.

One grabbed her from behind, attempting to pull her to a side street; the other snatched Onyx's reins from her hands. Maggie tried to scream, but the man covered her mouth with his palm.

Onyx went insane, rearing up, snorting, and knocking the man, who was trying to take him, to the ground, using the opportunity to land a hoof right down on the man's stomach.

The man's howl of pain caused several of the people close by to take notice.

Maggie's self-defense training that her father had insisted upon kicked in. She grabbed the man by the arm, stomped his foot as hard as she could, and as he leaned over, she seized the chance to throw her elbow backward, making perfect contact right in his groin.

He bent over in agony, screaming, "You bitch!" while wildly grabbing at her arm.

Seeing he wasn't on the ground and was still coming after her, Maggie turned, slamming the heel of her palm right into his nose, sending blood pouring from his nostrils, all over him and herself.

The assailant yelped, stumbled, and ran for the alley.

His partner in crime managed to crawl towards the same direction, following close behind.

They both disappeared.

Maggie began to shake so hard that she couldn't think straight. Reaching over, she hugged Onyx who had immediately come to her side and nuzzled her, doing his best to offer up comfort.

Shouting came from the direction of town, men running past her towards the alley after her attackers.

The adrenaline rush waned, and Maggie felt faint from the shock. Just as everything started to go black, a pair of arms encircled her, lifting her off the ground, and a voice said, "It is all right miss, I've got you. You are going to be fine."

The next thing Maggie was aware of, was a horrid smell right at her nose. She pushed it away before even opening her eyes. When she did open them, she realized the smell was coming from a bottle being waved around in front of her face by a rather pleasant-looking man smiling at her.

"Oh good, you're awake. The smelling salts did their job."

"Where am I?" Maggie tried to sit up.

The man stoppered the bottle, set it aside, and gently pushed her back down.

"Not so fast miss, you have had a terrible fright."

He poured something in a cup and told her to drink. The amber-colored liquid hit her throat, and she started to cough. Whatever it was, it was extraordinarily strong—stronger than anything she had ever had before.

The man took the cup and looked her over.

"I am Dr. James Carter. My brother, John, found you on the street and brought you here to my office. How are you feeling?"

"I'm alright, I think." Maggie tried to sit up again, and this time, Dr. Carter helped her.

"It's best if I check you over. You have quite a bit of blood on you."

Maggie looked down and discovered her dress was completely splattered with it. "It's not mine."

The doctor looked at her and raised a quizzical eyebrow, waiting for further explanation.

"The man who attacked me, I...um...well...I hit him in the face. I think I may have broken his nose," Maggie said the words timidly.

"Well," the doctor offered a little grin, "I'd say he got what he had coming."

A face popped around the door, one that looked a great deal like the doctor's.

"Is she well, brother?"

"I think she'll live," said the doctor. "Miss, this is my brother, John, the one who brought you in."

Maggie looked at him gratefully, "I don't know how to thank you. Everything happened so fast."

John smiled at her. "No thanks necessary. I am simply happy you are not hurt, and I am deeply sorry that this happened to you. This is not THAT sort of town, but market days and a rapidly growing area seem to bring some of the riffraff in more often than we like. I contacted the guard posted on the outskirts of town, and they are out looking for the men now. They will want to talk to you as soon as you are up to it... I failed to get your name."

"Oh, it's Bishop, Maggie Bishop. I'm new here."

"A pleasure to meet you. Would you like me to send for your husband?"

"Well, that would be interesting," Maggie's tone was sharper than she liked; she was growing weary of saying it, "I'm a widow. It's just me."

"My condolences, Mistress."

Maggie nodded.

How many times had she heard THAT today?

"Wait, my horse," she said as she remembered Onyx.

"He's fine. I just got back from putting him in my stable. A fine animal you have there. You two made quite a team giving those two miscreants what for."

James looked at his brother with an inquisitive look.

"I'll tell you later," John said to his brother, glancing over at Maggie.

Maggie looked at John, a nagging urge to explain bubbling, since she was, at least attempting, to keep a low profile.

"My father wanted to make sure that his only daughter could defend herself. He...hired...a teacher..." thinking and making it up as she went, "that specialized in... teaching young women how...to... protect themselves...from unwanted advances. He was a very proficient instructor and my horse...well...he is extremely protective of me."

Whew! She hoped they believed her.

She had no other answer to offer, and it wasn't entirely a lie.

John looked at her. "That must have been some tutor. I'd say your father got his money's worth, in choices of teachers and horses."

Maggie breathed a sigh of relief and smiled. She would have to be incredibly careful how she acted and with what she said. This was a time when witches were still hunted, and any modern, independent woman would be considered just that.

A door opened, and John turned to see who it was. He disappeared a moment and reappeared with a British soldier. "This is Captain Horace. Captain, this is Mistress Bishop."

The Captain removed his hat and bowed his head to her. "Begging your pardon Mistress, I just wanted to see to your well-being, and to let you know that my men are searching tirelessly for the scoundrels that attacked you earlier. We will not rest until they are brought to justice. I want to personally apologize to you for this incident. A lady being attacked on the streets of our fine city is reprehensible and inexcusable. I hope you were not terribly injured."

Be a proper colonial lady Maggie.

"Thank you, Captain, for your concern. I am fine, and I have no doubt that you and your men will locate them." Maggie smiled at him. She had a feeling that smiling was the way to go, getting in or out of any situation for a woman in the 18th century.

"Mistress Bishop," the Captain said, "after what happened and seeing that these men are still at large, I will not rest until you are home safely this evening. Please allow me, and some of my men, to escort you home."

"Thank you, Captain, but I have just purchased a place nine miles outside of town, and I would not want to trouble you."

"I really must insist, Mistress Bishop," replied the Captain. "My conscience will not allow me to sleep tonight if I do not."

"In that case, Captain, thank you. I shall be ready to leave shortly."

"Very good! I will wait outside." The Captain tipped his hat. "Gentlemen, good day."

Maggie stepped outside the door of the doctor's office only to realize that it was a mercantile as well.

"You have a shop?" she turned and asked.

"Actually, the store part is mine," answered John, "the doctor's office and apothecary belong to him," pointing at his brother. "We just opened a few days ago. You are lucky, or unlucky enough, to be one of his first patients."

John and James both broke into huge grins. There was no doubting these two were brothers, judging by how much alike they were— same hair color, build, even sharing those boyish smiles. Age seemed the only thing that separated them.

Maggie looked around. She thought she had found a little piece of Heaven in 1765.

Candy! They had candy.

She walked around like, well, a kid in a candy store. Picking out several types to try—knowing it wouldn't be like 2018—but she thought it was better than nothing. She wandered around, finding so many other things, like soap, tooth cleaning powder, and even a primitive toothbrush. She was amazed by the sheer number of items packed in this tiny place. After filling up the counter, she paid one brother while the other bundled everything up. They seemed incredibly pleased with the sale.

As she prepared to leave, she looked at both of them. "Well, you have a fine establishment here. As soon as I get my house set up, I will be back for more. Thank you again for all your assistance. I am in your debt."

Both brothers bowed their heads to her. John started towards the door and said, "I'll get your horse for you. By the way, you said you just bought a place. Which place is that?"

Maggie had stuffed a piece of candy in her mouth, "Oh, a place called... 'Beechcroft'."

John and James exchanged grave looks but said nothing.

John went out the door and Maggie looked at the doctor, who seemed more than a little concerned. Before she could ask him why, several customers came in. Not wanting to bring it up in front of anyone else, she smiled, waved 'goodbye', and left.

Yep, if the looks of concern she had been getting all day were any indication, she had, without a doubt, bought the biggest shithole of a house in the worst possible part of Williamsburg.

Captain Horace and three of his men escorted Maggie out of town. They made small talk, while sharing candy along the way. Captain Horace and most of the men in his command had arrived in Williamsburg only a month before and were still getting accustomed to the ways of the Colonies. They had an encampment set up on the edge of town to help protect it since the area was growing so fast. His regiment had been stationed there because a few other people had been attacked and robbed in the same manner that Maggie had.

He asked Maggie questions, and she answered as vaguely as possible.

Once she got somewhere quiet and collected her thoughts, she was going to have to come up with a more solid backstory and hope to God that no one decided to investigate it too closely. She told the Captain that she had purchased the house and land unseen, and that she was more than a little nervous about what she had gotten herself into.

He assured her that even if the house was basically unlivable, that she had still gotten a great deal. The land alone was worth what she had paid and that made her feel a little better. He was a very personable, friendly young man and she appreciated his attempt to reassure her. She was even more grateful for his company. If her newly acquired house was unsafe and she had to camp under the stars, she would at least have someone to assist her on the first night.

After what seemed like an eternity on the road, the small group reached a sign on the road that indicated the 'Beechcroft' home was at the end of a row of trees.

Maggie took a deep breath and looked at the Captain. "Moment of truth." She started down the tree-lined path with Captain Horace right on her heels.

Halfway down the entrance path, something drew Maggie's attention to the side yard. It was well maintained with a large oak tree in the center, lovely, and yet, troubling at the same time.

Maggie had times in her life, when she had been in places where she picked up on different energies and could tell if spirits were sometimes around. She never actually saw one but could always FEEL if there was one around. It never bothered her, or scared her, just made her a little sad that they were Earthbound.

But in this place, and in this yard, something was different and, whatever it was, terrified her.

When she reached the house, she slipped out of the saddle, gave Onyx a rub, and stood in front of her new abode. Maggie was completely and utterly dumbfounded by what she saw.

Captain Horace followed suit, standing by Maggie's side, equally astounded.

They both stared without saying a word, then turned to look at each other and back at the house again.

Captain Horace was the first to break the silence by saying, "Well Mistress Bishop, I would say you did very well for your ten pieces of gold."

Maggie nodded, still in too much disbelief to speak.

The house was BEAUTIFUL!

It stood two stories —a red brick home bigger than anything in Williamsburg. The front steps led up to a portico with white Corinthian columns reaching to the roofline where, at the top, was a large triangle-shaped piece of stained glass in the cupola. Glass windows extended the full length, top to bottom of each story, big enough for two people to walk through. Shutters flanked each window and could be closed in the event of a storm; large house wings extended from both sides of the main building.

The front entrance was flanked with smaller columns; the door itself was about five-foot wide, containing a carved ivory inlaid piece with a lovely scene depicting heavenly angels standing guard over human charges. It also sported a large ornate brass doorknob and a 'lion-head' knocker, along with a small sign just to the side that read "Beechcroft".

This wasn't just a house, it was a mansion, and quite an advanced one for colonial Virginia.

Captain Horace looked back at Maggie. "I hope you have a key."

"Oh, yes!" Maggie, still in complete astonishment that this now belonged to her, fished through her pocket, feeling very relieved that her attackers had not gotten it. She held it up.

"Allow me," said Captain Horace. He took the key from her, turned it in the lock, and pushed the door open. He looked to the other men and instructed them to check around the house to ensure it was secure.

Maggie stepped inside while he was speaking to them, getting her first look.

Two steps down, into the foyer, revealed an open layout, extremely unusual for that time period. The floor was covered with white marble for as far as she could see. Straight ahead was an enormous fireplace that took up most of the wall — so large, in fact, Maggie could have easily stood up in it without bending over. Beside the fireplace, on the wall, were portraits that had been draped.

To the left was a grand, sweeping staircase that curved in a 'c' shape upward and led to a balcony on the second floor that overlooked the open area below. The only furniture she could see was a large round table in the center covered by a white sheet.

The whole scene was breathtaking.

Maggie stood there, absorbed in every single detail. She didn't even hear the Captain come in. He was suddenly beside her staring wide-eyed at the sight right along with her.

After a few moments, he looked at Maggie. "Mistress Bishop, I think it's best if I check the house to make sure there are no squatters here."

She nodded, and he headed up the staircase.

Maggie made her way towards the fireplace, veering to the right to discover another exceptionally large room that appeared to be a drawing room.

Everything in there was covered as well. It contained another large fireplace against the far wall, and to the left were glass doors that led out into a formal garden with a lovely sitting area that she could make out from the window.

Going back into the foyer, she noticed a door to the left side of the fireplace. Upon investigation, she found it opened to a fully stocked library, complete with reading chairs and tables. Directly under the staircase was the entrance to the formal dining room, with the kitchen just beyond that. The dining room contained a table that accommodated twelve chairs, with some extra seats against the wall, and three serving buffets, all covered.

Maggie heard the Captain coming down the stairs and greeted him at the bottom.

"Mistress Bishop, I checked the rest of the house, and everything is secure."

"Thank you, Captain. How many rooms are up there anyway?"

"Six large bedrooms, ma'am, and a third-floor attic. I checked everywhere, and it's all clear — everything appears to have been locked up tight."

Maggie scratched her head. "Captain?"

"Yes, Mistress?"

"Why would anyone sell this amazing house, fully furnished with five hundred acres, for a measly ten pieces of gold? For goodness sakes, it looks like they just walked away one day and never came back."

Captain Horace gave her a strange, troubling look as he replied, "Ma'am, I have NO idea."

They both jumped a bit— startled — when the front door suddenly opened. The Captain's men came in and assured them that the house was secure from the outside as well.

He thanked them, told them to wait with the horses, and turned to Maggie. "Mistress, it will be nightfall soon, and I'm afraid that I must get back to the encampment, as I am expected back in the morning for a meeting. I can leave one of my men behind tonight if that would make you feel better."

"That won't be necessary, Captain. I will be perfectly fine here, and I have inconvenienced you and your men enough for the day. Besides, this is my home now, and I must get used to it. I can't thank you enough for all your help."

Captain Horace regarded her, trying to decide if leaving her alone was a good idea, but the resolution on her face told him that insisting was pointless. "Very well, Mistress, but I will send someone to check on you in a few days, just to make sure you are well. We will get your horse settled for the night and then, be on our way."

They walked outside; the other men were already getting hay and water for Onyx and their own horses. The stables were just behind the house, and even they were magnificent — clean, well-maintained, and fully stocked— with a rather large fenced area for the horses to stretch their legs at their leisure.

Onyx seemed pleased, and that was good enough for her.

After bidding the soldiers farewell and wishing Onyx a ‘good night’, Maggie went back inside her new home. It would be dark soon, so she needed to take advantage of the daylight while she still could. The house had plenty of candles, but she had no way to light them. Darn! She should have gotten the Captain to start a small fire for her before he left.

Oh well, that was tomorrow’s problem. It had been an extremely long day, and Maggie needed rest more than anything. After all, it wasn’t every day that you bought a mansion in the 18th century, got attacked by muggers on the street, and managed to snag a military escort home.

She looked around the house.

Why in the world would anyone desert a place like this?

It had to have been someone’s dream home, and it seemed, they had just disappeared into thin air. Hindsight being 20/20, the attorney WAS in a God-awful hurry to sell this place and based on the remarks made by the people at the sale, he had been trying to get rid of it for a while. Then, there were all the warnings from the good citizens of Williamsburg that caused Maggie to shiver just a little. Captain Horace didn’t mention anything, but, of course, he hadn’t been here very long. He wouldn’t have known what may have happened before he came.

What have you gotten yourself into Maggie?

She made her way into the drawing room. Pulling sheets off the furniture, she found a nice couch and loveseat, a coffee table, end tables, and a buffet bar set, complete with empty glass alcohol containers. Around the fireplace were four large, overstuffed leather chairs, surrounding a sizeable round footstool that was far-reaching enough for all to prop up their feet at once. In the corner to the left, there was a desk, stocked with ink bottles, pens, and paper. The mantel held a tobacco pipe on a stand beside a couple of very nicely bound books, candelabras flanking each side.

Two of the large windows at the front of the house were in this room, heavy red drapes hanging on each side.

Maggie looked outside. It was almost dark. Her mind flash to every teeny bopper horror movie she had ever seen, and she pulled the drapes closed, so if someone or something looked in, she wouldn't see it. She made her way to the couch, taking off her shoes before lying down. Asleep in minutes, she found herself having the strangest dreams of falling through time, peculiar faces in windows, and of the attack from earlier that day.

The dream of the assault was what startled her awake the next morning— an older, rather robust, African American woman standing over her while jabbing her with a fireplace poker.

6.

CHAPTER SIX

"Hey, hey, what are you doing lady? Get that thing away from me!" Maggie pushed the piece of iron aside.

The lady narrowed her eyes and demanded, "Who is you and why you in this house?"

Maggie tried to sit up, but the woman pushed her back down with the poker, planting it in her chest.

Maggie raised her hands, more annoyed than anything and said, "My name is Maggie Bishop, and I am the new owner. Just who do you think YOU are?"

The lady lowered the stick. "My name is Hettie. I am the house help here."

"Oh! Hettie," Maggie was a little less annoyed and a little grateful to see someone else, "it is nice to meet you, I think. I didn't know anyone else was here. The attorney didn't mention you."

"I expect there was a whole lot that Shipman fellow didn't mention. He's a slimy little weasel, that one is," Hettie said, shaking her head. Hettie looked at her suspiciously. "You bought THIS place? Why in the world would you do something like that? Or did your husband buy it?"

"I have no husband; I am a widow."

"OH! So why did YOU buy this place?"

"I needed a place to live, and I got a fair price on it. I am more than pleased with the house. For what I paid, I wasn't expecting anything this grand."

Hettie looked at her matter-of-factly and sighed. "That's because nobody else will come within twenty miles of this place after what happened to the previous owners."

Maggie lowered her head as she asked the one question she was quite sure she didn't want the answer to.

"What exactly happened to the previous owners?"

Hettie looked Maggie straight in the eye and said, "They was murdered."

"Murdered?" It took Maggie a minute to comprehend. "What do you mean, they were murdered?"

Hettie sat down on the end of the couch. "Well, about six months ago was when it happened. You see, Mr. and Mrs. Rawlings, they lived here with their only son and Mr. Rawlings' only brother. Mrs. Rawlings was an orphan, so she had no family and the rest of Mr. Rawlings' other family had all passed on. The Rawlings, well, they weren't what you would call good people. Mr. Rawlings was a businessman that stole people's money and land every chance he got and then he'd laugh about it. He'd just as soon step on someone as help them up if they fell on the street. And Mrs. Rawlings, that woman was just downright mean. She would beat her slaves just for her own amusement. She just seemed to like it too much, and her son, well, he was the same way. He took a liking to some of the young girls here, and he did what he wanted to do to them. Mr. Rawlings' brother, he liked to watch what the rest of the family did. He would get to drinking and give ideas to the other two on how to be ugly to people. That whole lot belonged to the devil himself if you ask me.

"One night, all four of them got together, drinking, carrying on and such, and they decided to go down to the slave quarters, up to no good. That's the night people started to disappear and were never heard from again. It happened twice more before the folks they owned decided enough was enough, and that they was going to take matters into their own hands. So, one night, a bunch of the menfolk from down at the slave quarters broke in the back door of the house here, dragged all of them out of bed, out onto the lawn out there and murdered them. Some travelers headed into town were camping on the main road up there that night and saw what happened.

"The next day, they came back with the authorities. By then, most of the slaves had run off for fear of being hanged. When the people from the town were investigating what happened, they came in the house and found the diary of Mrs. Rawlings. That woman, she had wrote down everything they did. Horrible things! I watched one of the men who was reading it have to stop to go outside to empty his stomach. After finding all that out, they decided it was best not to pursue the ones who murdered them and just leave them be, so the townsfolk took the family over somewhere, they never said where, and buried them all in unmarked graves. That family lawyer, Shipman, has been trying to sell this place ever since, but no one within a hundred miles would have anything to do with it 'cause they all think it's cursed. Nobody in town talks about it. They don't want that kind of stain on their perfect little place."

Maggie sat there dumbfounded. She didn't know how to feel about what she just heard. Leave it to her to find the one plantation that belonged to the Williamsburg 'psycho family of 1765'.

Her heart ached for all those poor souls they had mistreated and the life that they were forced to live. History tended to gloss over the darker parts of everyday life. The fact that she had been attacked, and purchased a 'murder' house, all in the same day, was proof of that. No wonder she had a bad feeling about that side lawn on the way in. Who wouldn't?

Maggie looked over at Hettie. "Hettie, why did you stay? No one would have faulted you for leaving."

"Oh, Mistress, where would I go? This place is my home. I have been here for thirty years. I ain't got no money, and nowhere else to be."

"Aren't you afraid to stay here?" Maggie asked.

"Oh, no ma'am. I'm a God-fearing woman, and I ain't afraid of nothing, 'cause I know the good Lord is looking out for me and he's stronger than anything on this land."

Maggie smiled. She admired Hettie's faith.

"Well Hettie, I sunk a good chunk of money into this place, so I am not going anywhere, either. I would be honored if you would stay on and work for me, at a fair price of course."

Hettie looked at her with a deep frown and scratched her head. “I ain’t got no money to pay you to stay on here.”

Maggie laughed. “No Hettie! I would pay YOU to work for me.”

“Pay me? I ain’t never been paid before.”

“Never?”

“No, ma’am, never in money, just in food and with a roof over my head.”

“Well, Hettie, your life is about to change...for the better.”

Hettie smiled. She liked the idea of that. She knew the good Lord looked after her and must have sent Mistress Maggie Bishop to her for a reason.

Maggie’s mind drifted to the thought of the poor people enslaved at this time, simply because of the color of their skin. They were victims, merely of circumstance, and of the time they were born into. A sudden thought came to Maggie. While she couldn’t change the world, she could change the lives of the people around her, and she could make a difference to them. A grand idea took shape in her mind and she grinned.

“You hungry, Mistress?” Hettie interrupted her train of thought.

“Please, call me Maggie.”

Hettie thought for a minute. “Well, that wouldn’t be rightly proper.”

Maggie looked at her and sighed. She needed to trust someone, and Maggie couldn’t think of a better person than this warm, gentle soul in front of her.

"Confession time Hettie, I am not exactly what you would call a 'proper woman'...I mean, I am not really sure how to act like a lady should. I...um...grew up away from town and didn't learn everything a young lady of standing should have. I was hoping maybe...if you would... do you think... you could help me out with some of this stuff? I mean, you have been here a long time and you have seen how wealthy people act, and you would have learned a thing or two from watching them."

Hettie looked at Maggie, thought for a moment, and replied, "Well, I reckon I could help you out some."

Maggie felt an enormous amount of relief. "Okay then, Hettie, how about this? You call me Mistress when we have company, but when it's just you and me, you call me Maggie."

Hettie smiled. "I think I could do that. Yeah...I like that idea." The woman's face lit up. "Now, come on, let's get you some breakfast. I have got some pay to earn."

Maggie watched Hettie rattle around the kitchen.

"We are running a little low on things around here. After, well, what happened, there won't no money for the usual things in the kitchen. No one would come near this place, so we have kind of been on our own out here. We have been living off things from the garden, eggs from the chickens and milk from the cows. I have been stretching out the other stuff. I hope this bread I made yesterday is alright for you to eat."

Maggie took a seat and put her hand up to her chin with her elbow on the table. "Whatever you have is fine Hettie, and I stopped at Mr. Holt's store yesterday. He is delivering a bunch of supplies today. He said I would be needing a great many things. I thought it was because the place was in such bad shape, but I see now, it was because this place is so enormous."

Hettie looked relieved. "Thank the Lord! Things were getting mighty thin. I wasn't sure how we were gonna make it through the winter."

As she cooked, Hettie looked around. "Yeah, this, sure enough, is a fine house, one of the finest in town or anywhere from what I hear. Mr. Rawlings, he had things brought in from all over the place for it. Had men working on it 'round the clock for three years to get it done. Said he wanted everyone to know how wealthy he was and didn't want them to ever forget it or him. Kind of funny, now he is laying in an unmarked grave and everyone is doing their best TO forget him."

Maggie looked over at Hettie and frowned. "Hettie, how were Mr. Rawlings and his family to you?"

"Oh, they were alright to me. Mostly because I took care of that boy of theirs, and if something happened to me, they would have had to do it themselves. That child, he was a bad seed from the day he come into this world, screaming bloody murder, covered in blood and with the blackest eyes I ever seen. Should have known how that one would turn out. Besides, wouldn't nobody else step foot in this house no way...everyone said something evil was on this land, that it was cursed 'cause Mr. Rawlings ran the Indians off it."

"He ran them off?"

"Oh yes, they lived on near twenty acres on the edge of the property line, but he pushed them down into a small area out by the creek. Him, his brother and son, they would harass them, shoot at them and do awful things to their women if they caught them out alone. The townsfolk just looked the other way 'cause they was afraid of what might get done to them. He terrorized that town as much as he did the people on his property."

"Oh my God! That's horrible. What happened to them— the Native Amer —I mean, Indians?"

"Well, they still here, just on a couple acres on the west side edge of the property."

Maggie had never wished anyone dead, but she thought this world was much better off without the Rawlings family in it.

Hettie put a plate in front of her and waited for Maggie to eat.

She took a bite and said, "This is wonderful. Thank you, Hettie."

Hettie looked pleased. "You're welcome Mistr...I mean Maggie."

Maggie suddenly remembered something Hettie said.

"Hettie, you said 'we' had been living off what was here? How many people are left?"

"Well, there's only five of us and the two children. Near on fifty or sixty people ran off after what happened. There's me, and Harm—he took care of the horses and he took care of yours this morning by the way. There's Abel, who has been tending the garden. He looked after the crops before things went bad. Joshua and Cecile are still here and their boys Thomas, who is about twelve, and the baby, Abraham. She was too far along with child when everyone ran off to leave. They have been tending some of the other animals and helping me."

That was five adults and two children Maggie now had to look out for. A minor panic attack was headed off when she heard a banging at the front door.

She and Hettie got up and went off towards the sound.

Maggie opened it to look out and see a wagon, being pulled by a horse and rider at full gallop, engulfed in a dust storm of their own making, moving away from the house at lightning speed. The front landing was filled with all the supplies she had purchased from Mr. Holt.

"Thank you?" Maggie called out to the far-gone rider, raising her hand in a weak wave. She had no idea she had gotten that much stuff.

Hettie eyed all the supplies like it was Christmas morning. "Looks like we are eating good today," she said happily.

Just then, a tall, slender, older man came around the corner, looking towards the fleeing delivery driver. When he saw Maggie, he took off his hat and bowed his head.

"Come on up here, Harm, and meet the new owner, Mistress Bishop."

Harm hesitated.

"It's all right, Harm," Maggie said gently, "It's nice to meet you."

He peered up at her, unsure of what to expect.

"Harm, I understand you took care of my horse for me this morning. I am grateful to you for that. Thank you."

"You ain't gotta thank me, ma'am."

Maggie looked at this poor man who had obviously been traumatized by the previous owners. She stepped around the supplies and down the steps, coming face to face with him. "Harm, I know the Rawlings weren't particularly good people, but you have my word, you will have a better life here with me if you want it. No one will hurt you, as long as I am living and breathing, and I won't force anyone to stay here who doesn't want to be here. I promise you that."

He glanced over at Maggie with a look of disbelief on his face, not knowing what to say or think. He wanted to think that she meant what she said, but he had been lied to before, so only time would tell if that were true, but he had a strange feeling that this lady was somehow different.

Maggie turned back to Hettie. "Hettie, do you think we can get everyone left here together for supper tonight in the dining room, I mean, if you have time to get a meal together?"

Hettie looked around with her hands on her hips and a broad grin on her face. "Sure, I can, Maggie. With all of this, we gonna eat like kings."

Maggie decided it was time to get to know her new home. She had not been upstairs yet, so while Hettie was busy in the kitchen, she decided to look around. The floor-to-ceiling windows let in a glorious amount of light throughout the whole house. She started up the stairs, made of the same marble as the floor below. At the top of the staircase, the first door was to the left. Inside was the master bedroom, an enormous room with a lovely four-poster bed, draped with heavy red fabric curtains on a rod that could be pulled closed. There was a second rod on the inside that had mosquito netting attached to it to keep out the bugs and let in the air. A little step stool led up to the bed; nightstand tables were on either side of it, along with a wooden chest at the footboard. The mattress was extremely soft for the 18th century.

Maggie saw why when she pushed down on it and a small goose feather popped out—the entire mattress was stuffed to the brim with them.

On the other side of the room was a nice-sized fireplace, with two leather chairs like the ones that were downstairs, and a small, rose-colored settee, with a small round table in front of it, was against the wall. A wardrobe was in the corner, full of the previous owner's clothing. She would make sure all of that was disposed of.

While she had no problem using the furniture and household items, mostly out of necessity, Maggie would not have the personal effects of those horrid people anywhere near where she slept.

The windows had heavy red curtains pulled to the side, letting in streams of sunlight, and another set of drapes revealed two glass double doors. They opened out onto a balcony with a breathtaking, scenic view of the property, and Maggie was pleased to see that it overlooked the stable that housed Onyx.

The fence around the stable looked to be a good size, and Onyx was taking advantage of it to run around in a circle, kicking up his heels, neighing. She made a mental note to have it enlarged, never wanting Onyx to feel boxed in. He was a free spirit and she wanted him to stay that way.

Maggie looked back around the room. These people may have been psychotic, but she had to admit, they had great taste. It was then that she noticed a small door in the corner beside the fireplace; she had an uneasy feeling about what was behind it.

"Please don't be full of dead bodies, please don't be full of dead bodies," she kept repeating, turning the door handle and pushing it open.

Peeking around the corner, waiting for something to jump out at her, Maggie couldn't believe what it held — a big, beautiful copper bathtub. She stood there staring at it in disbelief.

"There is a God!" she shouted aloud with her hands in the air above her head.

The fireplace in the bedroom, she now noticed, was open on the backside as well, to heat the room with the bathtub. She circled around the tub, touching it to make sure it was real. It was on casters, allowing it to be moved. A full-sized, draped window was on the opposite wall and a small table held a pitcher and basin for hand washing.

"Hello, you beautiful thing you," she said as she caressed it lovingly. She had never been so happy to see a bathtub in her entire life.

It really was the little things that meant the most.

Maggie noticed another door against the wall. "So THAT must be where the dead bodies are."

She walked over and made a face. "Let's see what's behind door number two," she muttered while pushing it open slowly, with extreme caution.

"OH...MY...GOD!" Maggie exclaimed.

Her jaw dropped. It was a real, honest to goodness, working toilet — a primitive one— but she had indoor plumbing, just the same. She examined it a little closer. It was actually what was referred to as a 'water closet', like the ones she had seen in books. She knew they had existed in Europe for a long while, but she had never heard of one mentioned in colonial America, at least not for a few more years.

There was a marble 'seat' with a basin underneath that had a hole in the bottom. A trough was hooked from the back of the basin up to a storage tank behind it. There was a pin you pulled out to let the water drain down to 'flush' and then you pushed it closed when everything was gone. The pin was also attached to a rod that went down and held another pin that sealed off the hole the waste went into after the 'flush' to keep the smell from wafting back up. Dried herbs were in a bowl on the floor next to it.

"Early air freshener maybe?" Maggie chuckled.

But this water closet was ingenious. Nothing but the best for good ole crazy-man Rawlings. He must have sent for supplies from all over the world for this house — and Maggie was glad for it.

Maggie explored the rest of the upstairs enthusiastically.

There were five more bedrooms, a little smaller, but very well furnished, and a similar, central bathroom for the rest of the bedrooms against the back wall of the second floor. There was an attic above, on a third level, with some trunks, pieces of furniture, a few other items, and plenty of dust, but Maggie decided to save going through all of that for another time.

She stood on the balcony overlooking the downstairs. If she had to be thrown back in time, she was glad it was with a few luxuries, even if the previous owners of them were insane nutjobs.

Maggie spent the rest of the day going through drawers and closets, cleaning out the personal effects of the Rawlings', mainly clothing. She wanted none of them and figured no one else would either, at least not right now. Anything of value, like jewelry and weapons, were already gone, probably taken by fleeing slaves or that lawyer Shipman.

Just as well, it was that much less to deal with. She piled it all up and moved it up into the attic. Maggie knew what the future held and in a few short years, the war would be upon them. There would be people who would need those items and many, many more. She was fortunate enough to have notice of what was to come — others were not — Maggie decided that she would make the most of that time to be as prepared as possible.

Hettie was singing hymns in the kitchen as she cooked.

Maggie stuck her head in to see if she needed any help and was promptly shooed out. Grabbing an apple off the table, she headed out to see Onyx.

Onyx greeted her with a nuzzle, only to slip his head down and snag the apple.

Maggie laughed. "Oh, I see how it is. You only love me for my apples." He happily munched away.

She noticed that his saddle had been put up and he had fresh hay and water.

"That's a fine horse you have there, Mistress Bishop. What should I call him?" Harm asked softly.

Maggie hadn't heard him walk up. "His name is Onyx and, yes, he is. He's a good horse and my best friend. I don't know what I would do without him." She rubbed Onyx's ears.

"Where did you get him from, if you don't mind me asking?" Harm walked up next to her, putting his arms along the top rung of the fence.

"Actually, he found me. I was completely lost, and he just kind of showed up."

Harm looked surprised. "Just out of nowhere?"

Maggie hadn't really given it much thought until that moment, but in hindsight, it did seem a little out of the ordinary. "Well, yes, I guess he did show up out of nowhere."

Harm looked over at Onyx, who appeared to be smiling back at him. "He doesn't act like most horses, does he?"

Maggie giggled. "No, I suppose he doesn't. How many horses were here, Harm?"

Harm looked over at the stable. "There used to be ten, but they are all gone now. A couple was taken by people who ran away and the rest, well, they just ran off after…well, they just ran off."

"I know what happened to the Rawlings family, and it's alright. You can speak freely around me."

Harm hesitated a moment before he spoke, lost in thought. "That night, the horses, it's like they knew something was gonna happen. They were rearing up, kicking at the stables, and crying to get out. I tried to calm them down, but they wouldn't settle down for nothing. I have been around horses my whole life, and I ain't never seen anything like it."

"You like working with horses, Harm?"

His eyes lit up and he smiled. "Oh yes ma'am! I love them! They are a whole lot nicer than most people."

"I suppose they are. How would you feel about taking care of them— just taking care of them, nothing else and getting paid for it?"

Harm frowned. "Whatcha mean?"

"Well, we will talk about it more tonight, but I am going to need someone to take care of the stables and Onyx, and I guess, I will need to get some more horses."

Onyx looked up with wide eyes in protest.

"Oh, relax Onyx, you will always be my number one horse."

Onyx huffed back in response.

"I guess a place this big will need horses to get things done, and you seem like you would be good at it. I will pay you, of course."

"You gonna pay me to just take care of horses?" he asked incredulously.

"Well, yes, if you think you would like that."

Harm looked around. "I think I'd like that very much."

Maggie was pleased. "Good, now how about you show me around out here."

Harm gave Maggie the grand tour.

The stable was more massive than she had noticed. There were twelve good-sized stalls, all well-maintained and open to the fenced pasture. There was a tack room full of saddles, bridles, and blankets. Outside was a large fire pit with a shade shelter for horseshoeing.

Maggie noticed a separate building off to the side that she hadn't seen from her balcony and was delighted to see that it was a carriage house with three stalls. One contained a supply wagon, the next a small riding carriage for two, and the biggest stall contained a beautiful, grand carriage lined on the inside with the finest and plushest of fabrics. It also had several lanterns hanging around on each side for evening travel and was big enough for six people. She could not believe her luck. She had hit the jackpot, for someone who had been thrown back in time over two-hundred years, anyway.

They walked and chatted, as Harm told her all about the property, what was grown there, how many people had been here and giving her the lay of the land.

Coming around a bend to inspect a grove of fruit trees, Maggie noticed some ramshackle structures on the edge of the woods. "What's that?"

"Oh, those are our houses."

Maggie rounded the corner and what she saw made her heart drop.

Twenty-five to thirty, of what could only be referred to as shacks, in various states of disrepair, squatted in a circle on a ridiculously small area of the land. They were all tiny and built within just a few inches of each other. Roofs had caved in, walls had holes in them big enough for animals to crawl through, and the stench was overwhelming. Chickens and little baby pigs roamed free. Maggie felt sick to her stomach.

"You live here?"

"Yes ma'am, the ones of us still here do. Things really started to fall down after folks left, so the ones of us who stayed took over the better houses."

Maggie was disgusted and appalled that the Rawlings family lived in such opulence on the hill, while the people who did all the work lived in such squalor and filth. She turned and looked at Harm, choked up with tears in her eyes.

"Harm, you won't have to live like this anymore. I will make sure of it. No human being should ever have to live like this."

Upset and infuriated, unable to speak anymore, Maggie angrily traipsed back to the house, leaving Harm to watch her go.

7

CHAPTER SEVEN

Maggie stomped back into the house, straight into the drawing room, closing the pocket doors behind her. She went over to the desk and slammed her fists down hard on it. How dare they?

How DARE they live like this when those poor people were living the way they were?

Hettie had removed all the sheets from the furniture and straightened up. Maggie's gaze fell upon the glass decanters on the buffet that had been refilled. She made her way over to it, poured herself a glass and drank it down in one gulp.

Rum! It was the rum she had purchased from Mr. Holt.

She poured herself another glass and had a sudden thought. She went back to the desk, managing to locate paper, a feather quill and some ink. She started to write, putting her plans into words. She WOULD make things right, at least in HER little neck of the woods.

Leaning back when she was done, Maggie had seven pieces of paper in front of her, a cramped hand, and a pleased look on her face. She got up, poured herself another glass, and walked out into the garden.

The flowers were a little unkempt, but beautiful, nonetheless. A little brick path meandered through the courtyard filled with boxwoods, rose bushes, black-eyed susans, hollyhocks, foxglove, and several other types of flowers and herbs. The path led past several secluded spots, with benches, for privacy. It ended at an open gate that led out onto the lawn.

Maggie walked through it and ended up in the side yard. She looked toward the spot where the Rawlings family had been murdered.

Hatred surged from deep within her.

Still repulsed from her earlier tour of the slave quarters, she lifted her glass in a toast in the direction of the 'murder spot' and bellowed angrily to the empty lawn, "Here's a big 'FUCK YOU' to the Rawlings family. I will do my damnedest to make sure that you are rolling over in your graves when you see how good the people you treated like shit on this land will be treated from now on. Buckle up buttercups, it's gonna be one hell of a ride, and I hope you have a good front seat with the devil for the show." She downed the glass of rum.

A gust of hot wind from the yard blew straight up, swirling debris and wrapping around Maggie, as if the dead were voicing their anger. Maggie closed her eyes and stood firm until the dust storm had settled down, but the storm inside her would not calm that easily.

When she opened her eyes, she spoke calmly and firmly, "This place belongs to me now, and there is no place for you or your hatred anymore. Go back to Hell where you belong."

Silence.

Maggie turned and went back inside HER house, leaving the dead to their own damnable fates.

In the dining room, the table overflowed with plates of wonderful smelling foods. Hettie was right, they were eating like kings tonight. The cook came through the door with a large plate of carved meat.

"You did all of this Hettie?"

"Yes, ma'am. I love to cook, especially when I have so many ingredients to work with," she said with a wink and a smile.

Maggie was amazed at all this woman could do. "Everything looks and smells delicious. Will the others be here soon?"

"They should be coming along any time now." On cue, the doorway filled.

Harm was the first to arrive.

"Come in, come in, and sit down," Maggie said.

Harm didn't have to be told twice; Maggie could hear his stomach growling from where she stood.

Another slim, lanky man peeped around the door, unsure if he should enter or not.

Hettie broke the awkwardness.

"Come on in Abel, and meet Mistress Bishop, the new owner."

He looked down shyly, hunching over, clasping his hat with both hands, obviously afraid. "Hello ma'am."

Maggie walked over and touched him on the shoulder, causing him to jump like a wounded animal.

"Don't be afraid of me, Abel. I won't hurt you, not ever. It's nice to meet you."

He nodded, his head still down.

"I understand you have been taking care of the vegetable garden, Abel. You have done a marvelous job. Thank you."

"Go sit next to Harm," Hettie instructed Abel and he readily obeyed.

Maggie heard voices whispering outside the room. She met a little boy at the doorway.

He was skinny as a rail, far thinner than any child his age should ever be, with the biggest, brownest eyes she had ever seen.

Maggie's heart melted. "You must be young Thomas. He nodded his head.

"My name is Maggie, and I am very pleased that you are here. Hettie has told me all about you."

His smile was a bashful curve of his lips.

Maggie reached in her pocket and pulled out something, handing it to him. "Go on, take it. It's candy." She popped a piece in her mouth to show him.

He looked at it, unsure if he should try it, slowly raised it to his mouth and put it in. The taste hit him, and a grin broke out on his face.

Maggie had just made a new friend.

A woman, carrying a little baby, and a man, came up behind him, placing his hands on the boy's shoulders. Thomas looked up at his father, still grinning.

"Joshua, Cecile and Abraham, I presume?" Maggie nodded to the pair.

"Yes ma'am," Joshua said softly.

"I am Mistress Bishop, the new owner, and you folks look hungry. Let's take care of that."

After everyone was seated, Maggie welcomed them all and invited them to eat. They all looked at each other unsurely, as if the food might be poisoned until Maggie started scooping some out of bowls, putting it on her own plate, and encouragingly passing it around.

They slowly followed her lead.

"I worked hard cooking up all this food, so ya'll better eat up," Hettie broke the silence and got things moving.

In a few short moments, they were all eating and thoroughly enjoying it. It was clear that no one at the table had eaten a decent meal in a good long while. Maggie took a great deal of joy in watching them fill their bellies. She made small talk about the weather and the farm, hoping to break the ice. A short time later, after a scrumptious cake that Hettie brought out at the end of the meal was served, they found themselves all happily stuffed.

Maggie cleared her throat. "I brought you all in for supper tonight because I wanted to talk to you."

The room fell silent.

"I know the previous owners were not good people, in fact, they were horrible people, and for that, I am sorry. I am nothing like them. I want a better life for you, and if you are willing to help me, I can help you. I want to make you all an offer that I hope you will accept. Please, just hear me out."

She started moving the plates out of the way. “If you can help me clear these dishes, I have something to show you.” They all pitched in and made some space.

Maggie spread the seven pieces of paper out on the table, placing one sheet in front of each person.

“What’s all this?” Hettie squinted at the page before her.

“These are your Freedom Papers.”

They all stared down at the paperwork in front of them even though they could not read them.

“If you want them, they are yours to take and leave any time you wish. All I ask is that you listen to my proposal first. But, before that, I need your word that what is said here tonight never leaves this room. It would be extremely dangerous for all of us.”

They all solemnly nodded in agreement.

Maggie nodded back. “Good! Now here’s what I have in mind.”

No one in the room made a sound, not even the baby, while Maggie laid out her idea...

“This place, this farm, can make a great deal of money, but I can’t very well run it all by myself. I need help to do it. I do not believe in owning people. Slavery is wrong, but unfortunately, a way of life here in the Colonies. I can’t change that, but I can change the way things are done on my own land. So, if you are willing to stay and help me, I can make life much better for each of you. First, these so-called houses that you are living in... you need better ones. Ones that aren’t falling apart. I am fairly sure I can get lumber and if everyone pitches in, we can build each of you a better house. I want each of them to be built on a three-acre lot that will be deeded to you.

You can do whatever you want with the land, grow your own food, farm things to sell, whatever you like, it will be all yours. I also cannot in good conscience let you work here for free, so if you choose to stay, you will receive a weekly wage. As long as I can make enough money to keep this place going, I will make sure you are taken care of and protected. You will be safe here. No one will beat you, or mistreat you, and I want you to feel free to talk to me, tell me how things really are, or if there is something that you need. I don't want anyone to be afraid here. But and this is the only way this will work, you cannot tell anyone about what we are doing here. If anybody finds out, they will run me out of town and sell all of you off to the highest bidder. I will do everything in my power to protect you, but I will need you to do the same in return."

When Maggie was done, she looked around the room, letting her gaze pause on each person in turn.

No one moved or spoke, but just sat there, solid as stone.

"Well, what do you think? Again, if anyone wants to leave, your papers are in front of you. You can take them, walk out that door, and no one will stop you."

Hettie was the first to speak.

"I ain't got nowhere else to go. This is my home and I plan on staying."

Maggie smiled at her.

After a few tense moments, Harm was next.

"I'm still gonna be your horseman, right?"

"Yes. You will handle all the horses and the stables," Maggie agreed.

"Well, it all sounds pretty good to me. I think I'm staying too." Harm grinned and touched a gentle finger to the corner of his paper wistfully.

Two down.

Abel was next.

"What would you have me doing?"

Maggie thought for a moment and said, "You have been taking care of the garden, right?"

"Yes, ma'am."

"Are you good at raising things, crops I mean? Would that be something you would like to do?"

"I know how to tend to stuff like that —what and what doesn't do well here on this land, and I do like watching things grow. I wouldn't mind doing that. If you don't mind terribly, I would like to take care of the gardens up by the house too. They look like they could use some work and I love watching flowers that bloom."

"Abel, I would be proud to have you take care of *all* of the flower gardens."

His weathered face lit up. "Well, I guess you got yourself a gardener then."

Everyone turned to look at Joshua and Cecile. Joshua still looked uncertain.

"If you have any questions, please ask me," Maggie said encouragingly.

"What would Cecile and I do, and what will my children have to do?"

Maggie shrugged. "Well, what would you like to do?"

Joshua looked at Cecile and back at Maggie, "Well, I don't know. No one ever asked me what I *wanted* to do before. I always just worked in the fields as I was told."

Cecile spoke up, "He likes to fix stuff, build things out of wood, like, furniture and toys, for the children."

Maggie looked back at him and smiled. "Do you want to be in charge of building things? You can help lay out and build the new houses and, I am sure, there will always be things that need fixing around here."

Joshua bobbed his head up and down. "Yeah, yeah, I think I'd like that," he said as the idea settled well with him.

Cecile looked over at Maggie and Hettie. "And I can help Hettie with the chores up here if she wants me to since all the other house help ran off. I can also sew right well, too."

Hettie readily agreed, "Yes, that would be really nice, and Cecile, she's a better dressmaker than any of those women with the shops in town."

"What about the children, Mistress?" Joshua asked as he took his wife's hand.

"Well, they would be— children— like they are supposed to be. They should not have to work like adults. They can play — and learn. They could go to school, get an education— learn how to read and write."

The room went quiet and everyone turned to gawk at Maggie.

"School? They could learn?" Cecile asked, her voice full of utter shock and disbelief.

"Why yes! We should be able to find a teacher for them and for the rest of you, that is, if you would like to learn."

They all looked around at each other, eyes wide.

Joshua went to answer, but Cecile beat him to it. "Yes ma'am! We will be more than happy to stay!"

That was it. Everyone was in. Maggie could not have been more pleased. She had a house, a plan, and a room full of people to help her.

They spent the rest of the evening planning for their future.

They decided which crops in the field were still harvestable, since the end of summer was coming up soon, what they needed to lay in for the fall, and what money producers needed to be added for next year.

Maggie had the advantage. She knew what the profitable cash crops were in Virginia and which ones would sustain them when wartime came. She made a list of things they needed from town to get things started. Her college business training kicked in and new ideas filled her head at a rapid rate. She also wanted to build things up, to keep them completely self-sufficient in the years to come.

Being nine miles from town would play to their advantage when the revolution hit. Maggie had already decided that she would do her best to stay out of the war. After all, her merely being here may have already changed the future in ways she could never imagine. One little shift could erase the future she knew, and she did not want to take any chances.

Yes! She decided her main goal would be to keep her head down and to make sure the people she was responsible for were out of harm's way. The rest of history would have to take care of itself.

The evening ended on a cheerful, optimistic note. It had been a good day, especially given how it had begun.

That night, Maggie would move into the master suite, so long as the bedclothes had been changed given the previous owner's hasty expiration and their less than desirable karma.

Hettie assured her that they had.

She took a bottle of rum and a lit candle up to her new room. Everything was coming together perfectly except for one thing. She needed more help for the farm and had no idea where to get it. She could hire some men from town, but she wouldn't be able to trust them with the secrets they were keeping here. Besides, judging by how fast that delivery boy peeled out, no one wanted to work on the murder farm anyway.

Then again, that might be to her advantage. The memories of the carnage and the rumors of the place being cursed might just keep nosey people away.

Oh well, that was tomorrow's problem. Today had been a huge success. She downed a glass of rum and headed to bed.

Damn! That was really good rum.

8

CHAPTER EIGHT

At her desk the next morning, Maggie worked on a list of things she needed, while Cecile and Hettie set the house back in order, occasionally calling out things for her to add to the list. She was so lost in thought that she didn't hear the knock at the door.

Hettie appeared in front of her, closing the pocket doors behind her, looking concerned. "Maggie, there's a soldier at the door to see you. He says his name is Captain Horace."

"Oh yes, he did say he would be checking in. I will be right out."

Hettie did not move but cleared her throat.

Maggie looked up questioningly.

"Don't you want me to show him in and then you tell me to get some refreshments?"

Maggie looked at her, confused.

"Cause that's what a PROPER lady of the house would do." Hettie winked.

Maggie smiled, finally understanding. “Yes, thank you, Hettie.”

Hettie grinned and went outside to get Captain Horace.

The Captain removed his hat as he entered the room. “Good morning Mistress Bishop.”

“Captain Horace, how good to see you. Hettie, would you bring in some refreshments for our guest?”

Hettie nodded and headed off.

“Captain, please have a seat.” Maggie waved in the direction of a chair as she moved to sit down across from him.

“Thank you, Mistress Bishop. I wanted to come by and see to your welfare.” Captain Horace settled in the chair, balancing his hat on his knee.

“That was exceedingly kind of you, Captain. I am very well, as you can see. I was fortunate enough to find a few servants had been left behind to tend the house. They have been taking good care of me.”

Hettie returned, setting a tray on the table in front of them and pouring, before turning back to the door and taking her leave.

“I am glad to hear that. I was rather concerned about leaving you here alone the other night.”

“Yes, well, things have turned out better than I hoped for.”

Captain Horace took a sip of tea. “I also wanted to let you know that the men that attacked you have been captured. They are awaiting trial in the public gaol. As it turns out, you were not their first victim. They had robbed several residents, although their usual prey had been drunkards coming out of the tavern. They were becoming more brazen when they attacked you. You will, no doubt, be pleased to know that the one man, with the horse print in his stomach, is still going on about being attacked by that 'demon horse'."

Maggie laughed over her own cup of tea. "Oh, that is good news, Captain, and I am sure Onyx will be very pleased to hear that he left such an 'impression'."

They chatted a little while longer, before the Captain announced that he had to leave.

Maggie saw him to the door.

Before he left, he turned, took something out of his coat pocket and handed it to her. "I almost forgot about this. An attorney in town, when he found out I was headed this way, asked me to deliver this to you. He said it had something to do with the estate. Good day, Mistress Bishop, and if I can be of any service to you, please, let me know."

"Thank you, Captain."

Maggie carefully opened the paperwork as she returned her desk.

Mistress Bishop,

My name is Peyton Randolph, Esquire Attorney of Law.

I have been informed by one Mr. Silas Shipman, Esquire, that you have purchased the entire estate of one Mr. Hubert Rawlings. Mr. Shipman, before his rather hasty departure from the colony of Virginia for London, asked me to forward to you the paperwork with a complete account of the estate. I have enclosed said paperwork.

Please let me know if I may be of any assistance to you.

Sincerely,
Peyton Randolph, Esquire

Maggie read over the accounting.

In addition to the house, its contents, the five hundred acres, everything on it, and the slaves with the house and land, there was an additional line that gave Maggie pause. The estate accounting included a business by the name of 'Williamsburg-Jamestown Trading Company', including a building with a small office and storage, along with all its contents, on Francis Street, along with three cargo ships.

Wait...what?

If she read this right, she had just become a business owner?

What the hell was she going to do with that?

"Hettie!" Maggie shouted out.

The housekeeper rushed around the corner. "You alright, Maggie?"

"Hettie, do you know anything about a trading business that Rawlings owned?"

Hettie frowned. "Well, he never talked about that stuff around me, but come to think of it, he did get big shipments of things from all over. He always had the finest things brought in for his wife. Why do you ask?"

Maggie looked up at her in astonishment. "I think I just became the owner of a shipping company."

A few days later, Maggie rode Onyx into town. She made a mental note to herself that she needed to find a better way to ride a horse in these damn dresses. They were big, bulky, and just too much darn trouble. She was a little nervous about riding out alone after the attack, but found the main road had a fairly good number of people on it during the day. As the main road between Williamsburg and Richmond, it was very well-traveled.

Plus, she had the 'demon horse' to protect her. After telling Onyx what the Captain had said, she could have sworn he laughed.

The town wasn't nearly as busy as it was her first day here and she easily made her way up the street. She needed to find Mr. Randolph and she knew exactly where the house was. She had been creeped out by it every time she passed it on her morning walks—in 2018. It was rumored to be one of the most haunted houses in the country. Maggie had not been able to get anywhere near it without feeling nauseated. A negative energy just rolled off the house. But that was in the future.

Standing before it in 1765, the place just gave off the feeling of being a plain old ordinary house. Something extremely bad must happen in it between now and 2018 to turn it because today, it seemed perfectly fine.

Maggie located Mr. Randolph, a rather pleasant man, who did, in fact, confirm that the trading company and three ships were indeed hers. He directed her to her new acquisition, bid her good day, and assured her that he would answer any questions that he could, but that he had not actually been Mr. Rawling's attorney, so his knowledge was limited.

Maggie located the building. It was locked up tight, and she had no idea how to get in. A crazy thought entered her mind as she stood there with her arms crossed staring at the front door.

What are the chances?

She searched around the building, on the ground, anywhere an extra key might have been hidden. No luck. A small bench sat in front of the store. Maggie pulled it over to the door, stood on it and ran her hand along the top of the doorframe.

JACKPOT!

Some things never change.

Maggie held up the key in triumph, jumped off the bench, pulled it back to its place, and unlocked the door.

The inside of the office was a mess. The desk was covered in loose papers, mostly bills and invoices, and there was a desk, chair and a cabinet. The cabinet held several items, including a full bottle of Scotch. Maggie pulled off the top and took a swig. Smooth.

Maggie came to the conclusion that the 18th century was turning her into an alcoholic. Oh well, being a little buzzed, considering all that she had been through, probably wasn't such a bad idea after all.

Searching through the drawers, she found a set of keys and a ledger book; she would examine that later back at home. The keys must be to the storage shelter outside.

Making her way out, she found that it was more of a cellar, with a locked door at ground level. She tried all the keys until she found the one that worked. Maggie started down the stairs and grabbed a quick peek. The cellar was dark, and she had no light, but from what she could see, it held wine—large casks of them.

Interesting. Had Rawlings been a wine merchant? And if so, why had no one mentioned it?

Weird! Of course, 'weird' was becoming the new norm as of late.

She relocked the cellar and the office, pocketed the keys, and headed to the stores with her list of things for the house.

By late afternoon, she had ordered additional supplies from Mr. Holt, picked up items from some other stores Hettie had asked her to grab, set up accounts in all of those stores for Hettie and Cecile to pick up anything the house needed, ate dinner—complete with some of that wonderfully spiced rum from the Raleigh Tavern—and was on her way to Carter's store.

John Carter greeted her at the door.

"Mistress Bishop, it's good to see you. How are you?"

"I'm well Mr. Carter, and you?"

"Oh fine, fine. Hey, I understand they caught the men who attacked you."

"Yes, the Captain told me they were in the gaol. I must admit, I feel much safer." Maggie grinned at the young man.

"Yes, but do continue to be careful Mistress. There are still plenty of others lurking around."

Maggie shuddered. He was right. This was a dangerous time especially for women who roamed around alone. She would have to be more aware of her surroundings.

They made small talk while Mr. Carter bagged up some candy that Maggie planned to take back to young Thomas when something in the fabric section caught her eye. She was surprised to see that it was leather— tanned dark, almost black.

He noticed her stare. “Very nice, isn’t it? I just got it in this morning. It would make a grand saddlebag.”

“Yes, it would.” But Maggie had another idea in mind. “I’ll take all of it.”

If Mr. Carter was surprised at the purchase, he didn’t show it.

With all the items paid for, Maggie gathered up her things, loaded them in her saddlebags, and headed out of town on Onyx.

As she rode, memories of her attack flashed through her head when she passed the spot where it had happened. How was she going to protect herself? It was a necessity, not a luxury.

She was lost in thought and at least a mile out of the town limits when Onyx’s neigh broke her concentration.

Coming towards them was an old man dressed in ragged clothes, wearing shoes that had seen a great many miles, pushing a rickety cart.

Onyx halted when they got to where the man was.

The old man stopped, wiped the sweat from his face and greeted Onyx. He rubbed his muzzle, then handed him an apple. “Afternoon ma’am.”

Maggie nodded.

He was very old — too old to be pushing that cart. How did he even move that thing? It was completely loaded down.

She took a closer look at him, and it struck her that there was something about him that looked oddly familiar. Was it his eyes? They were truly kind, cheerful and even, full of a little bit of spark. They were not the eyes of an old man.

"Have we met?" Maggie asked without thinking.

"Oh, we may have seen each other somewhere. I peddle my wares around here now and again. Say, weren't you that lady that was attacked a few days ago back in town?"

"I am afraid I am, but thankfully those men were caught."

"Good, good! It is a shame that a lady cannot ride down the street safely anymore. You know what, I may have something here that would be helpful for you to have around."

He rummaged through his cart; it was packed with everything from household items, to horse bridles, and even jars with some very strange-looking contents.

Maggie slid off her horse and watched him.

Onyx nuzzled the man's back, as if he knew him, working his way up, until he playfully grabbed the old man's hat off his head from behind. Onyx looked delighted with his accomplishment.

"I am so sorry! My horse tends to forget his manners," she said and tossed Onyx a side glare while attempting to take the man's hat back, resulting in a rather lively tussle between the two, until Maggie whispered in a demanding voice, "Stop it! Stop it, now! Give me that!"

Maggie won the tug of war, holding up the hat by the corner, cringing because it was covered in horse drool.

The old man's back was still turned, so he missed the whole incident. "Oh, it's all right," he called back, still searching, now underneath the bottom of the cart, "I'm rather fond of horses. They are very special creatures. Each has their own unique, individual personality. Ah, here it is."

The man pulled out— a sword.

Maggie was taken aback. She knew nothing about swords, how to hold them, how to use one, or even what a good one looked like. She wasn't even sure she would be able to use one on someone if she needed to.

"Go on," the old man said, "take it in your hands and see how it feels."

Maggie shook her head. "I don't think I could—"

"Oh, nonsense," the old man cut her off, "you mean to tell me that if someone was about to kill you or someone you cared for, that you wouldn't do anything you could to protect them?"

Hettie, Harm, sweet little Thomas?

She had given her word to keep them safe, and that she would do whatever it took to do so. Looking at the old man, then down at the sword he held out, she took it in her hands. Maggie felt a little surge, like a static shock. It was amazing how good it felt, how right. It did not look like anything Maggie had seen in the museums from the colonies.

It was a shorter sword, a great deal shorter, and the blade was very wide. The hilt was smaller too, fitting her hand like a glove. It must have belonged to a shorter man who had it specially made.

Maggie swung it in the air with ease, finding it much lighter than she expected. She turned it back and forth, looking at it closer. The hilt was ornate, engraved with swirls that included embedded tiny flowers, and in the middle was a little emblem. It looked like a coat of arms, but it was too small for her to make out, and above that, a single black stone containing flecks of red, as if it were splattered with tiny specks of blood.

It was very impressive.

"Would you look at that? Looks like it was made just for you." The old man beamed at her.

"I don't know how to use one."

He stopped to think for a moment and winked. "A pretty lady like you with all of the soldiers in this town? Why, I would be amazed if they weren't beating down your door just looking for a reason to come by and see you."

Maggie blushed. Oh, this fellow was definitely a salesman, and he was good. Something about it did feel right, and the old man looked like he could use the money. Besides, Onyx did just defile his hat.

She cut her eyes over to him like she was thinking hard. "Alright, I'll take it."

"Wonderful, and my dear, know this old man will sleep better tonight knowing that he did his part to keep a lady safe," he said with a bow.

Maggie paid him far more than the asking price and told him to keep it for the hat.

He thanked her, gave Onyx a good rub on his muzzle—while slipping him another apple—and started off down the road with his cart.

Maggie slid the sword down in the side of the saddlebag, leaving the hilt sticking out, mounted Onyx, and prodded him into a walk. A couple of minutes later, she remembered the emblem on the sword, and curiosity got the better of her. She turned around to ask the peddler about it, but he was gone.

The road was a straight shot, clear of trees on both sides. He was nowhere to be seen.

She shrugged it off. The old man must have been faster than she thought.

It was late evening when she arrived home.

Harm met her outside the front door, taking Onyx from her. She took off the saddlebag to take inside.

Hettie met her just inside. "Got your supper all ready and waiting for you."

"Thank you, Hettie! Has everyone else eaten?"

Hettie led her to the dining room. "They sure have. Everybody is so excited about what you plan to do, they have been running around taking care of things all day. I just left a stew pot simmering, so they could come in and eat whenever they wanted. Seemed the easiest way."

Maggie sat at the dining room table alone, eating her supper and looking over the ledger from her new shipping company. The numbers looked good— a little too good. They balanced out perfectly, which seemed a little odd. Knowing what she knew about 'ole man Rawlings', she had a strange feeling this was the book he wanted to be seen, not the one with the real numbers. She flipped to the back where the ship notes were. According to that, all three ships were sailing overseas, and one was expected back any day. She closed the book; the Captain would, no doubt, head here first, and she could get some more information when he did.

Hettie stepped in. "You need anything else, Maggie?"

"Is the rum decanter full in the drawing room?"

"Yes, it sure is. If you want something different, you know we have a whole wine cellar, right?"

Maggie looked up. "What? We have a wine cellar? Where?"

"Mr. Rawlings had it built under the house. The entrance is in the kitchen. It's a secret door that you have to pull a latch for. I know about it 'cause he would send me down for some late at night. Only me, the head of the kitchen and the family knew about it. He didn't want any of the other help knowing about it 'cause he was afraid they would steal it."

Maggie stood up. "Show me."

The latch was under a bottom shelf that held dishes in the kitchen. Sure enough, when Maggie pulled it, a little door popped open on a sidewall, in a little hutch area, where pots and pans were kept.

Taking a lit candlestick, Maggie followed the steps down, with Hettie on her heels.

At the bottom, Hettie took the candle from her and lit two large glass lanterns on the wall.

The room was about thirty feet wide and stretched back about twenty-five feet. Half of it was full of bottles —what looked like wines of all kinds, from all over the world. Some were on shelves; some were stacked in wooden boxes on the floor. Taking a closer look, Maggie found bottles of scotch, brandy, whiskey, and several small casks of ale. At the very back of the cellar, Maggie discovered a locked door. “Where does this go?”

Hettie walked up behind her. “Well, I’m not really sure, but I did overhear Mr. Rawlings tell that brother of his once to make sure he was at the cellar door for the ship captain to unload later that night.”

More convinced than ever that Rawlings had been doing some shady business dealings, Maggie had a sneaking suspicion that this house had a few more secrets to give up.

Later that evening, Maggie was alone in the drawing room. The house was so quiet. In 2018, there was always noise like the TV in the background, music playing, even the hum of the refrigerator.

Here, it was just deafening silence.

She took a glass and the decanter of rum, planting herself in front of the unlit fireplace. The room was bright; Hettie had lit lanterns and candles, making the room seem as if it had electric lights. A soft breeze blew through the windows, billowing the mosquito netting ever so slightly. Maggie did miss air conditioning, especially during the day, but the nights weren’t awful. She downed a glass of rum, thinking about the whirlwind of the past few days. She had accomplished a great deal, but there was so much more to do.

“Baby steps,” she said to herself, “Rome wasn’t built in a day.”

She looked over at the sword she had left on the desk. Pouring herself another glass, she walked over, picked it up and settled back down in the chair, laying it across her lap to give it a closer inspection.

The steel blade was exceptionally clean and polished, not a nick or spot on it, as if it had never been used. The hilt was a soft, golden color or was it…wait…it appeared to be ACTUAL gold. She peered closer and scraped it— definitely gold.

Who owned a gold sword?

Who could afford it, unless it was ceremonial, which would explain the crest and jewel on it? She ran her finger along the blade, and it drew a tiny amount of blood from the cut it made; it was razor sharp. Maggie stuck her finger in her mouth to suck the blood like a papercut. Once she had stopped bleeding, she held the sword up in one hand, turning it from side to side. "Where did you come from and how did you end up on the cart of a poor peddler?"

Just another question to add to the ever-growing list for the universe. Maggie watched the candlelight bounce off the blade of the sword. Shifting her gaze to the fireplace, something caught her eye. It was only noticeable if the light was just at the right angle and you happened to be looking in that direction at the exact, perfect moment, but she saw it.

Maggie got up. There was a little separation from the wall at the base of the fireplace. She knelt for a closer look. The floor appeared to go all the way to the wall, with a piece of molding along the top, but the piece of molding wasn't attached. It just lay flush against the wall.

She followed it with her finger, and it was the same, about four feet across, right up to where another piece of molding ran up the wall, laying flush as well.

Maggie went back the other way towards the fireplace. Laying her face against the wall, she looked back that way, and saw it —a piece of molding, so perfectly lined up against the fireplace that wasn't attached, so that she could see the slight glimmer of a hinge behind it.

The hidden door in the kitchen came to mind, so Maggie grabbed a candle. At the bottom of the fireplace, where the hearth hung over the floor, at the furthest part against the wall, she found it. A tiny latch, that when pulled, she discovered popped open a door.

Maggie moved cautiously as she approached it. She pushed the door open all the way and used the candle to light the lamps on the wall inside the room that it led to. Pivoting to get a better look, Maggie became aware she had found Hubert Rawlings' secret room, or rather, his man cave?

Against the far wall to the right was a vast collection of guns, everything from flintlock pistols like pirates carried, to hunting rifles, muzzles and bayonets, along with a few swords and knives. It was a collector's paradise, hidden from thieves by a—probably—very paranoid owner. Along the wall to the left, were shelves. The bottom-most contained bottles of fine liqueurs, scotches, brandies, bourbons, and assorted other choices; fine tobacco pipes made of silver, brass and even ivory were on the top ones. "Only the finest," Maggie said sarcastically.

A long desk and chair were against the longest wall facing the door. Ledger books and papers were scattered over its surface. Maggie set the candle down and sifted through them.

"Gotcha!" The real shipping ledger books were in front of her. "Let's see what you have been up to."

An hour or so later, Maggie sat back in the chair, sickened and disgusted. While Rawlings did indeed ship in legal items from all over the world, they were only a small part of his cargo hauls, just enough to cover up what he was really trading—human flesh and illicit goods.

According to his notes, his primary source of income came from his pirate captain's hauls and crews kidnapping people from other countries and selling them into slavery. That was bad enough, but it got so much worse.

Maggie found stacks upon stacks of detailed sales receipts where Rawlings had been supplying buyers up and down the colonies, for enormous amounts of money, with kidnapped slave children, mainly young boys and girls, between the ages of ten and twelve. He'd kept a book with buyer's names and their specific 'preferences', along with some other damning details that could be used as blackmail if he needed something from them.

"You skeevy fucking bastard. Hell is entirely too good for you."

Maggie's heart shattered thinking about all those poor children, what they had been through, being ripped from their families and homes only to be sold into— the thought made her want to vomit. Her anger grew, surging and swelling more so than it ever had before in her entire life. For the first time, she understood the phrase 'seeing red'.

She screamed and raked everything off and onto the floor. If that bastard weren't already dead, she would have strangled him to death with her bare hands. She slapped her hands flat on the desk, needing to hit something, balling up her fists to pound on it, over and over, needing to release the anger somehow.

Each time her hand made contact, she heard something— a jingle coming from the desk. Anger finally waning, her breaths coming in panting gasps, fists red and hurting, she ripped open the drawer only to find blank pages. She threw them on the floor and smacked the desk again—and heard the jingle again.

What the hell is that?

It sounded as if it was coming from the empty drawer.

Maggie looked closer; she shook the drawer and realized the sound was coming from inside it. Reaching back as far as she could, she felt nothing. She looked all around the edges of the desk, but it wasn't until she peered underneath, from the floor, that she saw the tiny, inconspicuous latch.

She pulled it and a false bottom in the drawer popped up—an early version of a safety deposit box. Maggie took the top off, looked inside and was completely floored.

It was full of money—shillings, tobacco notes, silver, gold, and even a few jewels. A fortune, no doubt his profit from the sale of these poor, kidnapped people. Maggie's first thought was that she wanted nothing to do with his blood money, but on the second, she decided that it may be more fitting to use that money to undo some of Rawling's ungodly misdeeds. She couldn't think of a better way to spend the money than on helping the people whose lives he had destroyed—poetic justice, if you will.

Maggie took another look around the room and decided it was best to keep its existence to herself. The guns would come in handy for the future. With the war coming, they may indeed need to defend themselves and this was a perfect hiding place for them, no one being the wiser.

She gathered the papers off the floor, stacking them into piles on the desk. These papers contained the names of some of the vilest people in the colonies, along with some of their deepest, darkest secrets, and with the kind of knowledge Maggie gained tonight, she might be able to use it against them in the future. Knowledge was a good thing to have, especially during wartime. Blowing out the flames, Maggie closed the door and went up to bed.

But it took her a long time, and several more glasses of rum, to fall asleep after the disturbing information she learned that night.

9

CHAPTER NINE

A few weeks later, things on the estate were progressing nicely.

People in town were warming up to Maggie, and she to them. She was slowly learning who they were and what they did. Maggie and Harm had gone in on market day, Maggie letting him pick out a couple of fine horses for the stables.

Harm was proud that Maggie trusted his judgment so much.

Onyx was gracious enough to allow the new horses to stay in the same stable, but he constantly reminded them, and everyone else who was around, that he was, indeed, the 'head horse' in charge. The additional horses allowed the men to take the wagon into town to pick up lumber and other supplies for the new houses, and since Maggie had set up accounts to be billed directly to her, they didn't need to check in with her all the time. She left them to their own devices, seeing more and more progress each day.

Hettie ran the kitchen, often singing religious hymns as she cooked.

Cecile settled in with the rest of the housework, ecstatic that she could bring the children up to the main house with her while she worked.

Maggie had picked up a few spelling books in town and sat down with Thomas every chance she could to help him learn, and he was an amazingly fast learner, soaking in knowledge and thriving in his new environment.

One afternoon, Maggie called Cecile to her desk. “Cecile, I need some new clothes made.”

“Oh, yes ma’am! I can make you some mighty fine dresses.”

“Yes, but I need something a little different.” Maggie grimaced as she pulled a drawing out of her pocket, showing it to Cecile.

“You want trousers...like a man?” Cecile looked at her with raised eyebrows.

“Yes and no. I want trousers, but I want the front to lace up like a corset in the front for a tighter fit.” Maggie ran a finger down a line on the rudimentary drawing. “They must be tight all over to work the way I need them to and so they aren’t bulky underneath the dress. And I want them made from this leather.”

She showed Cecile her purchase from Carter’s store. By then, Hettie had joined them, hands on her hips, looking over at the drawing.

"Lord have mercy! Proper women don't wear trousers, Maggie."

"I know, it's unusual, but I can't ride Onyx in these dresses the way I want to. It just doesn't work well. And I won't be wearing them in public, just when I am here, but I had another idea as well."

She drew it out for the two women, who looked on with furrowed brows. Maggie would get Cecile to make a skirt that tied on that she could wear over the trousers. That way, she wouldn't have to ride side saddle, but the tie-on skirt would conceal the fact that she was wearing pants.

And, if indeed she needed to move about more freely, she would only have to untie the skirt in one place, and it would fall away easily. Pairing it with a peasant shirt, the lace-up top would pull the whole thing altogether.

Once Hettie and Cecile saw what she was trying to do, and it started to make sense, they both grinned, nodding in agreement.

Cecile was anxious and excited to get to work.

The next morning, shortly after breakfast, a note arrived addressed to Hubert Rawlings. Hettie brought it into the drawing room and handed it to Maggie.

Hubert,
Your cargo has arrived.
You will need to be at the cellar door at 5 o'clock.
Captain Downing

It seemed that the first of Maggie's slave-trading scum captains was back in town, and he would be at the house tonight. Maggie had to be ready.

"Hettie, do you think you could get a late dinner together today for ten to twelve people? I think it's time to invite some company over, and I need Harm to deliver a note as fast as he can."

Maggie jotted down something, sealed it and handed it to Harm, who now stood waiting at the drawing-room door, hat gripped in his hands. "I need you to ride out as fast as you can to the army encampment. Give this to Captain Horace and wait for a response."

He nodded and was off, returning early that afternoon with a response that pleased Maggie very much.

A few hours later, Maggie turned on the charm for Captain Horace and eleven of his men at her dinner table.

"Captain Horace, I must thank you for accepting my last-minute invitation for such a late dinner. Imagine my horror, when I realized this morning, that I hadn't properly thanked you and your men for coming to my aid when those awful men attacked me." Maggie dripped with so much sweetness, she felt like Scarlett O'Hara in the picnic scene.

"Mistress Bishop, the men and I are grateful for your dinner invitation. It's not often we get to eat such delicious home-cooked meals."

Maggie raised her glass. "A toast, to you and your men for the excellent service you provide our little town."

Maggie had instructed Hettie to leave the false door in the kitchen open, and at 5 o'clock on the dot, Hettie—right on cue—ran into the dining room. "Mistress Bishop, there's a noise in the cellar. I think somebody might be trying to break in down there."

"Oh, my goodness!" Maggie played the shocked, helpless lady about to faint.

Captain Horace and his men jumped from the table. "Where is the cellar?"

Hettie led them to the kitchen and pointed.

Maggie remained sitting at the table, sipping her glass of rum, and heard the shouting. A smile crept across her face. As she had suspected, the ship's captain did indeed, have his own key, and had let himself in, right into the waiting hands of twelve British soldiers who thought him an intruder breaking into the house of a poor, unsuspecting widow. Maggie slid the chair back, taking her time and another sip of rum, before appearing in the kitchen, just as two of the soldiers dragged the apparent captain and three of his crew up the stairs from the cellar and out into the foyer. She put on her best worried, frightened face.

Captain Horace approached Maggie. "Mistress Bishop, do you know any of these men?"

Maggie shook her head. "No Captain! I have never seen these men before in my life. Who are they?"

"Probably associates of the previous owner. Looks like there was a door in that cellar that led down to the river." He looked at five of his men and ordered them to the river and to board any ship they might find.

"I took the liberty of inquiring about the previous owner after I escorted you here, and, well, I didn't want to frighten you in your new home, but I learned he was not a very good man."

"Oh my!" Maggie continued to play the unknowing victim, fanning her face with a limp hand. "Thank Heavens you and your men were here. What would I have done if we had been here alone? Captain Horace, I owe you my life. I cannot thank you enough."

One of the Captain's men returned a short time later, his hand resting on his weapon. "Sir, there is a ship and the paperwork doesn't appear to be in order. It carries smuggled goods."

Maggie acted astonished, hand flying to her mouth.

"Mistress Bishop, please stay in the house while we investigate further," Captain Horace directed, nodding to the men who restrained the intruders.

The soldiers dragged the Captain and his crew members, who, it seemed, had decided to remain silent given their current predicament, outside.

Maggie turned and headed for the living room, Hettie right on her heels, closing the pocket doors behind them.

Hettie was the first to whisper, "Laying it on a little thick, weren't you? But that sure was a mighty fine plan you had."

Maggie looked at her with a sly grin. "Worked like a charm." She poured two glasses, handed one to Hettie, and they toasted to a job well done.

When Captain Horace returned much later, he seemed pleased. "Well Mistress, the Captain of that ship is indeed a wanted man, as are many of his crew members. One of my men recognized him from an earlier incident. We must seize the ship's cargo, but my commander will be delighted to have these men locked away."

Maggie nodded. "I completely understand. And I just went back through my paperwork from the attorney. It seems there are some ships that I had no knowledge of, belonging to the estate that I purchased. It makes sense that this would be one of them, does it not?"

Captain Horace seemed surprised. "Oh, I suppose it does. Well, that is good news for you indeed. There is some cargo that is not illegal, and in that case, provided I can verify things, it will belong to you. Of course, you would have to pay the tax if you wanted to keep it, but it WOULD save me and the men the trouble of dealing with it."

"Oh, Captain Horace, whatever I can do to make things easier on you and your men. What is the legal cargo, out of curiosity?"

Captain Horace hesitated, looking down at his feet. "The cargo consists of thirty to forty slaves."

Maggie feigned shock. "Oh, I see...well...this IS a big farm, and I don't seem to have enough help, so, I think I will take them in. And, of course, I am more than happy to pay the tax. After all, look at the wonderful protection the government provides to us each day."

Captain Horace seemed pleased, puffing out his chest just a little. "Well ladies, if you will excuse me, the men and I have some work to do. What would you like to do with the cargo that you are keeping? I would like to hold onto the ship until we can take care of the smuggled items, if that's acceptable to you."

Maggie flashed him a smile. "Of course, Captain, whatever works best for you. And you can leave the cargo here. My people and I will take care of them. Again, Captain, I am in your debt. I don't know how to thank you."

"No thanks necessary, ma'am." He tipped his hat and bid them 'good night'.

As soon as he was out the door, Maggie turned to Hettie. "Gather everyone up, we have some guests to welcome."

Soldiers were posted to guard the ship until it could be sailed back into town the next day, leaving Maggie to the business before her. She stood before a frightened, huddled group ranging in ages from ten to fifty. They were all silent, terrified.

"My name is Mistress Bishop and I am the owner of this property. You have nothing to fear here, and if you are willing to listen, I have something to say that I think you will all want to hear. Anyone who wishes to leave need only to come to me and ask for your Freedom Papers, but for your own safety and the safety of everyone on this property, I must ask you to keep this all a secret." Maggie made them the same offer she had made to the original help.

When she was done speaking and asked if anyone wanted to go, not one soul came forward. She even saw a little light of hope in the eyes in front of her, making her heart feel just a little full. She asked Abel and Joshua to get them all settled for the night and to have supplies brought out to them in the morning, so they would be able to eat. She would leave it up to the current help to decide where the new ones would be best suited. With two more ships coming, Maggie hoped she didn't run out of land before she ran out of people to deed it to.

But that was tomorrow's problem.

A few days later, the new additions were settling in nicely. Hettie and Cecile added some of the younger girls to the house help list, taking all the heaviest work off Hettie. Cecile had taken a couple of them under her wing, teaching them how to take care of the house and how to sew. The youngest of the children were out on the side yard, running and playing with young Thomas, and taking care of baby Abraham for Cecile; kids being kids— as it should be.

More of the new houses were popping up each day, and with all the new help, they would be completed in no time along with the plans Maggie had added for a school and a central kitchen with dining area, so the work could be shared, along with good fellowship at meals each day.

The first completed house went to Hettie.

Maggie was there when Hettie saw it for the first time, so happy that she cried, making everyone else tear up, too. She had hugged Maggie so tight, telling her that God had heard her prayers and blessed her more than she ever imagined when He sent Maggie to her.

While Maggie missed her own family beyond belief, she had been blessed with another family in this time. Family didn't have to be the same blood; Maggie knew that in her heart, and she wished everyone in this time could see that as well.

The fenced pasture had already been extended for Onyx, and he was delighted with his new-found freedom.

In the two weeks following the first ship's arrival, two more notes arrived from Maggie's ship's captains—notes that Maggie had promptly forwarded to Captain Horace, so he and his men were waiting.

As before, the Captain took the smuggled goods to town and left the people. Maggie made her speech each time, and again, not one soul came forward to leave. The farm was now fully up and running, bustling with life, along with the rapidly growing little village not far from the house.

The crops that had survived were being harvested and sold, and new ones were being laid in. With any luck, they would be turning over a good profit by this time next year, but the strain was starting to show.

Keeping up with the people, the books, and three ships, sitting out in the water not making money, was overwhelming for Maggie and she knew that she needed help.

Her next trip into town, Maggie sought out Mr. Randolph, the attorney who had contacted her after the first one fled the country. She remembered that he was a man that was a fiercely loyal patriot. While she did not intend to get involved in the coming war, her best bet would be to walk a narrow line. If she had allies on both sides, each side believing she was loyal to them (all the while being loyal to America), it would only work in her favor. As long as she could keep up the charade of being the poor, defenseless widow woman who needed protecting, she and the ones she took care of would be safe.

She found the attorney at his office. "Mr. Randolph, I am in need of your assistance."

"Mistress Bishop, I am glad to see you. It will save me a trip out to your place." The man greeted her with a smile and waved her toward a chair.

"You needed to see me?"

He poured her a glass of wine. "Yes, but that is business that can wait until after you tell me what I can do for you."

Maggie sat down. "Mr. Randolph, I find myself in a bit of a difficult position. You see, I have purchased this large estate and between that, and the shipping company, well, I am afraid I am in over my head. I need help in the way of a full-time attorney, that will be paid very well for his attention and discretion, of course, and I would much prefer someone who is well, loyal to our colony first and foremost. I rather like handling my own business without having the Crown too involved, if you take my meaning"

Mr. Randolph stared at her and stroked his chin, as if in deep thought. After seemingly deciding she was, in fact, 'one of them', he smiled. "Mistress Bishop, I think I know the perfect person for you. I know a young man, who trained under me, that would meet all your...expectations. While he is young, he is a very bright lad, excellent with law and numbers, loyal to a fault, and his discretion is impeccable. His name is David Percy and he would be ideal for the position you are suggesting."

"Excellent, Mr. Randolph. I knew I could count on such a kind and compassionate soul as you."

Mr. Randolph's blush amused Maggie. She must be getting rather good at this role-playing thing.

"Wonderful! He is out of town, on an errand for me, but he should return late this evening. I will send him out to your house tomorrow if that is convenient for you."

"Yes, that would be lovely. Thank you, Mr. Randolph."

"Certainly…. oh, and the other business. I almost forgot. The landowner on the far side of your property has decided that he would like to sell a good deal of his land, and since you are the closest neighbor, it would only make sense to offer it to you first. He is willing to let it go for quite a decent price."

Talk about timing.

"Well, that is quite fortuitous indeed, because I suddenly find myself in need of some additional property for the farming plans that I have."

Maggie walked out of Mr. Randolph's office with a signed deal to buy an additional five thousand acres of land. With a total of seventy-eight people now working for her, that was a good thing. And, even better than that, the cost barely put a dent in the pile of money she had found stashed in the secret room.

She imagined the entire Rawlings family letting out a collective roar in Hell right about now, and she laughed. Deciding that a little dinner and some celebratory spiced rum punch were in order, Maggie headed for the Raleigh Tavern.

Gracie greeted her at the door, and a few more locals turned around to acknowledge her.

Maggie took the quiet table by the window, the same one she sat at the first time she visited. She liked that she could sit out of sight and take in everything around her. The people, the sounds, the smells— all reminding her that she was now a part of history. The items she only saw pieces of in museums, the speeches she only read about in books, the faces that went with the names, the original buildings, not ones that had been rebuilt—she was there. Despite the circumstances of how she got here, she always reminded herself that she was in an extraordinary situation and that she needed to take in every detail. She was honored to be a witness to the birth of a great nation—her great nation. She found it fascinating to 'people watch', while eavesdropping on their conversations; the rumblings of the colonists, the seeds that would lead to the revolution, the gossip about who was doing what—suspecting that she had probably become a part of that chatter. She listened to the old men nearby tell stories, about the glory days and conquests of their youth.

This particular day, a man that looked to be in his early forties, his face like leather from too much time in the sun, told a story about his ship in a horrible storm after they had just fought off a group of pirates. He spoke about how hard it was to keep afloat, but that he knew he had to because the lives of his crew and the thoughts of his dear Nadia, that he needed to get home to, kept him going. He had a far away, dreamy, but sad look in his eyes as he downed his ale.

"Gracie?" Maggie asked when the serving woman passed by, "Who is that man?"

"That's Captain Russell."

Captain?

"What's his story? Do you happen to know?"

"Oh yes! He was a sea captain, one of the best around and had a thriving little shipping business. He sold it after his wife Nadia became sick to stay home and take care of her. She passed a couple of months ago. He comes in now and again to visit with some of the menfolk. I think he gets lonely."

The wheels in Maggie's brain were turning. "And he is a good, honest man?"

"Yes, one of the best. He really is a good old soul."

"Thanks, Gracie."

Maggie waited around until Captain Russell got up to leave then followed him out. "Captain Russell! Captain Russell!" she called and waved.

He turned to look at her.

"Captain Russell, my name is Maggie Bishop, and I wish to have a moment of your time."

Ten minutes later, they were sitting in the shipping office having a conversation.

Maggie explained how she had come into possession of the ships and the company, all the unfortunate business practices of the previous owner, and that she needed a trustworthy captain that knew the seas and the laws. She wanted to make the business legitimate, well as far as the British were concerned anyway, and profitable, and she needed a captain who could put together crews, overseeing them while keeping them in line.

Captain Russell was more than a little intrigued. He thoroughly missed the life and indicated that he could handle all those requirements, but the overseas traveling was something he felt was more a young man's game and didn't think he could handle it on a regular basis.

"Thank you for the offer, Mistress, but I don't think this is the position for me."

Maggie looked at him and thought about it. If she wanted to grow the business and stockpile as many things as she could before the war, she might need to spend some time in the other parts of the Colonies.

"How about this? You can outfit and manage the other two ships with men you trust, and you captain the third ship for me, personally. I will keep it in port here and use it to sail up and down the coast only as I need it. That way, you can still sail, but the trips won't be as long, and I can give you the shipping part of the business to manage. If I have someone who knows the business, that I can trust, my only need will be to monitor things and, possibly, go to help open other offices in additional ports. You see, I want to trade with the other areas of the Colonies as much as possible. The less dependent we are on England for exports, the better. And did I mention that I pay EXTREMELY well?"

"I don't know. I think you should find someone else," he said as he started to leave.

"Please, Captain. I am all alone, I have no family to help me, and I have no idea what I am doing. I desperately need someone like you, and I am not above begging."

The Captain scratched his chin, deep in thought for what seemed like an eternity before he answered, "Oh, what the hell! Mistress Bishop, you have yourself a deal."

Maggie was thrilled. One more thing off her plate. "Wonderful, there is just one thing Captain Russell. I will require complete loyalty and discretion on your part. That is imperative and part of this agreement. You will garner both from me in return. Together, I think we will be able to make a great deal of money."

He tipped his hat. "I am both loyal and discreet to a fault, ma'am, and I am at your service."

Maggie wrote out the necessary paperwork for Captain Russell to claim the ships from the army. He would get to work immediately and send progress reports to the house. She included instructions for retrofitting the smaller ship. The Captain would, of course, have his own quarters, but Maggie wanted her own personal suite built on the ship that would be both comfortable and private.

On the way out of town, Maggie stopped off at the army encampment to see Captain Horace.

"Mistress Bishop, how good to see you."

"Hello Captain, it's wonderful to see you too. I came to let you know that I have found a captain for my ships. I have given him the necessary paperwork to claim them, and he will take them off your hands."

The Captain smiled. "That is indeed wonderful to hear! I have been meaning to come and see you. I have news of my own to share with you. My commanders were extremely pleased with the illegal cargo seized from the three ships at your estate. I have been promoted to Major." The soldier's face flushed with pride.

Maggie laughed and clapped her hands. "Oh, that is marvelous news. Congratulations, MAJOR Horace. We shall have to celebrate the next time you are near my estate."

"That would be lovely. Excuse me, Mistress, but duty calls."

With the tip of his hat, he was gone.

Maggie and Onyx headed home.

It had been an extremely productive day. Her new potential attorney would visit tomorrow, she had acquired another five thousand acres of land, the shipping company was set up with a new manager, and she was now in the good graces of a British major. Not bad for a 21st-century girl.

As they neared the house, a group of Native Americans turning down a path not far from the estate entrance caught Maggie's eye. She stopped, watching the scene. The group was moving away and were extremely thin, malnourished even. Small children who looked too weak to cry, asleep on their mother's shoulders; the mothers looking too tired to carry them.

Maggie remembered that Hettie had mentioned the tribe the Rawlings' men had terrorized, running them off their land. This must be some of them.

Mental note: another Rawlings wrong to correct.

Starting down the lane to the house, Onyx whinnied and pawed at the ground, even rearing up.

"Whoa boy! Whoa! What's wrong?" Maggie pulled the reins and tightened her knees to keep control of her mount, then rubbed his mane to calm him down when he stopped. With a wild look in his eyes, Onyx stared at the area where the Rawlings family had met their final demise. Maggie felt the evil heaviness oozing from that direction. It rolled across the air, a thick fog of anger and hate forming, detesting Maggie for her mere presence, loathing her for what she did with 'their' land, 'their' house, 'their' money, and 'their slaves'.

Maggie felt the weight of 'their' stares — a chill running down her back and every hair on her arms standing straight up. She talked, soothing Onyx, until they reached the house. Peering back toward the area, she could have sworn she saw the outlines of dark shadows ducking in and out from behind the trees.

The next day, David Percy arrived mid-morning, just as Mr. Randolph had promised. He was a young man, looked to be no more than eighteen or nineteen, scrawny, sandy-blond hair tied back, freckles on his face and a pair of wire-rimmed glasses on the bridge of his nose. They spent the rest of the morning discussing Maggie's estate, the shipping company, the new land she was buying and everything in between.

Mr. Randolph was right, he was extremely intelligent, having an answer and a plan for everything.

"Mr. Percy, I have to be completely honest with you."

He looked her directly in the eye, giving her his full attention.

"I am not your normal widow. I purchased this land and I intend to make it profitable, by any means necessary. The people on this property are my responsibility, and I do not take that lightly. I need an attorney to keep everything legal and above board. I also require absolute privacy and discretion, above anything else, and in exchange for your full-time commitment, I will pay you well above the normal rate. But you *must* understand that I cannot allow my personal business to leave this estate. Is that clear and acceptable to you?"

"Yes, ma'am, you have my word as an attorney and a gentleman. If I am in your employ, all of your information will be completely confidential."

"Well, Mr. Percy, if you want the job, it is yours."

He stood up. "I do indeed want the position Mistress Bishop, and I will do my best to make you proud."

Maggie waved to David Percy from the front door when he left. He looked uneasy, glancing towards the big tree in the side yard, trotting past that area quickly.

Looking over that way, arms folded, Maggie felt the heaviness, the darkness getting worse. It reached all the way to the front door now.

No one went to that side of the yard, not one person even glanced in that direction; even the grass was dying. The restless spirits of the Rawlings family were getting stronger, not weaker.

Maggie had to figure out some way to get rid of them before they were powerful enough to undo what she was doing here.

Later, after eating a quick dinner in the kitchen with Hettie, Maggie got news from the farm and filled Hettie in on all of her news from the past couple of days.

"Hettie, tell me more about the tribe on the edge of the property. I saw some of them yesterday and they did not look well."

"I don't suppose they did. They were a right quiet bunch. We never heard nothing out of them; they kept to themselves. They farmed over there by the river, had nice crops 'cause I'd see them in town selling sometimes, but these Rawlings men couldn't stand it. Called them savages, said they didn't deserve to be here. I heard them bragging one morning about burning all their fields, laughing, saying that should get rid of them. That was right before the Rawlings was killed. Why you ask?"

Maggie sighed. "Because I need to go right another Rawlings wrong."

Geez, why did these people have to be so utterly vile?

"Hettie, how many food supplies can we spare until I can send someone into town?"

Hettie tilted her head to one side, tapping one cheek with a finger. "Well, we are right stocked up, so we can spare a good bit I expect."

"Good, get Harm and Abel to load up a wagon with as much as we can. I'll be out in a few."

Maggie rode Onyx, as Harm and Abel followed with the wagon of supplies. Approaching the village, or what was left of it, Maggie was sickened by the conditions.

Everything around them had been burnt to the ground. There were no animals around, no children playing, only the dwindling smoke from a dying campfire in the middle of a bunch of small longhouses. Maggie dismounted, told Onyx to stay put, and motioned for Harm and Abel to wait.

A few frightened faces peered out from a couple of the shelters. From the direction of the creek, a young native American man came towards Maggie with a knife in his hand.

Onyx rushed to Maggie's side, nervously neighing.

Maggie held her hands up in a silent plea. "It's okay, I mean you no harm. I just want to talk. Does anyone here speak English?"

The young man eyed her through narrowed eyes, still holding the knife up. "I speak English. What do you want here?"

"My name is Maggie Bishop. I am the new owner of the house not far from here, Beechcroft. The previous owners that harassed you are dead. I am nothing like them, and I just want to help."

The young man just stared back at her suspiciously.

"I brought some supplies I thought you could use." She pointed toward the wagon.

The man glanced over, his eyes falling briefly on Harm and Abel, then moving back to Maggie.

"Please, I just want to help. What those men did to your tribe, it was wrong. You have my word that no one from my property will ever bother you." Maggie reached for her pocket, and the young man jumped, aiming the knife in her direction. She slowly pulled out a piece of paper as to not rattle him. "I brought this." She held it out.

He took a step towards her and snatched it from her hand. “What’s this?” he demanded as he looked it over.

“It says that I am giving your tribe one-hundred acres of land. No one will be able to take it from you either. I will make sure of it.”

He lowered the knife.

“What’s your name?”

He eyed her warily and said, “I am called Askuwheteau.”

“Askuwheteau, please take the supplies and use them so your people will not starve. My men will unload them for you.”

Something brushed against Maggie’s leg. She looked down; it was a beautiful little girl, with big brown eyes, who had taken her by the hand. Maggie smiled and knelt. “Hello, sweetheart.”

The little girl smiled shyly and ran back into the longhouse.

Askuwheteau called out some words in Algonquian, and a few people started to come outside.

She turned and called to Harm and Abel. “Bring the supplies.”

The two men eased the wagon closer to where Maggie stood.

Maggie walked to the back of the buckboard and pulled the cover aside. Hettie had added some baskets of fresh vegetables on top. Grabbing them, Maggie brought them around and held them out.

A couple of the women came forward, unsure of what to do, until Maggie urged them to take the baskets. They reached for them, nodding and smiling.

Askuwheteau walked around to the wagon, looking over its contents. He waved and motioned for some of the other men to come over. They started unloading it as Harm and Abel got down to help.

An old man came out to watch the scene and to study Maggie.

Askuwheteau spoke with the old man, who first looked surprised, then nodded at Maggie, and said a few words to the younger man.

"This is Mingan; he is our chief. He thanks you for your gift." Askuwheteau bowed his head in her direction.

Maggie nodded back and smiled as big as she could.

Another man came up, wearing beads and face paint, looking at her, then at Onyx—who snorted in response—then back at Maggie. He moved his hands as he spoke to the others.

Askuwheteau turned and said, "This is Powaw...Priest. He says your spirit is not of this world... but that your spirit is good... and he says your horse is strange."

"He's not the first to say that about Onyx, and I am sure he will not be the last." Maggie laughed. "Your English is very good."

"I went to the Indian school in town," he replied.

Maggie turned to see the wagon had been unloaded and the supplies were already being used. She turned back to Mingan and Askuwheteau. "Please, tell your chief, the land is yours to spread out on, farm on, whatever you choose to do. I know it is getting late in the season; I will send supplies each week until you can become self-sufficient along with some seeds in the spring for you to plant. If you need anything, please come to see me."

"Why are you doing this?" the young man asked.

Maggie looked around. "Because the Rawlings were horrible people, and no one deserves to be treated the way they treated you. Besides," she shrugged, "I need all the friends I can get."

She turned to go.

"Thank you, Maggie Bishop."

Maggie smiled; one more wrong was being struck off the list. But riding back, something bothered her. Powaw had said that Maggie's spirit was 'not of this world'. Could he tell Maggie wasn't from this time? She couldn't help but wonder.

The next morning, Maggie heard Hettie calling her name. She went into the foyer to see Hettie looking out the window. "What is it, Hettie?"

"There's Indians on the front lawn doing something strange. Lord have mercy! They are putting a curse on us."

Joining her at the window, Maggie looked out, narrowing her eyes, recognizing the scene playing out before her. "No Hettie, actually just the opposite."

Maggie went to the front door where Askuwheteau met her.

He greeted her as Powaw came up behind him with a large smoking oyster shell and a raven feather. "Powaw says that the evil spirits that were here are gone now. They will not bother you anymore."

The heavy, dark feeling that haunted Maggie was gone, and the entire front of the house felt... lighter. Maggie laughed, happy to not feel that evilness anymore, and to have the spirits of the Rawlings family gone once and for all.

"Thank you...my friends."

Askuwheteau and Powaw both nodded and left.

10

CHAPTER TEN

A few weeks later, Maggie was beyond miserable sitting on a settee in the middle of the Governor's Palace, dressed in a beautiful green gown that Cecile had made for her, completely surrounded by a group of ladies who clucked like a bunch of hens about the latest town gossip.

'This person was seen with that person.'

'So-and-so was cheating on his wife.'

'A servant was stealing.'

'Did you see that dress?'

It was like an endless soap opera. Who knew that colonial Virginia was such a hotbed of impropriety? These ladies seemed to have turned discussing the latest town scandals into a past time.

Maggie guessed that's what people did to entertain themselves before the television was invented. Downing her fourth glass of 'punch', Maggie tried to figure out how she ever let Hettie talk her into coming.

"It's time you started acting like the wealthy lady that you are, and wealthy ladies go to balls at the Governor's Palace!" Hettie had reprimanded.

Stuck in the middle of these ladies was not even the worst of it. Maggie had come to join them in an effort to escape the endless introductions and invitations to dance from every single male in the town of Williamsburg and the surrounding areas.

Word had gotten out that she was a wealthy widow, and since women were in short supply, Maggie had become the latest and greatest fare on the menu. She had feigned overheating to escape the dance invitations out of necessity, since she had no clue how to dance in the 18th century. She was mainly ignoring the ladies' scuttlebutt, nodding and smiling occasionally to appear interested, when she noticed the chit-chat had gone quiet. Looking up, she noticed all the ladies straightening their backs and putting on their best smiles as a gentleman happened by.

"Good evening ladies, you all look very lovely tonight."

Maggie detected the slight smell of sandalwood as she glimpsed a man in an immaculate British uniform wearing boots that had been polished to a shine.

The ladies all giggled and waved. Once he was out of earshot, they all started back up with a new topic of conversation.

'Such a handsome man', 'so well mannered', 'impeccable manners', 'can't believe he is not married', were all phrases used to describe him. It appeared that he was the only thing they could talk about now.

A much older lady fanned herself while watching him walk away. “If I weren’t married and a few years younger…”

Maggie stole a better look at him when he stopped to speak to a group of men. He was handsome. No! He was stunning!

Standing about six feet tall, he had light colored blond hair, tied back in a neat, straight ponytail, no powder or wig as the other men wore. He was a bit older than most of the men in town, appearing to be in his mid-thirties, with a finely chiseled nose and chin, the kind that came with age. His skin was flawless, his face clean-shaven, his smile revealing straight, white teeth.

No wonder the ladies were beside themselves staring —it simply could not be helped. When she heard him speak, Maggie heard the sexiest British accent she had ever heard before in her life.

“Who is that?” Maggie asked.

The ladies all stared at her in disbelief.

Charlotte White spoke up, “Oh, my goodness, you don’t know? Well, of course, you wouldn’t; you haven’t been here very long, and he has just returned from up north. That, my dear, is Colonel Gabriel Asheton, the most eligible and sought-after bachelor in the Colonies. Why, every unmarried woman around has been trying to land him for years. I should introduce you.”

Maggie shook her head, holding up her hand. “Oh no, please don’t trouble yourself. I’m not looking for a husband.”

The ladies all stared at her as if she had two heads, finding it hard to believe that she wouldn’t WANT a husband.

Maggie had royally messed up. She should have never said aloud in colonial Virginia that she didn't want a husband. Opening her mouth to do some damage control, she heard a voice clearing to her side.

It was Major Horace.

"Pardon me ladies! Mistress Bishop, you look as if you could use another glass of punch. May I escort you to the refreshment table?"

Maggie silently thanked God. "Oh, Major, yes please; that would be lovely."

He held out his arm and she stood, taking it, letting him lead her away.

He leaned over, whispering, "You looked as if you needed saving from the 'Ladies Gossip Brigade'."

"Oh, you have no idea. I find myself in your debt again," she said, accepting her glass, waiting while he filled his own, "It would seem the ladies are all abuzz about a recently arrived Colonel Asheton."

Major Horace choked a little on the punch he was sipping. He sputtered a little before swallowing it down. "Oh, excuse me...yes...well...I suppose they would be."

That seemed a little awkward.

"The Colonel just arrived back in town two weeks ago. He has been in Canada on military business."

"Oh, so you know him?"

Major Horace shifted on his feet. "Well, yes I do. We were... acquainted in England before I joined the army. We have since renewed ...our friendship."

The Major seemed to be choosing his words—a little too carefully—as he shot glances in the Colonel's direction.

"He is a fine man, comes from a good family, well-educated, an outstanding soldier, and the finest swordsman I have ever had the pleasure to watch."

Swordsman, huh?

The Major finished his drink, looked at Maggie, smiled and with the help of the little shot of liquid courage, kindly offered, "Allow me the pleasure of introducing you."

A few moments later, they stood before the man who was the center of attention. "Colonel Asheton, if I may? Permit me to introduce you to Williamsburg's newest resident, Mistress Maggie Bishop."

The Colonel looked at Major Horace, then at Maggie, flashing a million-dollar smile and taking her hand to plant a firm kiss on the back. "Always a pleasure to make the acquaintance of one of the fair ladies of Williamsburg, especially one as beautiful as you."

Wow! No wonder the women were swooning all around him.

Maggie smiled back. "The pleasure is all mine, Colonel."

He was asking her about her life in Williamsburg, when another soldier approached Major Horace, whispering to him.

"Ah, excuse me, Colonel, Mistress Bishop." Major Horace bowed and followed the younger soldier.

Maggie stood alone with Colonel Asheton, chatting about her newly acquired estate.

He was a charming man, but also a very personable and friendly. The energy Maggie sensed from the Colonel was one that she really liked. He was quite easy to talk to, and they seemed to really hit it off.

Mid-conversation, Maggie noticed a small hand come up over the Colonel's shoulder and make its way down the front of his chest from the side.

The Colonel turned, revealing that the hand belonged to a lady.

A lady by the name of Prudence Hunt.

Maggie knew this because the 'Gossip Brigade' had identified her as the one in 'that dress'.

That dress was made of a fine blood-red silk fabric, cut so low it revealed her more than ample bosom sitting so far up from the cinched corset that she could have balanced a plate on it. Her long blond hair was piled high on her head, several ringlets hanging down to brush her exposed shoulders. Her face was powdered, along with her chest. A lovely pearl choker encircled her elegant neck, and a tiny beauty mark dotted her chin.

According to the gossip circle, she was the widow of one Mr. Richard Hunt, her second husband, a wealthy merchant she had married when he was the ripe old age of seventy-nine —she couldn't have been more than twenty-five.

Her husband had only lived six months, though Maggie imagined it was probably a happy six months if he got to stare at those perky breasts for any length of that time. Unleashing those puppies, just one time, was probably enough to give the poor man a heart attack.

Prudence Hunt reached up with one hand, stroking the Colonel's face. "Gabriel," she purred, sticking out her lips in a pout, "I'm thirsty and there is no one to escort me to the refreshment table. Do you suppose you could help a poor lady in distress?"

"Of course, Mrs. Hunt." He turned to Maggie. "Please excuse me, Mistress Bishop."

Maggie nodded and watched them head towards the drink table. Shaking her head—and grabbing another glass of something from a passing tray—Maggie found a secluded spot by an open window with a blessed cooling breeze blowing through. Backing up against the wall, she took a minute to observe the room.

Everyone was laughing, talking, dancing, and having a wonderful time.

This was the calm before the storm. Although the signs of a revolution were there, they had not yet exploded in the way that they would in the years to come. A great many people in this room would not even live long enough to see the end of the war, making Maggie a little sad.

The scene unfolded, with Colonel Asheton and Prudence Hunt catching her attention. Judging by the placement of her hand on his back, slipping ever so slowly down his backside, it was obvious that Mrs. Hunt had her eye on husband number three. They were laughing and chatting with another couple when the Colonel, very discreetly, reached around and moved her hand back up. Maybe, he wasn't as into her as she was him; maybe he wasn't interested in becoming her next conquest, even though they did look very cozy.

Maggie was taking another sip from her glass when she saw it— an ever so slight stolen glance, across the room, directed at Major Horace. A glance that, in the five seconds it took, sent the silent message of 'I can't wait to be alone with you'.

At first, Maggie thought she had imagined it. Surely, she had too much to drink, and it was a trick of the eye, until she turned her gaze to Major Horace who was, in turn, inconspicuously sending back a very subtle, discreet acknowledgment.

Maggie lowered her glass in sheer astonishment.

Could it be that those two were having an affair? She saw the momentary affirmation directed back towards the Major. The two were, without a doubt, surreptitious lovers.

The most astounding part of the exchange was that the guarded conveyance wasn't coming from Prudence Hunt —instead, it was coming from Colonel Asheton.

Maggie stood dumbfounded, until the puzzle pieces fell into place. Colonel Asheton was unmarried at his age, brutally handsome, a perfect gentleman with impeccable taste and manners, very well groomed and the object of all the ladies' affections.

Of course — the man was gay.

In 2018, Maggie, being a single woman in the dating world, would have picked up on it immediately, since most people didn't have to hide it, but in 1765, the thought never even occurred to her. If the two were found out in this century, they would likely end up dead. Maggie felt a certain amount of compassion and pity for the two of them. In 2018, they wouldn't have to hide who they were, but here, in this time, they would never have the luxury of making that choice. They would never be free to be who they were.

It was too crowded and hot inside with so many people pressed together. Maggie refilled her glass, found the side door, and headed out into the garden for some fresh air. When the cooler temperature hit Maggie in the face, she realized she was drunk. She stepped towards a bench in the garden, tripped over nothing she could see, stumbled, and was well on her way to falling on her ass, when a strong pair of hands caught her from behind, steadying her. Maggie giggled, giddy.

"It's alright Mistress, I have you. Let's find you a seat, shall we?"

An arm wound around her back and a hand took her by the waist, leading her to the bench. When Maggie looked up, she was staring directly into the smiling, handsome face of Colonel Gabriel Asheton.

"Are you unwell, Mistress Bishop?" he asked with a great deal of concern.

Maggie giggled again. "I am perfectly fine, Colonel Asheton." She patted him on the chest, "It seems I may have had a wee too much to drink," using her fingers to indicate a little pinch.

"Yes, well, the host is known for adding a little... extra... to the punchbowl." He smiled at her. "Why don't I sit with you for a few minutes to make sure you are alright?"

Sweet Jesus, this man was even more handsome up close.

"Won't Mrs. Hunt be lost without you?" Her question seemed genuinely concerned, until a snort and another giggle, that couldn't be held in, escaped.

The Colonel laughed. "I think she can manage without me."

Maggie raised her finger. "I don't know about that. I think she may be sizing you up to become husband number three. Third time's a charm, you know?"

The Colonel was taken aback. "Yes, well, she will have to continue the search elsewhere. She isn't exactly my type."

"So, I noticed."

He eyed at her suspiciously, holding a breath in.

Oops, watch it, Maggie.

"What I meant to say is that you aren't really *her* type. She seems to prefer her husbands over the age of seventy, and well, you are certainly not there yet."

He relaxed, letting out his breath. "No, I don't suppose I am."

Whew! That was close.

They continued to chat until Maggie noticed couples drifting into the garden, looking for a little privacy. Maggie and the Colonel glanced over at each other.

"I should be getting home." Maggie started to stand, the Colonel helping her.

"Perhaps I should escort you there, Mistress Bishop," he offered.

"Maggie, please call me Maggie, and thank you, but I have my carriage and driver. He will see me home."

He nodded. "Maggie, and please call me Gabe. I am glad to have met you this evening. I hope I will see you again soon."

Maggie offered him a genuine smile. "Me too."

He escorted her back inside and bid her 'good night'.

Maggie located her hosts to thank them for the evening, and after saying 'goodbye' to a few others, boarded her carriage to head back to Beechcroft. She peered out of the window of the carriage, breathing in the cool night air. Lit lanterns on the sides illuminated the coach, making the front drive look as if it had modern-day streetlamps. When the carriage made a turn, she saw them: two people locked in an embrace in the darkness of a corner where they thought they wouldn't be seen.

There was no mistaking, it was Major Horace and Colonel Asheton.

Maggie saw them, and the Colonel saw her as her carriage sped away.

Maggie spent most of the next morning in bed, nursing a wretched headache. She made a mental note not to drink at the next Governor's Palace soiree.

By early afternoon, she managed to get dressed and make it downstairs, to the couch anyway.

Hettie appeared at the doorway. "There's a Colonel Asheton here to see you."

Oh geez, what fresh hell would this bring?

Maggie really hoped he hadn't seen her looking at them last night, but she knew better, and she had no idea what he thought.

"Show him in Hettie, and make sure you close the pocket doors behind you. I am guessing he will want some privacy."

Hettie raised an eyebrow but didn't say anything.

Colonel Asheton entered the drawing room, hat in hand, waiting for Hettie to leave before he spoke.

"Good afternoon Mistress Bishop, I hope I am not disturbing you."

"No, of course not," she said gently, "and it's Maggie."

He nodded, seeming very tense. “Of course, my apologies. I was not sure if you remembered that from last night.”

Maggie poured a glass of wine and handed it to him. “Please, sit down. Would you still like me to call you Gabe?”

He looked at her as if he had been expecting a much worse welcome. “I would like that very much.” He took a sip from his glass. Noticing Maggie did not pour herself anything, and how she seemed to not be feeling well, he looked at her and cringed as he said, “A little hair of the dog this morning?”

Maggie wrinkled her nose. “Just a little. I’m not sure what was in that punch, but I think I will skip it next time.”

Gabe chuckled and looked down. “Yes, I think you were not the only one who misjudged the potency of the refreshments last night.”

Maggie smiled at him as warmly as she could. “What brings you out, Gabe?”

He set his glass on the table. “I was concerned that, perhaps, you may have seen something last night that you misunderstood, and I wish to clarify, for the sake of all of the parties involved. I…”

Maggie held up her hand; she knew what he was referring to. She started to pretend that she didn’t see anything, but they would both know that was a lie, so she decided to take a chance. “Gabe, I know about you and Major Horace.”

His eyes widened and his face paled. “I... I don’t know what you mean…”

“Please, allow me to finish,” she interrupted.

He looked at her nervously with a tinge of fear in his eyes.

"Who you choose to have a relationship with is none of my business, or anyone else's for that matter. I would never judge you for being with another man. Love is love, and we don't always get to choose who we fall in love with. As long as the relationship is consensual and mutual, well, that's all that matters, and you shouldn't have to live in fear for your life simply for loving someone."

Gabe sat, unmoving, not speaking, as she moved beside him.

She placed her hand on his shoulder. "Your secret is safe with me. I would never put your life or Major Horace's life in danger for merely finding a little joy in this life."

Gabe looked up at her, hesitating before putting his hand over hers, letting out the breath he had been holding. "Thank you, Maggie."

She patted his shoulder with her other hand, before moving to the sideboard, picking up a glass while trying to decide if she could stomach a glass of rum. "Besides, it's not like I run, what you would consider, a normal place around here. I'm sure most of the townsfolk would consider how I live, if they knew, shocking as well."

Deciding to do without the rum, she put the glass down and turned, seeing that Gabe had regained his composure.

They spent the rest of the day talking and laughing, enjoying each other's company. Maggie had never been more comfortable with anyone in her entire life. He ended up staying for dinner and supper.

While enjoying an after-supper drink, Maggie had a thought.

"Gabe, Major Horace said you were the best swordsman he had ever seen."

"Well, I don't know about the best, but I can hold my own. Why do you ask?"

"Because I am in need of a huge favor. Can you teach me how to use a sword?"

Gabe looked at her curiously. "Why in the world would you want to know how to use a sword?"

"I just want to be able to defend myself and the people here if I have to. I know it's not the ladylike thing to do, but I really do want to learn, and it's not like I can go around town asking for a teacher."

Looking her up and down, Gabe shrugged. "Who am I to judge? Oh...why not. When would you like to start?"

Maggie was beyond thrilled.

At the end of the evening, as Gabe was about to leave, they embraced each other tightly as if they had each found a life preserver in the middle of the ocean after jumping off of a sinking ship, and they both realized that they had found something special in each other— an epic friendship bond that would stand the test of time.

Maggie and Gabe saw each other a great deal in the weeks to come, becoming so comfortable with each other they felt more like family than friends. He would come out to the estate a few times a week for her sword lessons, teasing her endlessly about her leather trousers. The first time he had seen her in them, his reaction was priceless. He gaped, his mouth hanging open, squinting his eyes as if he did not trust them.

"What the bloody hell are you wearing?"

Maggie patted the soft leather on her thighs. "They are my trousers. What? Only men can wear trousers? Please!"

Gabe shook his head and grinned; he no longer tried to argue with her.

11

CHAPTER ELEVEN

They talked about anything and everything, nothing was off limits. On the evenings he came out for lessons, he would often stay for supper and drinks. Sometimes, they stayed up so late talking, they fell asleep leaning against each other on the couch.

Maggie had one of the extra bedrooms made up especially for him, at his disposal when and if he needed it. She even had Major Horace, now calling him by his first name, Jonathan, over for supper on sword-lesson nights when his schedule allowed, giving the two gents some time alone.

She picked up how to use the sword quickly, practicing every day, loving the power she felt when she wielded it.

The days Gabe couldn't make it out, Maggie would try to make it into town, so they could have dinner in between meetings on his busy days. They would often dine at one of the taverns, strolling the streets, arm in arm, afterwards, back to his office.

The townspeople took notice. Whenever Maggie was in a store, the 'Gossip Brigade' would surround her, asking about her relationship with the Colonel, and even though she insisted they were merely close friends, the rumor mill churned.

One day, while waiting for their dinner, Gabe seemed as if he wanted to ask her something, but hesitated.

Maggie rolled her eyes, knowing him well enough to read his body language. "What's on your mind?"

Gabe fidgeted with his sleeve, then spoke, "Well, it seems I, and several other members of the army, have been invited to a small dinner party at Tandy Hall, the home of John Sherman, tomorrow, and I was hoping you would accompany me. These things are terribly boring and …" he trailed off.

Maggie looked at him knowing there was more to the story. "I see, and who else will be there?"

"Myself, a couple of other colonels in town, a few townspeople…"

"And?" Maggie continued.

Gabe looked up. "A few ladies in town…"

Maggie slowly pulled it out of him. "Which ladies?"

Gabe huffed. "Oh, alright! Prudence Hunt will be there, and she tends to get rather...handsy."

Maggie folded her arms across her chest and made a face. "So, I noticed at the Governor's Palace."

"Yes, well. She seems to have an unhealthy fascination with me, and I thought if you accompanied me to the party, that perhaps she might behave herself. Between you and me, fighting off women all the time is absolutely exhausting," he complained.

Maggie scoffed and leaned in closer. "You're telling me? You should try being the new wealthy widow woman in town. Every man from sixteen to ninety-five has made it a point to introduce himself, ask me to take a stroll and stopped short of dropping to one knee and proposing on the spot."

Gabe lifted his glass in the air and whispered, "I'll protect you if you protect me."

Raising her glass to his, Maggie clinked it. "Deal!"

The next afternoon, they arrived at a stunning house located on the south end of town. It belonged to John Sherman, who was an attorney fiercely loyal to England. The house had been built only a few years before and was one of the finest on the street.

The pair was warmly greeted and shown to the parlor for drinks and conversation until dinnertime. There were several other military men, accompanied by their wives, whom Gabe introduced to her, and a few residents of the town.

Maggie had taken a seat on the couch, chatting with the lady next to her, when she felt Gabe's hand on her shoulder. She reached up without looking, patted it and smiled. She would recognize his touch anywhere. Maggie looked around; Prudence Hunt was noticeably absent. She overheard Mrs. Hunt's escort for the party, another gentleman of a ripe old age, say that she was not feeling well and was spending the day at home.

The afternoon just got a great deal better.

Dinner consisted of a delicious meal with a pleasant mixture of conversation about the state of affairs in town, the weather, and the beauty of the house and gardens that Mrs. Sherman had spent a great deal of time perfecting. Everyone politely steered away from politics, which Maggie was grateful for.

Every so often, Gabe would take her hand under the table and give it a little squeeze, as if to say 'thank you' for coming along.

Eventually, the final course was brought out. It consisted of a bitter apple dumpling concoction soaked in a great deal of brandy sauce. Stuffed from the rest of dinner, Maggie felt like she would explode if she ate another bite, but not wanting to be rude, she took one small spoonful in her mouth before sliding the rest of it around on the plate to look as if she had eaten more. Everyone finished eating, got up, and filed into the parlor for after-dinner cocktails.

Out of nowhere, Maggie's mouth and throat began to burn, and then became excessively dry. She had just reached the doorway, Gabe behind her, his head turned speaking to another officer, when the room spun out of control. She reached back for him when she started to fall.

Gabe caught her before she hit the floor, easing her down. "Maggie! Maggie! What's wrong? Can you hear me?"

He touched her face as she felt the pain slam into her head, her heartbeat now racing, and her supper threatening to come back up. She curled on her side, pulled her knees up, and screamed out as stomach cramps ripped throughout her midsection.

Mr. Sherman grabbed a servant girl, telling her to run as fast as she could to bring back Dr. Carter.

Gabe scooped Maggie up in his arms and Mrs. Sherman led him to a downstairs bedroom. When Gabe laid her down, she started to vomit. Gabe turned her on her side to keep her from choking.

Her body trembled uncontrollably, her breathing having become rapid and uneven.

Mrs. Sherman and a servant pushed past Gabe, a bowl of water and rags in their hands, to bathe her face and clean her up.

Gabe stared down at her helplessly, wondering what would have hit her that fast.

He knew the answer before he reached the dining room because he had seen it before. He picked up the dessert plate Maggie had eaten from and smelled it. While it didn't smell like any poison, her uneaten dumpling had something green and ground up on top of it. He rushed the plate to Mrs. Sherman.

"What's on this?" he demanded and pointed.

Mrs. Sherman looked confused.

"The green stuff, what is it? It wasn't on mine, but it was on Maggie's."

Mrs. Sherman looked closer. "I have no idea. There was nothing like that in that recipe."

Dr. Carter rushed through the front door and into the bedroom. "What happened?" He felt her forehead and examined her eyes.

"She was poisoned." Gabe handed him the plate.

Looking at the dish and taking note of the odd bit of green, Dr. Carter pinched it with his fingers and smelled it. "Foxglove. It has Foxglove on it."

Mrs. Sherman looked aghast, rushing out of the room.

Gabe moved to the other side of the bed, taking Maggie's hand.

"Tell me exactly what happened," said Dr. Carter. Gabe filled him in.

"But she did indeed vomit?" he asked. "And how much did she eat?"

"Yes, and she only had the one bite that I saw," replied Gabe.

Maggie lay on the bed groaning and writhing in pain.

"Can't you do something?" Gabe said to Dr. Carter.

"Getting it out of her system is the best thing to do. If she only had one bite, on a full stomach and she vomited, most of the poison should have come out, but right now, all we can do is wait."

Maggie could hear voices shouting, but she couldn't understand what they were saying. Her body was wracked with pain, her head throbbed, and her stomach churned; she was sure she was dying. After what seemed like an eternity, everything went dark and she fell into a deep sleep.

Gabe held her hand, smoothing her hair back as he whispered in her ear, "Please wake up Maggie, please. I'm sorry, this is my fault. I shouldn't have brought you here. I need you to be well. Besides, we have a lesson tomorrow. You know you don't want to miss a chance to whip my arse," saying anything that might possibly give her what she needed to fight for her life.

He stayed by her side the rest of the night, sitting in a chair he pulled up with his head lying on the bed and refusing to relinquish her hand.

The next morning, he felt something touch him, waking him up.

Maggie had opened her eyes and was running her fingers through his hair.

He had never been so relieved to have a woman stroke any part of his body in his entire life.

"Hello, beautiful."

Everything on Maggie hurt, from the top of her head to the tip of her toes — even thinking made her brain ache. Gabe smiled at her as he gently brushed some loose strands of hair out of her face.

This was the last damn dinner party she was going to as his date.

She was so thirsty.

"Water," she croaked, despite the pain in her throat.

Gabe held a glass up to her mouth and helped her to drink.

That was better.

"What happened?" she managed to ask.

His expression became grim. "You were poisoned."

Poisoned? Seriously? How? Why? So many other questions came to mind, but she was too weak to ask them aloud.

She turned her face towards her friend. "Hey Gabe?"

"Yes, Maggie?"

"Don't ever invite me to another dinner party."

Gabe grinned. "Never again, you have my word." He laughed and kissed the top of her head.

Two days later, she was able to go home.

Dr. Carter said that he had never seen anyone recover so quickly, attributing it to the tiny amount she must have ingested, but she was still very tired and weak.

Mrs. Sherman had seen to her every need, apologetic, horrified and dumbfounded as to how this could have possibly happened under her roof. The military men at the dinner had questioned everyone in the house, from every guest down to each servant who had been there that night. No one knew anything.

For lack of any other reason, they had decided that it was just a terrible accident, that somehow bits of flowers from one of the centerpieces had dropped onto her plate.

But neither Maggie nor Gabe were buying into that.

For one, there were no flower arrangements near Maggie's plate on the dining room table, and how did it manage to fall into just her dessert — only hers.

Riding in the carriage, Gabe beside her, his arm around her while she lay on his chest, she was just happy to be going home.

Jonathan sat across from them, still worried about her condition. He and Gabe discussed plans to keep an eye on Maggie as she dozed, both tremendously concerned about her safety. The carriage finally stopped as they arrived at the front door of the manor.

Hettie was pacing the floor when Gabe carried her inside. "Oh, thank the Lord you are home, where we can take care of you. How are you feeling Maggie?"

"Tired and in desperate need of a bath," she replied as she caught a whiff of herself.

Hettie barked out orders to the other servants, while Gabe carried her upstairs to sit her on the small couch in her room.

Jonathan was right on their heels. He poured her a glass of water, handing it to her, while he and Gabe continued to make plans.

Gabe would stay the next couple of days, working from the house, since Jonathan needed to get back to his men. Gabe had more leeway, since his duties were mainly handling paperwork now, whereas Jonathan had to physically be there to command his troops. Jonathan would be back as soon as time allowed.

By the time Maggie's bath was ready, it was time for Jonathan to leave.

He took Maggie's hand. "Feel better, Maggie, and get some rest." He kissed her on the cheek, then turned his head to kiss Gabe on the cheek as well. He held Gabe's hand for a moment, and he was out the door.

Maggie smiled. "You two are so sweet, and it makes me a little jealous."

Gabe blushed.

Hettie appeared at the door. "Want me to help you to the tub?"

"No, thank you, Hettie, I'll manage, but, if you could whip up some kind of soup, it would make me very happy. And could you close the door behind you?"

Nodding, Hettie headed downstairs.

Maggie went to stand, finding herself a little shakier than she thought.

Gabe wrapped his arm around her waist. "Let me help." He walked her to the bathtub.

She held onto the edge of the tub, a little dizzy. "Gabe, can you help me out of these clothes."

Gabe's eyes widened, and he froze.

Maggie looked back seeing his hesitation, his sense of propriety clearly stopping him. She stared at him a moment. "Gabe, look, you are my best friend, the best friend I have *ever* had. I know it isn't proper for you to see me with no clothes on, but let's face a few facts, shall we? The sight of a naked woman does absolutely nothing for you, so what difference does it make? And I have no problem with you seeing *ME* naked because you know very well that I am not like other women. Modesty is not really my thing, in case you haven't noticed."

Gabe thought a moment and shrugged his shoulders. "No, I suppose it's not."

Maggie flashed him a weak grin. "Besides, isn't there something in the soldier's code about coming to the aid of a lady in distress? And, right now, I am really in distress."

The sight of Maggie about to collapse moved him into action. He stripped off her clothes, picked her up and set her into the tub. Kneeling beside the tub, he helped her wash her hair and get the rest of herself cleaned up.

She offered him a grateful smile, silently thanking the universe for putting them in each other's paths.

An hour later, they were sitting on Maggie's bed, each eating a bowl of chicken soup. Clean, with food in her stomach, Maggie felt a great deal better. She napped the rest of the day and even managed to make it downstairs for supper.

The next day, she was up and moving around, much to Gabe's chagrin. He was playing the role of a hovering mother when a message arrived stating that he was urgently needed in town. After a bit of back and forth, Maggie convinced him that she was fine and that he should go take care of his business. Gabe was not comfortable leaving her but was forced to admit the message did seem important.

She walked him to the door.

He hugged her tightly and kissed her on the top of the head. "Make certain you lock this door behind me. I will be back as soon as I can."

Assuring him she would be well, she waved him off. She spent most of the day napping in her chair. Later that night, sitting in front of the fireplace in the drawing room, listening to the sound of a thunderstorm outside, Maggie sipped a glass of her favorite rum. She'd slept too much; her mind now churned in overdrive.

Hettie had left for the night, as had everyone else, so she was completely alone. Thoughts of the previous few days replayed in her head.

She didn't believe for one second that she had been poisoned by accident; there were just too many things that would have had to come together perfectly for that to be so.

But who would want to poison her?

She hadn't been in town long enough to make any enemies, and as a matter of fact, she had gone out of her way to be as nice and helpful to everyone in town as she could. It had to have been someone in the Sherman house because that was the only way it would have worked, but Gabe was the only one at that dinner party that she knew.

None of it made any sense. A noise from the back of the house broke Maggie's train of thought.

"Hettie?" she called out.

There was no answer.

"Cecile, is that you?"

More silence.

Maggie set down her glass, getting up to investigate. She picked up a lantern, holding it up, looking around. Approaching the kitchen, she noticed broken glass from the window on the floor with a small tree limb in the middle of the mess. This storm must be worse than she thought.

She set the lamp on the table and searched for something to clean up the mess with. Out of the blue, something slammed into the back of her head and everything went black.

When Maggie woke up, she was lying face down in the kitchen, next to the pile of broken glass with her hands tied behind her back. She managed to heave herself upright. Her head throbbed from where she had been hit and her eyes were having trouble focusing. She heard things being knocked over in the drawing room and out in the foyer. Blinking, her eyes cleared a bit just as she heard a voice.

"Oh good, you're awake."

Maggie looked up.

Prudence Hunt stood in the doorway of her kitchen.

She was dressed in a black cloak, her hair tied back, with a wild look in her eye, holding a flintlock pistol in her hand. She strolled over to Maggie and crouched down next to her.

Maggie shifted a bit. "Prudence, what are you doing?"

The other woman stood up, sneering. "The same thing I have been trying to do all week. Kill you."

Maggie shook her head trying to comprehend what was happening. "You were the one who poisoned me?"

"Well, not me personally. I paid a servant girl to slip the Foxglove into your dessert and to keep her mouth shut, but the stupid little bitch screwed the whole thing up. Usually, the poison works so well— at least it did on my first two husbands. But you! You had to go and be the exception."

"Me? Why me? I have done nothing to you," said Maggie as she slyly shifted herself to one side to grab a shard of glass that was near her.

Prudence squatted back down. "But you have! You took Gabe away from me. I was well on my way to making him husband number three, and I would have kept him around for a while. After all, he is rich and devilishly handsome. I can only imagine how he is in bed..." her mind drifted for a bit before she continued, "but then you came along, and it was like I didn't exist, just pushed to the side like yesterday's whore. But don't concern yourself about Gabe. Once you are gone, I will be there to comfort the poor grieving soul. Of course, he will be upset, distraught even, but I will offer him the comfort of my shoulder for his tears and the comfort of my bed, well, for the rest of him. He will fall in love with me and forget all about you before the worms have even started to devour your flesh."

Maggie couldn't believe how delusional this woman was. "You crazy bitch! Gabe will never fall in love with you, especially when he finds out that you killed me."

Prudence got right in her face. "Oh, that's the beauty of it. He will never know. You will be found out on the front lawn, in the same place as the Rawlings family— dead. Everyone already thinks this place is cursed, and they will just assume you fell prey to the same fate, just another victim of circumstance. They will think a slave that had been hiding out decided to do away with the wealthy owner and rob the place blind. I've already trashed the other rooms to make it look just like that. It's the perfect plan. No one will give it a second thought."

Prudence stood up and started knocking things off the table onto the floor.

Maggie looked up at her. "There's just one little problem with your plan."

Prudence turned around scowling at her. "And what's that?"

"I'm not dying tonight."

In one quick movement, Maggie snapped the ropes on her wrists, blood dripping from where she had cut into the skin with the glass shard, grabbed the tree limb, and smacked Prudence right in the side of the head. She used the same limb to knock the pistol out of her hand; it slid under the table, out of Maggie's reach.

Prudence was on the floor, rolling and stunned. She pulled herself up using the table where the kitchen knives were stored.

Maggie was making a break for the foyer when a hand grabbed her leg, pulling her backward; she fell flat on her face. Rolling on her back, Maggie used her free foot to kick Prudence in the face, but Prudence refused to turn her loose, and seized Maggie's free leg with her other hand, pulling her back even further.

Still weak from the poison and additionally stunned from the hit to the back of the head, Maggie could not stop her.

Prudence crawled on top of Maggie, a knife from the kitchen in her hand, straddling her.

Maggie pushed back.

Prudence raised the blade that she gripped with both hands, and brought it down, aiming at Maggie's heart.

Getting a hold of the other woman's wrists, Maggie held them back as much as her strength would allow. Feeling the tip of the knife close to her heart, Maggie felt a sudden burst of adrenaline, screamed, and pushed back with all her might.

Prudence fell backward and the knife fell to the side.

Maggie scrambled, grabbing the blade, coming up on her knees and holding it in front of her at her chest, aimed outward in a defensive position.

Blinded by rage, Prudence screamed and lunged at Maggie, never noticing the knife in Maggie's hand. Her eyes went wild with anger and disbelief, she looked down to see the blood pooling on her own chest.

She lingered a few seconds before she fell to the side, lifeless, her eyes still open.

Maggie sat there on her knees, panting, taking in the scene. When she knew that Prudence was no longer a threat, she lay on the floor, trying to calm her breathing along with her heartbeat and the nausea in her stomach, as she watched the ceiling spin. She closed her eyes.

There was a loud banging at the front door and lots of shouting, just before she heard it being kicked open.

Gabe stared at the horrific scene, his heart in his throat. Maggie was lying on the floor, covered in blood, unmoving, her eyes closed. Beside her, Prudence Hunt was in another pool of blood, dead with the hilt of a knife sticking out of her chest. Gabe rushed to Maggie's side, patting her face while calling her name. He checked for a pulse.

Oh, thank God, it was there.

Maggie fluttered her eyelids.

Gabe pulled her to him, holding her, and looking for wounds he couldn't find. "Maggie! Where are you hurt?"

"My head," she groaned.

Gabe reached around, feeling the back of her head, and located a large bump concealed by her hair. She also had several cuts and bruises that were forming on her face, arms, and hands.

Harm appeared at the door. "Lord have mercy. I wondered why Onyx was trying to kick down the stable." He looked around, shocked. "Is Mistress Bishop alright?"

Gabe looked up. “I think so, but Harm, I need you to get my horse out front. He is accustomed to riding at night. Take him into town to the encampment where Major Horace is and tell him to bring several men and the army doctor.”

Harm nodded and disappeared.

Gathering Maggie up in his arms, Gabe moved her to the couch in the drawing room. By then, she had started to come around. He poured her a glass of brandy, held it up to her lips and ordered her to drink it.

After she had downed it, he asked her what happened.

Maggie explained the entire story.

He sat in silence as she spoke, in complete disbelief of all that had transpired. When she was done, he pulled her to his chest, embracing her, thanking God that she was alive. He didn’t know what to say, so he didn’t say anything.

It was Maggie who broke the silence. “Hey Gabe?”

He pushed back a little to get a better look at her face.

“I am starting to see why you prefer men to women. Women are batshit crazy.”

He stared at her a long moment, registering what she was saying.

She started to giggle a little.

He shook his head in amazement that she could make a joke at a time like this and pulled her back into his embrace —she was still giggling, and he was convinced that she was in shock.

" Yes, well, I guess maybe it does have its advantages." He couldn't help but chuckle himself.

Jonathan and his men arrived before dawn. After hearing what happened, Jonathan had his men remove the body, while taking Maggie and Gabe's statements.

Gabe explained that when he got to town, he discovered the note he received was a trick, so he rode as fast as he could back to Beechcroft, knowing something was terribly wrong.

After being told the rest of the story by Maggie, Jonathan assured her that this would not cause any trouble for her since she was merely defending herself against a mentally unstable woman, especially since that woman had confessed to killing two husbands. He would handle everything.

The army doctor checked Maggie over, proclaiming that she would be fine after some rest.

Hettie appeared, nervous and concerned for the welfare of her mistress. She took charge, having everything cleaned up and put back into place as soon as the soldiers were done and even making sure everyone was fed breakfast while they were working.

Once everyone had left, Maggie changed clothes and climbed into bed, wanting nothing more than to rest and forget. When she woke up later that evening, she found Gabe asleep on the bed beside her, his arm wrapped protectively around her. She turned to look at him as he slept, not knowing what she would do without this man, her best friend, hoping she never had to find out.

12

CHAPTER TWELVE

1772

Seven years had passed since that unforgettable night.

Gabe continued to be a constant in Maggie's life. He was always there for her, just as she was always there for him, but never more so than the day he received the devastating news.

Jonathan, who had been sent elsewhere in the Colonies for his duties, had contracted pneumonia and died.

When he received the letter, Gabe was heartbroken. He would not eat, could not sleep—completely unable to function in any form. He wouldn't leave his bed, only lay there and grieve, until the day Maggie marched in, ripped the bedcovers off him and ordered him to get up. He had told her to just leave him alone, which of course, she hadn't...not until she had moved him into her house, temporarily, to get him back on his feet, nursing him back to health, body and soul.

Slowly, but surely, her stubborn determination had paid off and she succeeded.

Things had changed for Maggie, too. She had become a force to be reckoned with, an extremely wealthy, sought-after woman, one of the richest in the Colonies, a shrewd businesswoman and, after promising herself she would never be a victim again, a warrior. She had spent every day practicing with her sword, getting better and more precise as the days passed, never leaving the house without it, concealed in a holster strapped inconspicuously to her back, along with two boot daggers that she had made special.

Gone was the naive girl with a soft body and a baby face, replaced with a woman who was strong, confident and in control of her surroundings. She had gained the respect and admiration of everyone who encountered her, American and British alike, whom she had been careful to build good relationships with.

The estate had grown from the original five hundred acres to over ten thousand, now completely self-sufficient. She had two hundred sixty-eight people in her employ, who all enjoyed freedoms that they would have nowhere else. A church and a school had been built to educate their children, and them, if they wished to learn, giving everyone the chance at a better life. She had arranged internships in town—at a premium price of course—for the people on her estate, so that she now had her own personal blacksmith, tanner, shoemaker, brickmaker, gunsmith, and even a doctor in training — every occupation they had in town.

A variety of crops thrived in the Virginia soil; Maggie had as many different types added as she could, creating an abundance for use and for sale through her shipping companies that now included offices up and down the east coast. Secret cellars had been built in several locations on the property for hiding supplies for the upcoming war, so that, no matter what, her people would be taken care of.

Plans had been put into place so that if strangers showed up on the property unexpectedly, everyone would move into playing a part that would not seem suspicious. A bell at the school would be rung if trouble approached, alerting the children, who would then either run to the fields, picking up farming tools that were placed close by, or to the central kitchen, taking up utensils, as if it were their daily jobs. The youngest children had hiding spaces they could be corralled into.

While a few chosen slaves belonging to the other townsfolk were being educated in town, they were few and far between. Anything on the scale that Maggie was doing would attract attention and trouble, so she did everything within her power to keep it a secret.

She had built a great relationship with the Native American tribe, trading with them, helping to provide for them, and even allowing them to send their children to the school. Maggie was even surprised to learn that Mingan, their chief, had attended a few days a week himself. He seemed extremely happy and content to sit with the children, learning right along with them.

Maggie would have dinner with the kids at the big dining room every now and then, always as delighted to see them as they were her. She soaked up every peaceful moment available. Maggie stole off every chance she could, riding out with Onyx to a special little spot tucked away in a grove of trees she found on some of the lands she had purchased. It had a small babbling brook that, as it reached the circle of trees, went over a cliff about ten feet high, turning into a beautiful waterfall, puddling into a dammed-up little lagoon at the bottom before it turned back into a little stream. It was quiet, peaceful and secluded and had become her own little personal oasis. Maggie savored her time with Onyx, when it was just the two of them again, like in the beginning, before the world became so complicated.

By the end of 1772, Maggie knew it was time to start laying in some contingency plans. Word had already reached town about the colonists who had burned a British schooner that had run aground in Rhode Island a few months before, inflaming tempers with England. The Boston Tea Party, being brought on courtesy of Sam Adams and John Hancock, would only be a year away, and was really going to piss off the British, leading to major problems with port service once the British shut it down the following year. The Revolutionary War was approaching faster by the minute.

Maggie had walked an exceptionally fine line so far, just as she had planned. She had made powerful friends on both sides, allowing her to slip through the lines unnoticed. Anyone that traveled for her always carried paperwork, carefully worded and signed by her. If they were to ever get in trouble, they were to ask for the commander and give them the papers, which could be read in support of either side, signed by a wealthy lady known to be great friends to their cause, whichever one that happened to be at that given moment.

Calling Captain Russell to the house for a meeting, Maggie explained that she was concerned there may be some trouble with the ports, and being a fear that he shared, he listened carefully as she laid out 'Plan B' for him. It involved pulling the crew members off one of the ships and making them into a land group that could travel parallel to the coast, supplying the other towns by wagon. Maggie had laid out the easiest routes while pointing out, that it should, not only, keep them in business, but be of great benefit to the other colonists when things were sure to get difficult for them.

The Captain liked the idea but was concerned about being stopped by troops on both sides. When Maggie showed him a copy of the traveling papers she used and explained how they worked, he broke into a broad grin.

"Mistress Bishop, this might just be crazy enough to work."

And it did.

Maggie spent as much time during the next few years away from town as possible. Gabe had been sent to New York, so she hadn't seen him in a couple of years, and she missed him terribly. They wrote letters back and forth, but the mail had become sporadic.

Colonist militias were being formed in the taverns in town; no longer places of joy and merriment, instead becoming hotbeds of political discussions and discourse. It took only one instance of seeing a man tarred and feathered for Maggie to decide that it was more than enough for her.

The worst part was that the person rolled there on the street, screaming, writhing in unbearable pain and reeking of burning flesh. The lucky ones would die instantly. The other poor bastards eventually would die, but only after several days of monumental pain, fever and agony. It was a horrible way to go.

Maggie chose to focus on taking care of her little neck of the woods, trying her best not to change history, at least the major parts of it anyway.

April 19, 1775

Maggie sat by the fire in her drawing room, alone that day, sipping a glass of rum. And so, it had begun. Even though she knew the news would not reach here for a couple of days, the American war for independence was underway. 'The shot heard round the world' would have already been fired, though strangely, no one would ever know for certain, by who or by which side.

Looking down at her glass, Maggie wondered if that shot was simply a mistake, a misfire, a mere miscommunication, or was a deliberate act of fate, inserted precisely at that exact moment in time, to ensure that this war, would indeed, begin. She had been thinking about fate a lot these days; the fate of the people around her, the ones she loved, and of her own. Maggie said a silent prayer for Gabe.

July 4, 1776

The Declaration of Independence was ratified in Philadelphia.

January 1777

Maggie heard a knock at the front door. When she opened it, she was surprised to see there was no one there. Just as Maggie was turning to close the door, she noticed a package on the porch. She picked it up and brought it inside. It was in a brown paper wrapper, tied with string, with 'Maggie Bishop' written on the outside.

Maggie tore open the parcel to reveal a book. It was a collection of Scottish Faerie Tales. She flipped through it to find there was no letter, no note and no kind of acknowledgment.

How odd.

The book itself was beautiful. It was larger than a normal edition, bound in an exceptionally good leather and the pages even appeared to have gold on the edges. Who would send this to her? She had mentioned to Gabe that her mother was Scottish, but that she didn't know much about Scotland itself. She was willing to bet it was a gift from him. There probably had been a letter attached, but, if it were on the outside, it wouldn't surprise her in the least if it hadn't made it.

With the state of the mail these days, she was amazed she had even received the book itself. She put it on the table next to the fireplace, reading it each evening while enjoying her nightcap.

13

CHAPTER THIRTEEN

September 1777

Hettie came into the living room where Maggie was sitting at her desk. “Maggie, a messenger just left this for you.” The housekeeper held out a sealed letter.

Maggie ripped it open and read it quickly.

Damn.

“Hettie, send Thomas into town to the shipping office. Tell him to inform Captain Russell that we will need to sail to Philadelphia immediately.”

“What’s wrong, Maggie?”

“It seems our men manning the wagons have gotten themselves into some trouble. I will need to go take care of it personally.”

Hettie started towards the door. “I’ll go get Thomas right now.”

Maggie sighed, wrote out instructions for David Percy, who had turned out to be an enormous help to Maggie over the years, and went upstairs to pack.

A week later, Maggie and Captain Russell stepped off the ship in Philadelphia and were immediately surrounded by British soldiers. The Captain in charge demanded their papers, as he sent men on board to search.

Captain Russell looked at Maggie nervously.

"Of course, Captain. Here is my paperwork and I think you will find everything in order."

"What is your business here, ma'am?"

"Well, Captain," Maggie said sweetly with a big, flirty smile, "I own a little shipping company here, and it seems that some of the men in my employ may have gotten themselves in a tiny bit of trouble. I merely wish to sort out the whole affair and be on my way. I understand they have taken up residence in your local gaol. Would you be kind enough to point me in that direction?"

The Captain looked at her, his eyes stern as he considered her request.

The soldiers returned from the ship. "Nothing on board, sir, and with a minimum crew."

The Captain nodded. "Very well ma'am! The gaol is that way." He pointed down the street. "Captain Francis is in charge. He should be able to help you."

"Thank you so much Captain for your help."

They started away, sure they were in the clear when they heard a voice shouting from behind them, "Mistress! Mistress! Wait!"

Damn it.

Maggie turned around with her best smile. "Yes, Captain?"

"Mistress, I just wanted to warn you to be careful. There was a battle nearby recently and the place is crawling with enemies of the Crown."

"Oh my! Well, thank you for the warning, Captain. I feel so much safer knowing you and your men are looking after things."

He tipped his hat.

Maggie turned, and they moved away quickly. She instructed Captain Russell to find a good tavern and to secure some rooms for the night; she wanted to go to the gaol alone.

The Captain protested, but Maggie assured him she would be fine.

She found the gaol with relative ease, straightened her dress, patted her hair and went inside. Two soldiers greeted her, asking her business. She indicated she was looking for Captain Francis and was escorted inside. In front of her, sat the most disgusting pig of a man she had ever met.

He was short, with a big round belly that kept him from getting anywhere near his desk. He was completely bald, his powdered wig sitting askew on his head. He held part of a turkey leg in one hand, most of which was on his face, and had a greasy linen napkin stuffed in his shirt collar. He reeked of putrid body odor and bad whiskey.

Maggie vomited a little in her mouth, swallowing the bile to speak. "Captain Francis, I presume?"

"Yes!" he spat the word, spitting food out of his mouth. "Who are you and what do you want?"

This was going to be harder than she thought. "My name is Mistress Bishop, and I have come to see about some men in my employ that you are holding here."

"What men? I'm holding a lot of men here."

"They were..." Maggie covered her nose with a handkerchief, "transporting some supplies in wagons. I don't know any more details than that."

"Oh yes! The pissers!"

"Excuse me?" Maggie asked, wondering if she had heard wrong.

"I said, the pissers— they got drunk in the local tavern and decided to have a pissing contest."

"And is that illegal?" she asked, confused.

"It's only illegal if you get so drunk that you turn around while you are doing it, completely miss your target, and manage to piss all over the newly purchased boots of a British major."

Oy.

He slapped the turkey leg down. "The Major was not amused!"

"I see," she said when she realized that there was only one thing that would work with this fellow. Maggie planted her hands on his desk—into something sticky. She raised her hand with a disgusted look on her face and wiped it on the back of a nearby chair, really not wanting to know what it was. "Okay, Captain, let's cut to the chase. What is it going to cost me to get my men out?"

He eyed her up and down with a lustful look upon his face as he picked at his teeth with his dirty fingernail.

"And not THAT either!" She shot him a nasty look. "I mean in terms of money. Let's make a deal."

Maggie walked out less than an hour later with all her men, a much lighter pocketbook, and a still sticky hand.

Captain Russell met them outside the tavern.

"Captain, get these men out of town as fast as possible."

"What about the wagons and horses?"

"Don't even bother wasting your time. I'm sure the British have seized them already. We will have to count them as lost. At least the cargo had already been unloaded and sold. We can acquire more once we are back at the estate. Take this money, buy some more horses and see them home. When you return, we will take the ship back to Williamsburg."

"Why don't we take them back on the ship?" Captain Russell asked, confused.

"Because Captain, your men decided it was a good idea to get drunk and have a pissing contest all over a British major's boots. It's probably best if they take the low road out of town."

Captain Russell rubbed his face, clearly irritated. "Son of a…. We will have a nice long chat on how to conduct ourselves in public on the way back home."

"I think that is a marvelous idea, Captain."

"But what about your safety here alone?"

"Don't worry about me, Captain. I will be just fine, and maybe I can do a little damage control in the meantime."

Maggie was sitting in a quiet back corner at the tavern where she had taken a room, sipping on a glass of ale, taking in the scene around her. The place was crawling with British soldiers, drinking and celebrating. The tavern owner had mentioned that the town had literally just been taken over after the Battle of Brandywine.

They were laughing, talking about how they would take the rebellion down in no time, showing these colonists who were in charge. These men had no idea who they were dealing with. Maggie was looking out the window lost in thought when she heard a cough. It was the tavern owner.

"May I refill your glass ma'am?"

"Yes, thank you."

"You aren't from around here, are you?"

"No, Williamsburg...I am here on business."

He pulled out a chair and sat down. "Ma'am, please forgive the intrusion, but I ask that you listen to me. This place is not safe for fine ladies such as yourself. These soldiers are getting rowdy, destroying everything in sight during the day and accosting women at night. They have taken over the entire town, including the room I had set aside for you for this evening. If you must stay, may I suggest you head out of town a bit? There is a little place a few miles away from here that has a nice tavern. I know it is safe because my brother and his wife run it; nobody will bother you out there. It's too far away from here for them."

"That's truly kind of you," said Maggie as she glanced at the soldiers getting drunker by the minute, "maybe I will take you up on that offer."

He seemed pleased. "I'm sending my wife and son out there with a couple of our horses for safekeeping. You could ride out with them. They are leaving in just a few minutes."

Maggie thanked him for his kindness, left a note for her captain, and two hours later arrived at the Rising

Sun Tavern. It was a quaint little place— a decent sized establishment, with a big fireplace, supper in the pot, and a few good, clean rooms upstairs. The tavern itself appeared to be on a well-traveled road, but back a little ways out of sight. If you didn't know it was there, you could easily miss it.

Maggie paid for her room for the next couple of weeks and went upstairs to drop off her stuff before it was time to eat. The room was much nicer than she expected. A nice, clean bed in the middle, a bench at its foot, a table and chairs in the corner, and its own fireplace. There were even picked flowers in a glass vase on the table.

She rather liked it.

Supper was a vegetable stew with a big chunk of cornbread that was particularly good, especially paired with a nice bottle of rum. Maggie relaxed in the back corner as she happily sipped from her glass. There were a few other people eating, mostly Quakers it seemed, the tavern being rather quiet.

Maggie was thankful for the peace. She was trying to concentrate on recalling her American history from high school. Remembering what happened around Williamsburg and Yorktown was easy, since she lived there with its living history museums, bringing it to life right before her eyes, but the rest of the details of the war were a bit hazy. She remembered the basics, but the small battles and skirmishes just weren't coming to her. She was just wishing she had paid more attention in history class and less attention to the cute guy who sat in front of her when THEY came in.

Five men, dressed in plain clothes, all wearing wool cloaks, doing their best to not draw attention to themselves. They took a table in the other back corner, across from Maggie, ordering food and ale, talking in hushed tones as if they didn't want anyone to hear.

Maggie stole a few good looks. The oldest man seemed to be the one in charge, having a commanding presence even though he only appeared to be in his forties. He was in exceptionally good shape with broad shoulders, like those of a man who worked hard and was proud of that fact. His cheekbones were high, a little rosy, highlighting what looked like chicken pox scars, his nose straight and prominent, accented by his dark brown hair tied back, and his bluish gray eyes.

There was something oddly familiar about him, but Maggie couldn't quite put her finger on it.

But it was the youngest man in the group that Maggie found herself drawn to. He was tall, maybe early twenties, with blond hair, blue eyes, a rather strong muscular body and a very handsome face.

Normally, Maggie just admired attractive men from afar. They were constantly parading themselves in front of her, cornering her at parties and in town, telling her how lovely she was, while touting all their finest qualities in hopes of courting her, dollar signs being the main thing they saw. Maggie paid them no mind. She had far too many secrets and responsibilities to let herself get distracted by a man, and honestly, she hadn't met anyone that even remotely interested her.

But she did miss sex. Oh God, did she miss sex, especially lately!

She had considered taking a lover — most of the widows in town took one discreetly on the side, but being wealthy, she wasn't sure she would be able to find anyone she could trust, so she had pushed the thought from her mind long ago.

The man across from her, however, had her having all sorts of improper thoughts. She must have been looking a little too much because he raised his head, meeting her gaze, and locked eyes with her, a stern look on his face.

Busted.

Maggie was about to direct her attention in another direction until his stern look broke into a very, subtle sly smile. She smiled back, and they locked eyes for several seconds. It was broken when three of the men at the table got up, bid the rest 'farewell' and departed. The one in charge and the handsome young man remained for another half an hour, continuing their hushed conversation.

Maggie couldn't hear what they were saying, but she had grown accustomed to seeing these confidential meetings in taverns in the past few years, not giving it a second thought. She was finishing her drink, thinking about turning in when the front door of the establishment burst open.

Three British soldiers strode in, heading straight to the tavern owner, asking him a bunch of questions. Most of the people eating didn't even raise their heads in acknowledgment, used to the drill, but the two men across from her lowered their heads, pulling their cloak hoods up and tight around their faces. The younger man scanned the room. She noticed that he had reached into his boot, pulled out a knife and laid it across his lap.

The soldiers moved from table to table, pulling people back to get better looks at their faces. The had checked everyone else and were headed straight for the two men.

The younger man tensed, tightening the grip on his knife, ready for a fight.

Don't get involved, Maggie; Don't get involved, Maggie.

"Excuse me, sir, may I help you?" Maggie put herself between the soldiers and the two men.

"Out of the way ma'am. We are searching for two traitors to the Crown that were seen coming this way."

"Oh my!" Maggie put on her best-shocked face, raising her hand to her mouth.

She really did deserve an Oscar for all the acting she had been doing lately.

"Well, thank goodness that you and your men are out here keeping all of us safe."

The soldier was impatient, looking around her at the two with their heads still down. "We need to check these men."

"Oh, Captain, is it? I can personally assure you that these men are no threat. You see, this one," she said, pointing to the older man, "is my father who has been very ill recently."

The man started to cough on cue.

"And the other one is my brother who is...well...he just isn't...right if you take my meaning. He is calm right now, but any little upset to his routine causes him to go into fits. Why, the last man that upset him...well, there was nothing the doctor could do to save him. He said it was the worst carnage he had ever seen inflicted on one person in all of his thirty years of being a doctor."

The young man shook the table and stomped the floor with his foot for emphasis.

At least I have good back up dancers.

Maggie gave him her best concerned expression. All three soldiers looked at each other unsurely as they shuffled their feet.

"Yes, well, just the same, we still have to check."

The younger man was about to lunge when Maggie motioned behind her back for him to stay. "I completely understand, but I know my dear friend Colonel Asheton would be so disappointed to hear that my father had been bothered when he was feeling so poorly. Why, he thinks of my father as his own."

The Captain blinked. "Colonel Asheton, you say?"

"Oh yes! He is like another brother to me." Maggie nodded. "You know him?"

The soldier stuttered, "I know him...that is...I mean to say ...I know of him…" He turned to his men. "Let's go. There is no one here." He tipped his hat respectfully to Maggie. "Ma'am, safe travels to you and give Colonel Asheton my regards."

"Thank you, Captain, and thank you again for ensuring the safety of our citizens." Maggie smiled and waved at them their whole way out. When she was certain they were gone, she turned around to see the two men standing and pushing their hoods back.

The older man spoke. "My dear lady, I don't know what to say except that I am forever in your debt." He bowed slightly.

Maggie looked at him and crossed her arms. “You really should scout your surroundings a little better before you sit down, sir, especially if you are a hunted man. You should always have an easily accessible escape route in place.”

He touched his chin and appeared rather amused by her advice. “Yes, that is something I will have to keep in mind for the future. Please, can you be so kind as to tell me the name of the lady I am so indebted to?”

“Mistress Maggie Bishop of Williamsburg.”

He was slightly taken aback. “YOU are Mistress Bishop? The one I have heard so much about? Allow me to introduce myself. I am General George Washington, Commander-in-Chief of the Continental Army.”

Maggie stood there, flabbergasted, her mouth gaping open, speechless. She could barely believe what she had just heard. The myth, the man, the legend; General George-freaking-Washington was standing right in front of her, and she had just saved his life.

“Permit me to introduce my associate, Major Benjamin Tallmadge.”

The young man bowed with the same shy grin on his face he’d had earlier.

Maggie nodded, even more stunned. For a war she went out of her way to not get involved in, she somehow managed to do it anyway, and with two of its key players.

“Please Mistress Bishop, sit and join us. It’s probably best we delay our exit while the soldiers are searching, and we appear to be safe here, thanks to your quick thinking.”

Maggie considered the invitation.

Oh, what the hell? How many people can say they had drinks with George Washington?

She took a seat.

The General called for more ale for himself and the Major, and more rum for Maggie.

Major Tallmadge spoke. “Mistress Bishop, what on Earth possessed you to do what you just did?”

Geez, even his voice was sexy.

Maggie shrugged. “You looked like you could use the assistance and besides, I was enjoying a quiet evening that I didn’t care to have interrupted.”

Both men found her explanation entertaining.

Washington regarded her with admiration. “Mistress Maggie Bishop, I am amazed we have not met sooner. You are a very well-known and respected lady throughout all of the Colonies.”

“So, I understand, General. I don’t leave my estate often, only if the shipping business takes me away. I have plenty at home to keep me busy.”

“Yes, I have heard of your estate, how self-sufficient and prosperous it is. They say you started out with a few acres and have grown it into quite the little domain.”

Maggie nodded and took a sip. “I started out with five hundred acres of ‘cursed’ land. I now have over ten thousand acres with my own personal little village, everything I, and the people on it, need to get by. I very rarely even have a need to go into town anymore.”

He looked fascinated and intrigued. “I am a farmer, as well, with a small estate, and I am always in search of new ways to improve and make things more efficient. I would very much like to hear about what you have done, and perhaps glean a few ideas for my own little corner of the world. I am looking forward to returning to the farm life once this war is over."

Maggie could tell that he loved being a planter more than anything, using the thought of it as an incentive to get him through the war. It broke her heart to know that this man would never be left alone, to be 'just' a farmer again. The survival of this country would demand on him spending the better part of his remaining time in this world putting her needs first and his own desires last.

"Well, General, you are welcome at Beechcroft at any time. I would be honored to host you."

He seemed very pleased with the idea.

"What about you, Major Tallmadge? What's your pre-war life story?"

He looked up from his ale. "Not much to tell! I was born in Setauket, graduated Yale in '73, was superintendent of Wethersfield High School for three years and ended up enlisting in '76."

"A high school? Really?" Maggie was surprised by that. "I would have never taken you as a superintendent of a school. The military life seems more... befitting."

He smiled, even blushing a little as he and Maggie exchanged an extended, lingering look.

General Washington seemed to notice the 'look', as well. He cleared his throat, breaking the trance, and they both looked away. "Major Tallmadge, it appears to be getting late, and since we are uncertain as to where the soldiers from earlier are, perhaps it's best if we stayed here tonight."

The Major gave the General a peculiar look. "I thought…"

The General lifted his hand and cut him off. "Mistress Bishop has provided us with a well thought out cover story, so no one will bother us here tonight, and the thought of sleeping in a bed is rather appealing at the moment,"

In her mind, Maggie could already see the placard reading 'George Washington slept her'.

"I think we should retire here for the night and get an early start in the morning."

Major Tallmadge replied, as if he were a little confused. "If you think that is best, General."

Washington looked at him and nodded, an impish look in his eyes. "I do, and I find myself very tired this evening. I think I shall retire early." He put his hand on Major Tallmadge's shoulder as he got up, patting it several times, looking over at Maggie and back at the Major. "I'll arrange the rooms; you take your time and enjoy your…ale."

He turned to Maggie. "Mistress Bishop, once again, I offer my gratitude. If you are ever in need, and it is within my power, I will be happy to return the favor. Good evening." He nodded and was gone, leaving Maggie and Major Tallmadge alone.

The pair spent the next few hours talking about everything and nothing. He talked about his father, who was a clergyman and his four brothers, the oldest who had been taken prisoner in the Battle of Long Island and died in a prison camp. He spoke of his love of learning, his years at Yale, his friendship with Nathan Hale, his years managing the high school and, finally, his promotion through the ranks in the Continental army.

Maggie spoke about her parents, as close to the truth as she could anyway, telling him that she had no one left, but the people she took care of on the estate. She told him about her best friend, Gabe, leaving out the whole 'he's a gay British Colonel' part. She glossed over the widowhood thing as well, since, truthfully, there was no husband. She spoke of her love for Beechcroft and for Williamsburg.

They laughed and talked until the tavern keeper told them he was blowing out the lanterns, but that the lamps in their rooms had been lit for them, neither realizing it had gotten to be that late. By that time, they were on a first name basis.

"I'm sorry Maggie, I have kept you up late. Let me escort you to your room."

They crept upstairs quietly, as to not disturb anyone else, until they reached her home for the night.

"Well, here we are. This is my room." Maggie stalled, even if it was just for a few more precious minutes.

"Yes," Ben replied, pointing at the door, "there it is."

They gazed at each other longingly, Maggie preparing—hoping—for a good night kiss. He leaned in close, inches from her face. Maggie could smell the scent of ale on his breath, and just as she was sure he was about to kiss her, he opened his mouth; she closed her eyes, turning her head ever so slightly…

"Good night, Maggie." And he stepped back.

Maggie took a few seconds to comprehend what was, well what wasn't, happening and composed herself.

"Good night, Ben." She turned to face her door and then right back again before he had a chance to move, "Ben?"

"Yes, Maggie?"

"I hope to see you again...soon."

A slow smile spread across his lips, as he reached out to gently touch his fingers to hers and whispered. "I would like that, as well."

He nodded, turned and headed down the hall to his room.

She was still standing there when he looked back before going inside.

Entering her own room, Maggie closed and bolted the door, pressed her back to it and slapped herself on the forehead for getting herself so worked up. Ben was a great guy; she really liked him.

He was handsome as hell and happened to have the nicest little ass she had seen since she got to the 18th century. Maggie was getting all hot and bothered thinking about him, about what she could do to him and what he could do to her.... but he was also from 1777 and the son of a preacher, no less. Men in this time were vastly different than in 2018. They were gentlemen, they wanted wives; they considered one passionate kiss grounds for marriage.

Maggie didn't want a husband; she didn't need one. She had managed to do just fine all on her own, but she certainly could have used a good, long night of fuc.... She shook her head.

"Put him out of your mind, Maggie, you are only torturing yourself," she said to herself, crawling into bed.

She spent the rest of the night tossing, turning and thinking about Ben.

The next morning, she was tired, cranky and horny...and that was not a good combination.

General Washington and Ben had already left by the time Maggie came down to eat, which was closer to dinnertime.

It was probably for the best. It would be easier to not want Benjamin Tallmadge if she didn't have to look at him. Besides, Ben would, without a doubt, complicate her decision to stay out of the war. She needed to focus on her number one concern: keeping everyone at home safe.

It would be a few weeks before the Captain would arrive back to escort her home. There wasn't much to do out where the tavern was— nothing really, since there was JUST the tavern, and a few weeks was a long time to stay holed up here, but she needed to deal with it until then.

She was eating dinner the next evening in her corner when she overheard a group of traveling Quakers that came through tell the tavern owner that the British had shut down the main roads going south out of Philadelphia just that morning —everyone was being searched, and having their papers checked. The soldiers were being very thorough inspecting all documentation.

Shit.

That meant that, while the Captain and her men had likely made their way out of town in time, getting back in could be a problem. This could delay his return, possibly by weeks or months. Captain Russell was very resourceful, but even he may not be able to get around the army that had Philadelphia locked up like a drum.

Even if he were here, she was sure the British would not release her ship, not at the moment anyway. She would just have to lay low.

The following night, she was sitting back, savoring the last bottle of rum in the tavern, listening to a storm rage outside. The place was about half full of people who were part of the mass exodus of the remaining few loyal to the colonists, and they were getting out while the getting was good. Most were headed for Lancaster, hoping for a warmer greeting, farther away from Philadelphia.

The wind blew open the front door, bringing a hooded figure in with it.

The figure went to the front, ordered and paid for an ale, and headed straight for Maggie's table by the fire. She had reached down, placing her hand on one of the daggers in her boot, when the person slid the hood back slightly.

There, staring back at her with a wide grin, was Ben.

Maggie was incredibly happy to see him.

"What are you doing here? It's not safe for you," Maggie asked, annoyed that he had put himself in danger.

"I came to see you."

"Me?"

He took a sip of his ale. "I came to warn you."

Maggie became concerned. "Warn me, about what?"

Ben leaned in close, whispering, "You need to be out of here soon. There will be a battle not far from here in a few days' time. It will be a little ways up the road, but I don't want you anywhere near it."

Maggie knew there were several skirmishes the first couple of years of the war, and while she couldn't remember names, dates or details, she did know that they did not go well for the Continental army. "But I can't go anywhere."

He looked confused. "Why not?"

"My ship is docked in Philadelphia and my captain is on his way, over land, back to Virginia. The British have blocked off the southern route out of the city, checking people and papers."

Ben seemed surprised. "When did they block off the southern route?"

"Yesterday, according to some of the people passing through."

He nodded. "They are probably trying to cut off supplies coming in. I'll let the General know, so we can plan around it

Please let that information that I just gave him not change anything in the war.

It was harder than she thought it would be to stay away from all of this.

"Ben, does the General know you are here?"

He looked down at his ale. "He knows that I had to come this way to deliver some information, and I may have suggested that we owed it to you to make sure you were safe since you saved our hides. He agreed and said that as long as I was back by morning, it would be alright."

Maggie glanced at the door. "I see. I am grateful for the information."

She looked over at his big, beautiful blue eyes. What was it about this man that had her so…? Maggie's left hand was on the table.

Ben reached over and placed his hand over hers, rubbing her fingers very lightly one by one with his thumb.

"Ben, was warning me the ONLY reason you came?" Maggie asked softly.

He looked up at her, trying to figure out how to answer and how to work up the nerve to say what he wanted to say. "I needed to make sure that you were safe...I wouldn't be able to live with myself if something happened to you that I could have prevented." He hesitated. "I know I have only known you a few days, but I do care about your welfare a great deal. To be completely honest, you are all I have thought about since the day we met."

A warmness flooded Maggie's heart, and spread a little bit lower. The door to the tavern opened again, and Maggie saw two British soldiers come inside; Ben's back was to them.

"Pull up your hood," Maggie whispered as she kept a cautious eye on them.

Ben did as he was told.

"Follow my lead."

He nodded.

Maggie took his hand in hers, his elbow on the table, and started running her fingers up and down the length of his arm. She giggled and touched his face, as if she had too much to drink and she couldn't keep her hands off him.

Standing, she tugged him to his feet and led him up the stairs by the fireplace to the rooms above, keeping his back to the soldiers —she herself walking up them backwards to keep a watchful eye on them. The soldiers noticed them and started moving that way. Maggie giggled and waved to them with a devilish smile.

"We were just married. It's our wedding night," she called to them behind her hand.

The soldiers did not move for a full minute, watching her intently. Finally, one of them waved her off with a wide grin, indicating they would not bother them.

She giggled all the way up the stairs. She led Ben to the end of the hall and pointed to the owner's back steps that led down into the kitchen and to a side door.

Ben took Maggie by both shoulders. "Go to Philadelphia. You will be safe there. Pretend to be a Loyalist if you need to and do whatever it takes. We have friends in town there. I will get word to you after the battle. Please be safe."

Maggie looked at Ben. "I'm not the one going into battle. Be careful and please come back to me, Ben. Now, go before you get caught." She pushed him towards the stairs.

He stopped, turned, cupped her face in his hands and kissed her. His lips were firm, pressing to hers, his tongue sweeping inside, laying claim. His fingers clung to her skin, like he never wanted to let go.

The heat from the kiss shot through Maggie's entire body and her knees went weak.

His smile afterward was huge. He turned and was gone.

Maggie stood there and watched him go.

What the hell have I gotten myself into?

She answered herself out loud. "Another sleepless, restless, horny night in bed alone —that's exactly what you have gotten yourself into. Where's a cold shower when you need it?"

The next day, Maggie managed to buy a horse from the tavern owner, one that she fully intended to return via his brother in town. On her way out, the wife of the tavern owner in town ran out, asking her to please take a basket of eggs to her husband. The woman was concerned about him not having enough to eat, since the British soldiers had taken over their business, running up bills without paying.

Maggie took them and promised to deliver them. She was stopped upon entering the town but told them she was just returning from the country after picking up some eggs. The soldiers bought her story, and they dared not pat down a lady.

A good thing too. If they had found her sword secured to her back or the daggers in her boots, she would have been in all kinds of trouble.

The town had turned into redcoat central; Soldiers were everywhere, filling the streets, the taverns, and the homes of the residents that had fled.

Maggie got off her horse and looked around. Where the devil was she going to stay? All the places for rent were taken over, and she just couldn't set up in someone else's house. She stood there, rubbing her temples, a stress headache starting to form. She seemed to be having a good deal of them lately.

With her eyes closed, she heard it. Turning her head, she thought it must have been her imagination, until she heard it again— a distinct, familiar voice.

Searching all around, her eyes locked on a man astride a horse. She would recognize that side profile anywhere.

She called out, waving. "Gabe! Gabe!"

He turned his head in response and saw her, taking a moment to realize that it was, indeed, his Maggie. He slid off the horse and headed towards her and she towards him. They wrapped their arms around each other, hugging and laughing.

"Let me have a good look at you. Oh God, Maggie, you look wonderful. I have missed you so much."

Maggie looked back at him. "I have missed you too. I am so happy to see you."

They embraced again.

"What are you doing here?" He held her at arms' length.

"I had some business to take care of. I am waiting for my captain to get back to get me home. What are *you* doing here? I thought you were in New York?"

He wrapped one arm around her, leading her off the street. "Army business brought me here. I handle a great deal of confidential information, and I must go where I am needed. Where are you staying?"

"I was just trying to figure that out. I stayed a few nights at a tavern outside of town, but I am looking for something here, in town, so my captain can find me when he returns."

He led her up the street and stopped in front of a house. "Well, look no further. The army has put me up here, and you will stay with me. We can catch up and you will be much safer under my roof."

Maggie smiled and hugged him again. "I am so glad to see you."

Gabe led Maggie in, introduced her to the servant of the house, Serena, and showed her around. "Make yourself at home. I have to go attend to some affairs, but I should be back by supper, so we will have plenty of time to talk."

He kissed her on the top of the head and left.

Maggie couldn't believe her luck. She had a place to stay, and it was with her best friend. She went into the parlor, poured herself a drink, and plopped down in a comfortable chair, looking around. It was a lovely house; the walls were painted a cheerful yellow, accented with light blue curtains and furniture.

Serena appeared at the door. "Can I get you anything, ma'am?"

Maggie looked up. "Oh no, thank you, I'm perfectly fine. Serena, who lives here?"

Serena looked to a family portrait above the fireplace of a man, a woman, and four children. "The Turner family. They were forced out with the rest of the supporters of the Continental army when the British arrived. The soldiers took over the houses of the families who were loyal to the Patriots. They called them traitors, said they could go live in the woods with Washington and his army. Didn't even let them take their personal items."

Maggie looked horrified, afraid to ask her next question. "Serena, did Colonel Asheton put anyone on the street?"

Serena thought a minute. "No, ma'am, at least I don't think so. He just arrived, and the other soldiers had already run people off by then."

"Thank you, Serena."

She disappeared.

Maggie gazed up at the portrait, grateful that Gabe hadn't turned these poor people out himself and wondering if he was the same Gabe she knew and loved.

A few hours later, Maggie and Gabe were talking and laughing over supper. She filled him in on the estate, how much it had grown, on the gossip in Williamsburg, and even on the never-ending shenanigans of Onyx.

He roared with laughter when she explained her reason for coming to Philadelphia because he knew the Major whose boots they had pissed on, and the man was a total prick. He told her about the past two years in New York, how things were going very well for him, career-wise, and how the change of scenery had been good for him since Jonathan had passed.

They remembered him fondly, even raising a toast to his memory. They steered clear of war talk. Maggie respected the fact that Gabe was a British officer, a title he was very proud of, and Gabe knew Maggie's loyalties, given her position in Virginia, would naturally lean towards the Patriots, though she never said it aloud.

Neither wanted to let their political differences come between their friendship.

The next morning, Gabe was gone when Maggie came downstairs. Maggie noticed the area around where they were staying was in a very bustling part of town, with lots of people and shops. She decided she could use a little distraction, so she left a note for Gabe and headed out on the street. Walking by one of the stores, Maggie noticed a window with several dresses in it. She had packed lightly, not planning on staying long, and decided that it would be nice to have some new things.

Philadelphia in 1777 was an enigma. Half of the town had evacuated, leaving in such a hurry that they left entire houses full of the precious items they had spent a lifetime collecting. The other half of the town acted as if it were just another ordinary day. The Loyalists of this town were out and about, shopping, dining and enjoying themselves, pretending as if the other part had never existed.

The whole scene was very strange, especially for Maggie, who knew that another battle was about to take place not far from here. She hoped Gabe wouldn't be involved; she wanted him safe, but she couldn't very well tell him about it without confessing that she had spent time with the General of the opposing army right after saving him from being captured.

Maggie still had no intention of getting involved in this war, she was too afraid of changing the outcome inadvertently, but it was proving more difficult by the day.

And then, there was the little matter of Benjamin Tallmadge. She tried her best to not think about him, but that was proving impossible. She had to find a way to put him out of her mind.

Maybe a little shopping would help.

Five dresses, three pairs of shoes and several boxes of other things later, he was on her mind more than ever.

Later that night at supper, Gabe seemed distracted.

"Gabe, what's wrong? You are so quiet."

He looked up from the peas he had been pushing around with his fork. "Forgive me, Maggie. I have a great deal on my mind."

Maggie slowed her chew, looking him over. "Anything I can help with?"

He pushed more of his food around. "I don't want to bore you with army matters. I'm just afraid another battle may be looming. There has been some movement from the other side, and we aren't sure what they are up to."

Maggie looked down, guilt gnawing at her conscience. "I'm sure you will figure it out."

Putting his fork down, Gabe propped up his elbows and looked her directly in the face. "So, Serena tells me that you bought out a store today."

Whew! She'd thought he'd figured something out there for a moment.

"Yes, well, since I wasn't planning on staying in Philadelphia very long, I didn't bring a lot with me. I can't very well walk around town naked," she teased.

He grinned. "Well, you could, but you wouldn't have anywhere to hide your sword."

They both laughed.

"Are you keeping up your lessons?"

Maggie smirked. "Of course, I am. It is a wonderful stress reliever. Although, I think Harm and Joshua are getting tired of making dummies for me to practice on. No bag of hay will ever dare cause trouble at Beechcroft." She waved her butter knife around in the air; Gabe seemed to be coming around. "Oh, and I added to my arsenal." Maggie reached to her boots and pulled out the two daggers that she had specially made, laying them on the table.

Gabe raised an eyebrow, picking up one for a better look, running his finger along the blade. "I'm impressed." He peered closer. "These are very nice."

Maggie took a sip of wine. "Thank you. I had my blacksmith make them just the right size to fit here," she said and pointed to her custom boots.

He looked down, feigning shock. "What happened to my sweet little Maggie?"

Maggie's smile faded. "She had to grow up. Too many people were depending on her to take care of them."

Gabe looked at her compassionately, knowing that she had much more responsibility than any one person should. "Uneasy lies the head that wears a crown." He reached over and laid his hand on top of hers.

Maggie laid her other hand on top of his, lowering her eyes solemnly.

"So," Gabe said, trying to lighten the mood, "any of those eligible bachelors in Williamsburg got their eye on you?"

Maggie laughed. “Yeah, all of them. Last month, one tried to propose, but he was so old he kept forgetting his name and what question he was trying to ask.”

Gabe chortled.

“Seriously, I can’t even go to town anymore. I get cornered everywhere I go by men aged thirteen to eighty-four. I’m a woman with land and money; I am more sought after than the Holy Grail these days.”

Gabe was in full belly laugh.

“Oh, laugh it up chuckles. Mess with me and I’ll tell everyone I come across that you are on the hunt for a wife...and that you’re hung like a horse.”

He tried to look appalled, but it just came out as a goofy face.

Maggie loved that they could talk and joke about anything and everything.

“What about you Gabe? Seeing anyone special?”

He shook his head, wiping the tears from laughing so hard from his eyes. “No, I haven’t had the time and it’s not like my type is on every corner.”

Maggie looked him in the eye. “You will find someone.”

He nodded. “But, seriously, Mags; you haven’t found anyone you are even remotely interested in?”

Maggie hesitated, a little too long, and Gabe noticed. “You ARE interested in someone.”

Sighing, Maggie shook her head, laying the napkin on her lap across her plate.

Gabe leaned back with a glass of wine in his hand. “Come on, Maggie, don’t leave me in suspense.”

She propped her elbows on the table. “I did meet someone at the tavern that I was staying at for a few days," she made sure to take her time and word it carefully, "we spent all night talking before he had to leave. It was nice. I felt something that I haven't felt in an awfully long time."

"And, you haven't seen him since?" Gabe asked quietly, rubbing his chin.

"I did, briefly. He couldn't stay long, but he did kiss me before he left, and boy, it was a kiss." Maggie sipped her glass again.

Gabe looked at her incredulously. "Well, well, well, would you look at that? I think Maggie is in love."

Maggie picked up the napkin and threw it at him. "Stop! I have seen him twice and probably never will again. Hardly time to fall in love, LUST maybe, but not love."

Gabe leaned forward. "For as long as I have known you, I have never heard you talk about anyone like this."

Maggie shrugged. "I have never had the luxury. Gabe, I have so many people who need me, who depend on me...I have worked hard to make a safe place for them and I can never do anything to endanger their lives, even if it means that I am alone for the rest of mine. But then, back in that tavern, no one knew who I was. No responsibility, whatsoever, and, for a little while, it was great. I was just a woman talking to a man, and enjoying the hell out of it, even if it was just for a little while."

Gabe refilled her glass. "You know, no one expects you to give up all of your happiness for them. You are allowed— no, you deserve to have something special."

Maggie looked at Gabe. "Doesn't matter, I'm sure he is long gone by now. Besides, right now, I would just settle for a night of really great SEX. God, I miss sex so much."

Gabe choked on his wine. When he was done coughing and sputtering, he looked over at her. "Well then, what did you say his name was? I may need to get a good look at this man."

"Ben, his name is Ben."

A few days later, a battle did indeed occur not far from the tavern Maggie had stayed at in a little area called Germantown. Gabe thankfully was in Philadelphia during the skirmish, which did not turn out well for the Americans. An unfortunate fog caused a great deal of confusion for Washington's troops.

Maggie was terribly worried about Ben, but she had no way of finding out about him without raising eyebrows; every night she sent up a silent prayer for his safety.

Gabe was busy meeting with army officials at all hours of the day and night, and Maggie was becoming more restless by the day. She decided to go out for a stroll. Passing an alley, she felt like someone was watching her. Maggie ducked into a store for a few minutes, and when she came out, the feeling was still there.

Over the years, Maggie's senses had become very finely tuned to what was going on around her, to the point of inexplicably being able to anticipate other people's actions. She turned down an alley as if she were on a specific path, knowing the person following her would, too. She leaned against a doorway, and as the cloaked figure on her tail passed by, she stealthily fell in a few feet behind, so that she was now the one following. Thinking it might be a robber, Maggie pulled one of the daggers from her boot and slipped it in the sleeve of her cloak. The person approached the end of the alleyway, turned right and was gone by the time Maggie got there. She looked up and down the street seeing no one. Standing there, wondering where in the heck the person went, an arm snaked around her waist and a hand covered her mouth.

Oh no, you don't.

Just as Maggie was about to elbow him and swing around with her concealed knife, she heard him whisper,

"Maggie, Maggie! Stop! It's me, Ben."

It took a few seconds for Maggie to register. He pulled her into a doorway, looked up and down the street, then released his hand from her mouth.

"Ben!"

They embraced, then she slapped him on the chest; his hands never released his hold on her waist.

"You scared me to death. What are you doing here?"

Ben looked down at her, saying dryly, "Well, it's nice to see you, too."

"Oh, of course, I'm glad to see you." She reached up and pulled him into a kiss.

Ben, looking happily stunned, grinned as Maggie cupped his face. "I was worried to death about you."

He pulled her in tighter. "I'm fine. It just took me a few days to get away from camp after the battle. It didn't go as well as we had hoped."

Maggie caressed the cuts on his face. “As long as you are safe, that’s all that matters.”

He kissed her. “We are pulling out soon, and I am not sure when we will be near Philadelphia again. Winter is coming, and Washington is planning on moving us to Valley Forge.”

Maggie cringed. She knew that part of history. Valley Forge would be far from a picnic for these soldiers. Images from portraits in museums flashed in her head. Men with no shirts, no boots, very few, if any, supplies, and lots of snow. It would be close to the breaking point for the Americans. The thought of Ben in those conditions broke her heart.

He pushed the hair back from her face. “If you can break away, I can get to the tavern this evening. I am not safe here in Philadelphia, but I can make it there if I am careful. I am not sure how much time we have left here, but I would really like to see you while I can.”

Maggie didn’t hesitate. “I’ll be there.”

Ben hugged her, whispering in her ear, “I have to go. I will see you tonight.” He kissed her hand and slipped away.

Oh, Maggie, what the hell are you doing?

Maggie stopped and did a little shopping on the way back to the house. By the time she arrived, Gabe had sent word that he wouldn’t be home until late. She left a note for him saying that she would be back for supper the following day, packed a few things—including her trusty egg basket for a cover story—and headed to the tavern.

When she got there, Maggie secured meals and drinks for two, and a room for herself for the night. She took the table in the corner near the fireplace and waited. A few people came in to eat, but no British soldiers.

Maggie waited, warmly buzzed by the time Ben arrived. He slipped in the side door, wearing the same cloak from earlier. After checking the room, he felt safe enough to lower the hood, flashing a smile.

That man is too handsome for my own good.

He took a seat next to her as the tavern keep brought over a tankard of ale for him.

He took her hand on the table. "I am so happy that you came, Maggie. I was afraid you might not."

She squeezed his hand. "Of course, I came. I wouldn't have missed it."

They had supper and were drinking, just enjoying being together, when the door opened. Two British soldiers entered. They seemed more interested in ordering ale than looking around the room, so Maggie and Ben took the opportunity to slip up the stairs unnoticed. They stood before Maggie's door, Ben holding both her hands.

"I suppose I should go."

Maggie looked at him, lowering her eyes. "Do you have to go NOW?"

"I do not have to be back until the morning, but…".

"But… I have a room, and we can talk without worrying about any soldiers coming in to interrupt us."

He looked at her, anguished. "It would not be proper for me to be in there."

Maggie looked at him with a devilish grin. "Good thing I am not much on propriety." She opened the door and pulled him in.

He looked around, as if afraid someone might jump out at anytime. Inside the room, the tavern owner had lit the fire and the lanterns for the night and had been kind enough to leave a bottle of brandy and a glass on the table.

Maggie led Ben over to the table and chairs, pouring the glass and they took turns sipping. She slipped her hand across the table into his.

Leaning in, he kissed her— a long, slow, passionate kiss that took on a sense of urgency. Maggie stood up and moved to stand in front of him. He took her by the waist, looking into her eyes with a deep longing. Maggie undid the ribbon holding her hair, shaking it out. She took his head in her hands and pulled him into another sensual kiss. He wrapped his arms around her pulling her tighter. Maggie pushed back just enough to untie his shirt, slowly, deliberately, reaching down to pull it up over his head and dropped it onto the floor. She ran her hands over his chest and down his back as he looked at her with an unmistakable hunger. Maggie started to untie the laces on her dress when he put his hands on hers to stop her.

"Maggie…"

Maggie froze wondering if she had misread the whole situation. She waited, thinking that this was the time that came the 'it's not you, it's me' speech when he said something that completely caught her off guard.

"Maggie, I don't know...I have never…"

She looked at him quizzically. “What is it? You don’t want to do this?”

He looked alarmed. “No, no! It’s not that. I want you, Maggie, I want you more than I have ever wanted anyone or anything in my life. I want to be with you... tonight.”

“Then, what’s the problem?”

He looked like he was at a loss for words. “I have never...been... with a woman before.”

Maggie tilted her head, astonished. “You are a virgin?”

He nodded.

Maggie blew out a long breath. “Are you sure you want to do this, that you don’t want to save yourself for marriage?”

He looked her deeply in the eyes. “I’m sure.” He pulled her to him, kissing her.

Maggie finished untying her gown, dropping it to the floor. She stepped out of her shoes and the dress, standing only in her shift, which she slowly, seductively lifted over her head, leaving her completely nude. Maggie took his head in her hands pulling his face to her breast, positioning him exactly right.

He lightly stroked one of her erect nipples before replacing his fingers with his lips, suckling as she guided his movements by pressing her body closer to his.

Maggie tossed her head back and moaned in response to let him know how much she enjoyed that.

Encouraged, Ben moved to the other, doing the same before tracing a path with his tongue down to her belly button.

Maggie reached down, took him by the hand, and led him to the bed. She kissed him tenderly, helping him to undress. She laid back, pulling him on top of her so they could explore each other with their hands and lips. She gently pushed him over on his back so that she was able to straddle him, teasing one nipple, then the other, until he groaned in delight. She slowly moved downward with her tongue, to the inside of his thigh, then worked her way back up to her ultimate goal.

Taking his manhood into her mouth, she started out licking slowly, watching his face as his eyes closed, and occasionally opening them to look down at her. She could tell that he was trying to hold himself back, moaning in ecstasy as it hit him in waves. She picked up a little speed and when he took her head in his hands, pulling her closer to him on the verge, she stopped.

He looked down, confused.

Maggie worked her way back up the length of his body and sank her tongue into his mouth, enjoying and exploring as she worked him up even more. She smiled as she positioned herself over him and lowered herself onto his member.

She watched his face as he gasped in delight, looking up at her, his mouth agape as she took him all the way inside. She moved, slowly at first, letting him enjoy the sensation until he was unable to wait any longer. He took over, moving faster and faster, pounding harder into her until satisfying his need was all that mattered.

Her orgasm built as well, and she called out to him as she reached that point. “Oh! Oh! Ben!”

He was making his own pleasurable exclamations as his momentum built and it wasn't long before he cried out her name with this final release.

Once they were both fully satisfied, Maggie collapsed on his chest. He pulled her face to his, covering her with kisses. Maggie's heart was pounding, and her breathing had become heavy. She slipped to his side and panted as she stretched her arm across his chest.

Ben looked over at her, seeing her out of breath and flushed, suddenly concerned. "Are you alright? Did I hurt you?"

Maggie laughed. "Noooo! You did not hurt me; believe me, you did not hurt me at all. What about you? How do you feel?"

Ben relaxed, smiling. "I…. feel…. amazing. I had no idea."

They both laughed, kissing and exploring each other, happy and content, even if it was only for the night. They made love twice more, until they both fell asleep, entangled in one another's arms, exhausted, and blissfully in love.

The next morning, Maggie woke to find Ben putting on his boots. He was still shirtless, so she reached over and stroked his back.

He turned around, leaned over crawling on top of her, kissing her. "I'm sorry. I did not mean to wake you." He went back to getting dressed.

Maggie watched him putting on his shirt, propping herself up on her elbow. "Here's a thought. How about you resign from the army and come with me to Virginia? We can lay in bed all day, making love."

He pretended to think. “What about food? I can work up quite an appetite.”

Maggie bantered back, “I have so many servants that they can bring us food all day long. We never have to get out of bed.”

“As tempting as that sounds, I have a war to get back to.”

Maggie made a sad face.

“But don’t worry, sweet Maggie, I will be back for you. Wild horses will not keep me away.”

He sat back down on the bed, pulling her close and kissing her. “But, if I do not leave soon, General Washington will have me up on desertion charges.” He gathered his things.

Maggie threw the covers back and walked naked over to the items she had brought with her.

Ben stopped to stare as she walked by. “God, you are beautiful.”

She came back to him with a pile of things. “You need to take these.”

He accepted the items. “What’s all this?”

Maggie sighed. “They are things to take to Valley Forge when you go— some blankets, some new shirts and socks, and a very warm wool cloak. There is also some money sewn into the bottom seam. Keep it for the trip to Valley Forge, in case I don’t see you before then, and buy food any chance you get.”

He looked at Maggie, taken aback. “I can’t take all of this from you.”

She insisted. “Oh, yes, you can, and you will. Valley Forge in the winter will not be easy, especially with the British cutting off supply lines.”

He looked at her, grateful. “Maggie do not worry about me. I will be fine.”

She moved closer to him. “I know, but if you find yourself in need of supplies or money, ever, send word to me and I will get you what you need. I will be in Philadelphia until my captain gets back, and in Virginia after that, but I have my ship on standby and can sail with very little notice.”

Ben set the things aside and pulled her close to him. “The only thing I need is for you to be safe and sound.”

She nodded.

“I have to go, but if I can get away again soon, I will somehow get word to you. I will think of nothing but you, my sweet Maggie.” He kissed her one last time and was gone.

The happiness from the night before was slowly replaced by the reality of what she had done. Sadness and guilt washed over her.

Nice going Maggie! You just did the one thing you promised yourself you wouldn’t do. You very well may have fucked up the future. All because you wanted to get laid.

The whole ride back to Philadelphia, Maggie’s mind was consumed with guilt. She had no doubt that she had fallen in love with Ben Tallmadge, a man that was to marry another woman after the war, going on to have a crapload of kids, all who would have important jobs in the developing new country.

She was not destined to be with him.

That one thing alone could have already changed the future. For all she knew, the simple act of giving him blankets for Valley Forge could have changed it. Maggie felt a very nasty, nagging headache coming on.

She reached Gabe's house just before dinner in a less than perfect mood. She went straight to the parlor, in desperate need of a drink.

Gabe sat on the couch, nursing a glass of his own, looking a little out of sorts.

"What are you doing home so early?" she asked, pouring her drink and plopping herself on the couch next to him.

"Oh, I have had a hell of a day. I spent most of it dodging the advances of a very merry, widow woman looking for husband number six —yes SIX! I had to leave the office and come home to work to get some peace and quiet. What about you? Where have you been all night?" He gave her a good look over, sipping his brandy.

Maggie frowned before answering. "Safely securing my spot in Hell —I just spent the entire night bedding a virgin."

Gabe stopped mid-sip, looking over at Maggie, stupefied. After a few seconds of registering what she had just said, he lifted his glass in a toast. "Oh good, we can share the same handbasket on the way."

They leaned towards each other and clinked glasses.

Gabe eyed Maggie. "So, are you going to share the details on this virgin deflowering willingly, or are you going to make me beg?"

Maggie looked down at her glass with a sheepish grin. "Sure, right after you share the details of your new...fiancé is it? What date should I make myself available for the wedding?"

Gabe rolled his eyes and his head toward the back of the couch, as if completely drained of energy, and sighed. "Oh, that woman, Mrs. Francis Bright, the last name of husband number five that she still goes by, or as she wants me to call her, Fannie."

Maggie covered her mouth, stifling her laughter. She was quite sure that 'Jingle Bells' hadn't been written yet, but she secretly wondered if it would be about this particular woman.

"Let me guess, is she a rather full-figured lady?"

Gabe looked at her, one brow arched. "Yes, how did you know? Have you met her?"

Tears came to Maggie's eyes; it was becoming harder to hold in her laughter. "No, I haven't had the pleasure...although I am very much looking forward to it. Continue, please."

Gabe shot her a disapproving look. "Yes, well, we were introduced at dinner the very first day I was here, at the Shippen's residence. The first night we met, she cornered me, wanting to be sure, that I knew she was available. Since then, she's come by the field office in town, waving through a window, or 'happened to be passing by' whenever I go outside — one of the reasons I have been working later the past few days. Even then, I have been leaving through the back door, just in case. She has no idea that I can see her waiting from the corner window. Today, however, she appeared at dinnertime with a basket of food and a picnic blanket, hoping 'we could enjoy an early dinner on this fine, crisp day before the weather started to turn colder'. I told her that I was expected elsewhere, came straight home and bolted the door. I have been hiding in here ever since. Serena has had to tell her three times already today that I was 'unavailable'."

Maggie could no longer hold back the laughter.

"I'm glad you find this so amusing," Gabe said dryly.

"So, have you picked out a china pattern yet, or should I just surprise you?" Maggie wiped the tears away.

He got up to bring the brandy tumbler over to refill her glass and his. Maggie was still laughing when Gabe sat back down and laid his arm on the couch behind Maggie's back.

"Your turn."

Maggie's laughter came to an end, her face became solemn and she pulled her feet up underneath her.

The look on her face caused Gabe to become concerned. "Maggie, did this man hurt you...or did you hurt him?"

She shot him a look. "It wasn't like that."

"Well, you don't look very happy for someone who spent the whole night with a man. Was he not... 'UP' for the challenge, so to speak?"

Maggie playfully smacked him. "He was...thank you very much. Ben was...wonderful."

"Ah, so it was the mysterious Ben you turned into a man."

She cut her eyes over at him.

He leaned toward her. "Maggie, what's wrong? I can tell something is bothering you a great deal."

Maggie looked at him, tracing the edge of her glass with her finger. "Oh Gabe, I think I have gone and fallen hard for a man that can never be mine." She leaned over on his chest.

He set his glass down and pulled her to him, smoothing her hair. "Well, obviously he isn't married if he is...*was* still a virgin, so what's the problem? Is he engaged to someone else?"

Maggie wanted to tell Gabe the truth, but she couldn't. She had thought about telling him about her past...well, the future she was from, but she was too afraid he would think her mad, and she couldn't lose him. She hadn't told anyone, and the truth burdened her, so she simply said, "It's just extremely complicated. There can be no future for us."

"There is no future for any of us really, Maggie. None of us know how much time we have with someone, so you just have to take the moments of happiness when you can, for as long as you can. Enjoy him, even if it's for just a little while."

She knew he was thinking about Jonathan when she saw a small tear escape his eye. Looking up at him, she wrapped him in a tight hug. "I miss Jonathan, too."

Three days later, Gabe announced that he had to go to New York to report on troop movements.

Maggie knew that part of his job was handling sensitive information, so she never asked details. The less she knew, the better. That way, there was a less likely chance of her interfering with the way things turned out— a thought, that every time it came to her, also came with a debilitating headache. The whole time-travel thing was way over her head; she would make herself crazy trying to work out every little detail of 'what if?' and frankly, it was exhausting.

Maggie thought about Gabe's advice. Maybe, she should enjoy what time she could with Ben and just remember to be in the moment, taking what happiness she could while it was there. Her future wasn't promised, and for all she knew, she might not live to see the end of the war. Her estate wasn't in the future; it would have been well known if it was. Maybe everything she worked so hard to protect and preserve would just fade away in the next few years, along with the rest of Williamsburg. The thought made her shudder.

Gabe left the next morning and Maggie received a note from Ben that afternoon wishing to meet at the tavern that night. The thought of seeing him made Maggie ecstatic and afraid at the same time.

Live in the moment, Maggie.

She couldn't help herself; she rode out, egg basket in hand, to the tavern. The whole 'needing eggs' charade had turned out to be a simple and ingenious way of getting in and out of town without any trouble from the British.

Maggie was in her room at the tavern before supper, when there was a knock at the door. Opening the door, Ben rushed in, picking her up in his arms, kicking the door closed behind him, and kissing her ravenously.

There greeting was raw, animalistic.

He pushed her against the back of the door, pinning her arms above her head with one hand.

Maggie laughed as his kisses moved down to her neck; he cupped one of her breasts through the fabric of her dress, causing her to moan. Lowering his mouth, he bit at her nipple with his teeth through the cloth as he kneaded and teased with his palm. Maggie's body was overcome with a desperate need for this man.

He released her arms so that he could free her from her restraints, undoing the top of her gown and pushing it down to her waist, freeing her swollen breasts as he roughly kissed her lips.

Maggie pulled his cloak and coat off, dropping them to the floor in one swift move; she removed his shirt in the seconds that followed. She ran her hands over his chest and up to his head, threading her fingers through his now loose hair, before pulling his head down to her bust.

Ben suckled her breasts as he rid her of the rest of her gown. He wrapped his arms around her bottom, picked her up and carried her to the bed, laying her down, his expression heavy with love and desire in his eyes. He disposed of the rest of his clothing and climbed atop her. He teased her nipples with his tongue before moving further down to begin his oral exploration of the crevice between her thighs.

She writhed with desire and pulled his mouth closer to her mound as he went about his mission of pleasing her.

He glanced up at her face to see how lost she was in the moment and was emboldened by the fact that he had the power to make her feel that way.

Her hips fell into a perfect rhythm with his actions; the pleasure building quickly within her. She cried out and gripped the sides of his head with her hands as her back arched, her body trembled, and she came hard.

She pulled his head up to hers. "I need you inside me! NOW!" she commanded.

Ben grinned, happy to oblige as he positioned himself between her legs and plunged deeply into her core. He moved in and out slowly at first, before his own urgent demands took over and he quickened his pace. When he could hold back no more, his seed erupted, filling her completely. He rested his forehead upon hers before taking the time to slowly and tenderly kiss her.

They rolled to one side, their bodies still connected and lay happily sated.

"I'm sorry, Maggie," he whispered.

"For what?" she asked and stroked his chest.

He kissed her forehead. "For being so rough. It's just that I missed you so much and I couldn't control myself. I hope I did not cause you any discomfort."

Maggie closed her eyes, snuggling in tighter. "You did not hurt me. It made me feel like I was the most desired woman in the world."

He ran his fingers lightly over her back, saying softly, "You ARE the most desired woman in the world —at least in MY world. I can't imagine I will ever want another."

Maggie opened her eyes, a familiar pang of guilt creeping into her conscious mind.

Be in the moment, Maggie. This may be the last time you get to spend with him. Tomorrow is not promised.

She closed her eyes and slipped her hand down the length of his body, all the way down, until she reached her intended destination. She gently stroked and kneaded him until he was ready for her once more.

He tenderly called out her name as he rolled her underneath him, and they spent the rest of the night living in the moment.

The next morning, Ben was getting dressed when he noticed Maggie's sword. "What's this?"

Ben had come in so unexpectedly the night before, that she hadn't had the chance to put it away. "It's mine. I carry it everywhere I go."

He looked a little taken aback.

Maggie noticed his reaction. "I was attacked when I first came to Williamsburg. I vowed never to let myself be that vulnerable again, so I carry it holstered under my cloak everywhere I go."

He picked it up for a better look, admiring the quality. "Do you know how to use it?"

She moved next to him and took it from his hand before putting it away. "Yes. Gabe taught me how to use it. He is a very good teacher."

He put his arms around her from behind, kissing her neck. "You are a remarkable woman, Maggie Bishop," he said and made love to her one more time before he left.

Maggie, back in town, and having delivered another basket of eggs to the tavern, headed back to the house. She had just finished dressing after a long and much-needed bath when Serena knocked on her bedroom door.

"Mistress Bishop, there is someone here to see you. I think it's important."

Maggie followed Serena downstairs. Standing in the foyer was an officer that Maggie recognized as Gabe's personal assistant.

He saw her coming down the stairs. "Mistress Bishop, I need a word alone with you," he said with a grave look on his face.

Maggie had a sinking feeling in the bottom of her stomach as she showed him to the parlor.

"Mistress Bishop, there is something I need to tell you."

Maggie swallowed hard, preparing for the worst.

"Colonel Asheton left instructions with me to notify you if anything should happen to him."

Oh God, not Gabe!

"Colonel Asheton left yesterday morning on a mission to New York. He did not arrive at the appointed checkpoint. We have evidence to suggest that he was captured and taken prisoner by the Continental army. We have men searching for him as we speak."

Maggie let out the breath she had been holding, leaning against a table. "But you don't think he's dead."

"No, ma'am, we do not. Colonel Asheton would be far too valuable for the information that he knows. They would interrogate him, and once they were satisfied they had extracted all pertinent information, they would likely hold him for a high-profile prisoner exchange in one of their prison camps."

Gabe must have been a much more important man in the army than she realized. A grim thought came to mind. "When you say 'extracted', what do you mean?"

The man looked down as if he didn't want to answer. "Ma'am, the information that the Colonel is privy to is extremely sensitive and would be very valuable to the other side…" he trailed off, leaving her to fill in the blanks.

Maggie grasped his meaning and very calmly stated the obvious aloud, "You mean they would torture him."

"Yes ma'am, they would not hesitate."

Maggie closed her eyes, the grim reality washing over her. This was war, and each side would do whatever they had to do to win— each desperately trying to hold onto their own way of life and doing anything they deemed fit in the process. Now, she had become stuck right in the middle, exactly where she had vowed to never place herself, because she had soldiers on both sides that she loved dearly.

"We will keep you informed of any information, Mistress. I must go back to the office, in case any word comes in. I will keep you apprised of the situation."

Maggie nodded, and he let himself out. She fell back on the couch, her arms wrapped around her middle, still in shock. The thought of Gabe being tortured shook Maggie down to her very core. He was the closest thing to family she had in this time, and she couldn't let that happen to him. He would move mountains for her; she would move worlds —her worlds— for him.

Maggie rode as fast as she could back to the Rising Sun Tavern. After getting directions from the tavern owner, she was able to locate General Washington's encampment. She was met by soldiers on patrol and she immediately asked to be taken to the General himself. She pulled up the hood on her cloak and kept her head down as they escorted her through the camp. They took her to a tent and told her to wait there. Her back was to the tent entrance when she heard someone come inside and a crisp voice say, "I understand you wish to see General Washington."

Maggie recognized that voice instantly.

Shit! Fuck! Damn!

Straightening her back, she turned and lowered her hood as she said, "Hello, Ben."

Ben was shocked to see her. He moved closer to her, taking her by the shoulders. "Maggie! What are you doing here? It is not safe for you to be out alone."

He could feel how badly her body trembled. "Ben, I have to ask you something."

He nodded, suddenly overly concerned about her appearance in camp. "What is it?" he asked, realizing the situation was serious.

"Did anyone in this encampment take a British officer into custody yesterday?"

He let go of her. "You know I can't tell you that. Maggie, I don't understand? Why would you even want to know?"

She pleaded with him. "Ben please, just tell me. Did any of the men here capture a British colonel yesterday? It's important to me to know the answer."

He looked down, kicking at the ground with his hands on his hips and simply nodded.

Maggie let out a hard breath. “Ben, please! I need you to release him.”

His eyebrows shot up in amazement. “Let him go? You want me to release him? Why in God’s name would I do something like that? That man has information that we need badly.” He touched her face when a tiny tear dropped from the corner of her eye. “Maggie, for the love of God, will you please tell me what is going on?”

She took a seat on a nearby cot and Ben sat down next to her, taking her hand in his. He could see how upset she was, how close she was to a complete breakdown. Something had happened since this morning that had turned her world upside down.

He kissed her hand and whispered, “Tell me.”

Maggie took in a deep breath and let it out. “Do you remember that first night, at the tavern, when we spent all night talking?”

Ben looked at her thoughtfully. “Every single word.”

“I told you about my best friend, Gabe, and that he was the one person in this world that I could depend on more than anything. He has been there for me when I had no one else and has saved me more times than I can count. He is closer than a brother to me. I told you all that, but what I didn’t tell you was his full name. You see, his name is Gabriel Asheton... COLONEL Gabriel Asheton...of the British army…. and he is the man that was taken into custody yesterday.”

Ben's jaw dropped in astonishment. He could not believe what he had just heard, and he had no idea what to say in response.

"Ben please! I didn't know before, but I know now that Gabe has access to a great deal of information that you need. I also know that I cannot allow him to stay here to be tortured or worse, die of an illness in a war camp. I owe it to him to do whatever I must to save him."

Ben closed his eyes and sighed, now having a truly clear understanding of her predicament and loving her even more for the loyalty in her heart. He would do anything for this woman, but he couldn't do the one thing that she asked of him. She had put him in an impossible situation, and he knew there was a good chance he would lose her because of it.

"Maggie, I would do anything for you; I would even step in front of a bullet for you, but I can't let him go. The truth of the matter is…. this war is not going well for us. We have lost the last few battles and discontent is spreading rapidly among the men; hell, there is even talk of replacing Washington. We NEED the information that this Colonel Asheton has, and if we don't get it, we could all very well find ourselves on the wrong end of a hangman's noose. Ask me to do anything else for you, anything, but please don't ask me to do this."

Maggie knew all those things were true, but she also knew that her mind was made up and she was getting Gabe out, one way or another, no matter what the consequences.

She got up, wiping the tears from her face. "Alright, I am asking you to do something else for me."

Ben stood up. "Name it."

Squaring her shoulders, she looked him directly in the eye, determined. "Take me to see General Washington."

Ben shook his head and looked down, before lightly touching her hand and quietly saying, "It won't make any difference. The General won't let him go."

Maggie looked straight ahead. "He hasn't heard my offer yet."

A few moments later, Maggie arrived at General Washington's tent, her hood up and Ben at her side.

He hadn't tried to talk her out of it, instead choosing not to say anything during the short walk. He knocked on the wood support beam, and when they entered, he scanned the room. There were several officers that the General was consulting, or rather, arguing with.

Ben cleared his throat and the General turned to acknowledge him. "Begging your pardon sir, there is someone here who wishes to speak with you...in private."

Washington looked at his guest quizzically, unsure what to think of the hooded figure standing before him. He turned to the other officers and said, "That will be all for the night. We will resume in the morning." He saw that they were all clear of the tent before turning to his guest. "We are alone."

Maggie lowered her hood.

"Well, Mistress Bishop, what a pleasant surprise. Please! Please come in!" He motioned to a seat for her that she took, while Ben remained hovering nearby nervously.

"Thank you, General Washington."

He poured her a glass of something and handed it to her. "It's not as good as what you are accustomed to, but it will help knock the edge off. Now, Mistress Bishop, what can I do for you?"

Maggie was so nervous that she drank down the whole glass. He was right. This stuff tasted a little like diesel fuel, but it did help calm her nerves a bit. "General, I am afraid I need to call in that favor that you owe me."

He stared at her intently, intrigued. "Go on."

She blew out a hard breath. "General, it has come to my attention that you took into custody yesterday a British officer by the name of Colonel Gabriel Asheton."

The General cut his eyes over at Ben scolding him with a silent, 'I wonder who told her that?' expression. The Major was looking down at the ground with his hands clasped behind his back, trying hard to go unnoticed.

"General, that man happens to be a very old and dear friend of mine, and I have come to plead with you to release him."

General Washington looked at her compassionately, knowing all too well that this war had split many friendships down the middle. "Mistress Bishop, I am very sympathetic to your cause, I truly am! However, that man has a great deal of knowledge that could help us win this war. As much as I would like to return the favor I owe, I cannot do it this way. I AM terribly sorry."

Ben offered Maggie an 'I'm sorry, but I told you so' look.

Maggie laid both hands on the table in front of her, gathering herself, and took in a deep breath. "General, I have a much better way for you to get information."

Washington and Ben stared back at her with intriguing, yet perplexed expressions on their faces.

"General, I can get you all the information that you need. You see, I am currently residing in the home of Colonel Asheton." She glanced over at Ben and noticed that his jaw had tightened, and his eyes had narrowed. "I have access to the same information that he does," she lied, "and I can obtain additional information from the other officers in town, as well. They like to talk business during supper parties, and they don't pay much attention to the ladies who might be listening."

Maggie avoided looking at Ben because she could feel the anger building from across the room. "You see, General, I have worked very hard to remain completely neutral during this time, my only loyalty being to the people that I wish to protect on my estate— they still remain my main concern above all else. I have walked a very fine line between both parties, being friends to all sides as a matter of survival, and to maintain a sense of peace at my home. But Gabe is like family to me, and if saving him means that I must pick a side to commit to—your side—then I will. You have my word that I will do everything I can to ensure that the Continental army wins this war if you release him. I have money, I have means, I have ways around these Colonies that no one else is afforded the luxury of. As long as I can remain anonymous, I can be the perfect spy for you. No one will ever suspect me."

General Washington leaned against a table with his arms crossed, regarding Maggie while pondering the idea laid out before him.

Ben was the first to speak. "General, sir, you can't seriously be considering this?"

Washington looked up at him. "Actually, Major Tallmadge, I am."

Ben's eyes widened. "But sir, what if she is found out? What if she is caught?" he argued.

Maggie spoke up, "I guess, I just can't allow myself to get caught."

Anguish blossomed across Ben's face. "Do you know what they will do to you if you are found out? Do you? Let me enlighten you. They will throw you in a prison camp, probably full of men to do what they will to you, then they will hang you by the neck until you are dead. Have you ever seen anyone hanged? It's barbaric. After that, they will take that precious estate, that you have worked so hard to protect, and burn it clean to the ground. All those people that you have promised to take care of will be turned out and God only knows what will happen to them. Is that what you want? Is it? What about..." he broke off, looking at her, his helpless expression finishing the sentence, '*What about me? What will I do if anything happens to you?'*

Maggie looked at General Washington while aiming the statement at Ben. "I would do anything for the people I love, even if it means risking my life. You can have no better soldier in your army, than one who is serving solely to protect the people that they love the most. Those are the ones willing to risk the most because they are the ones with the most to lose."

General Washington studied her as he listened to the determination in her voice. She was right. She would make the perfect spy, and he had no doubt that she would keep her word to be loyal. Something told him there was another person she would do anything to protect, and that person happened to be in this tent. If those two were put together as a team, they would do anything and everything to cover each other's backs.

"Major Tallmadge, have some men take Colonel Asheton, blindfolded, north of Philadelphia tomorrow, set up camp, and make it easy for him to escape."

"But sir…"

"That's an order, Major Tallmadge."

"Yes, sir."

"And as for this plan of Mistress Bishop's, I think you, Major Tallmadge, would be the most logical choice as her contact. No one else in camp will know about this, just the three of us. Why don't you escort her to the edge of town in the morning? You two can work out all the ...details. I think this evening would be a good time and away from the camp, of course. Perhaps at that nice little tavern we all first met in."

Ben clenched his teeth. "Yes, sir."

Maggie stood. "Thank you, General Washington. You will not regret this."

He stood and bowed to her. "I am certain that I will not. Good evening, Mistress."

Maggie raised her hood and stepped outside to catch her breath.

Ben grabbed her by the arm and pulled her into the nearest empty tent. "Just what the bloody hell did you think you were doing back there?"

Maggie could see how angry he was, and she jerked her arm free, stating, "Saving my friend, just like I said I would."

Ben raised both hands to his head. "No! What you just did was put yourself in the worst kind of danger. I know you think you can handle this, but it's not a game, Maggie. This is real life— war— it's ugly and it's costly. Men, who know exactly what they are getting into, lose their lives each day in battle, and you just signed yourself up for the deadliest spot on the field without giving it a second thought."

Sitting down on the cot, Maggie rubbed her temples, calmly saying, "What would you have me do? What would you have done if it had been your brother when he was back in the British prison camp, and you were able to make a bargain like this one to get him out safely instead of….? What would you have done?"

Ben softened as he sat down next to her and a whispered 'anything' was his resigned response; he took her hand. The weight of the deal weighed heavily upon her and his heart ached because of the anguish it was causing. He just wanted to protect her, to keep her safe and he wasn't so sure that he would be able to.

"Ben, I don't want to fight about this, not tonight, and not with you of all people. Right now, I just...need you. Can we get out of here and just go be together somewhere alone?"

He sighed and gingerly kissed her forehead. “That sounds like the best plan I have heard all day.”

Two hours later, they were together in a bed at the tavern, fiercely clinging to each other and what was left of their quiet moments. They didn’t talk, just alternated making love and holding onto each other for dear life.

Awaking early, they dressed and left before daybreak. On the ride back to Philadelphia, they talked about how they would be in touch, how they would signal back and forth, and when and where to meet. The tavern owner that had first warned Maggie away from Philadelphia and his wife were loyal Patriots. They could carry messages for them.

No one would suspect a wife visiting her husband in town or him visiting his brother outside of town where his wife and son were staying. No one would question Maggie stopping in for a meal once a week at the tavern.

If they needed to meet, Maggie could use the egg gathering story as a reason to go back and forth across the lines. And the beauty of the whole plan was that if the tavern owner or his wife were questioned, they wouldn’t actually know what was happening. Maggie and Ben were known lovers to them; they would just assume they were carrying love notes, and they would be — except certain phrases would have different meanings.

‘Counting the days’ would mean no new information, ‘missing you terribly’ would mean that Maggie had information but was unable to get away, ‘wanting to run away together’ would mean that she felt as if she was under suspicion and was being extra cautious and ‘can’t wait to see you’ would mean that they needed to meet at the tavern the following night. The phrase 'I want to marry you as soon as possible' would indicate that Maggie was in extreme danger and needed Ben's help as soon as possible.

That one was his idea and Maggie found it a little ironic given the circumstances.

Ben slipped her into town along a dangerous little pathway that she would have never been able to find her way through alone.

Standing on the edge of town, still concealed in the density of the woods, he pulled her to him, embracing her tightly and kissing her as if it were their last time. "Be careful, Maggie. Keep your safety the number one priority, above the army, above Gabe, above me, above everything else. I don't think I will be able to live if anything happens to you." He took her face in both his hands, gazed into her eyes lovingly and said, "I love you, Maggie."

Maggie was taken aback when he said the words. She was even more startled when she heard herself say, "I love you, too, Ben."

Maggie slipped back into the house and upstairs into her bedroom without seeing anyone. She closed the door, took off her boots and sword, putting them away, and threw herself on the bed. She could not believe the mess she had gotten herself into. It was bad enough that she had gotten herself involved in the war—she had vowed to remain out of it—but she had somehow managed to land herself right smack dab in the thick of it.

If Maggie made one mistake, hell, if she even looked at the right person the wrong way, she could very well end up singing 'God Save the Queen', sipping tea at tea time with her pinky sticking out, instead of eating hot dogs at a baseball game while listening to the 'Star Spangled Banner'. And the fourth day of July wouldn't be filled with picnics and fireworks to celebrate Independence Day if there was no 'Independence'. She had done everything she could to avoid it!

EVERYTHING!

Yet, here she was, up to her neck in it. She had even lied to General George-freaking-Washington, Mr. Honesty himself. She knew she had no access to the information that Gabe had about the British army, and she hadn't been to the first military dinner in Philadelphia. The only one she had attended was in Williamsburg, all those years ago, and well, that one hadn't gone so well. She would either have to rely solely on the information she remembered from school about the going ons around Philadelphia, which was frankly *none*, or she would have to find a way to get information from the people around her, an idea that she didn't like at all.

But what choice did she have?

Gabe meant the world to her and there was no way she was going to let him end up in a Continental army prison camp to rot, especially after hearing the way that Ben's brother had starved to death in a British prison camp years before.

And then, there was the matter of Ben.

He was handsome, sweet, loyal...and in love with her. Even worse, she realized that she was head over heels in love with him as well.

She had been alone for so long, and now she couldn't imagine her life without him—except that she had to.

A big part of history was that Ben's many children went on to hold major offices in the new government in the years to come. They were destined to help shape the young country into what it was to become. Even if he and Maggie were to get married, she would never be able to give him the children that he was meant to have. Maggie was now thirty-four, and even though Cornwallis would surrender in four years, effectively ending the fighting, the war wouldn't officially end for six more years with the Treaty of Paris, making her forty and well past childbearing age for that time.

Ben did not take a wife until after this was all over, being too wrapped up in winning the war and getting the nation on its feet. She also had to remember that Ben was still young at the tender age of twenty-three. That would make him only twenty-nine when everything was all said and done, leaving him many years to focus on settling down and having a family. She had been his first, and your first is not someone you easily forget, especially when you think you are in love with that person.

At some point, she would be forced to break his heart.

The dismal thought left Maggie despondent and with a feeling of self-loathing. She did not want to lose him, but she would have no choice in the matter. It would be the right thing—the only thing—to do.

Which brought Maggie to the most disturbing thought of all. Nowhere in history, that Maggie was aware of, was a woman by the name of Maggie Bishop mentioned during the Revolutionary War, which meant her contribution was either unimportant, forgotten or... that she wasn't around to take credit for it. She knew her house did not exist in the future, meaning that she would leave no legacy behind. Her untimely death would explain that. Without her, the life she had built at Beechcroft would cease to exist, and with no existing family in this time and no heirs, there would not be a single person in this world to take Maggie's place to ensure the people on the estate were provided for.

That thought was extremely dismaying to Maggie. She remembered something else that Ben had said— that if she were caught as a spy, she would be hanged, and her house burnt to the ground —that certainly would be one explanation, not a comforting one, but one, nonetheless.

The weight of everything on Maggie's shoulders was getting heavier by the day, and she didn't have a single soul she could talk to about it, making that burden ten times worse. But she had to do what she had to do now, to take care of the ones that she loved. Maggie didn't have the luxury of worrying about the future, because she had to somehow get through today.

14

CHAPTER FOURTEEN

Maggie spent most of the morning pacing the floor, looking out the window, and waiting for Gabe's return. If he 'escaped' just north of town, it shouldn't take him long to make his way home.

Suppertime approached, and he still had not appeared. Maggie was getting incredibly nervous that something had gone terribly wrong. She was just about to leave, and go search for him herself, when she heard a commotion at the door.

The door flew wide open and she heard men's voices saying things like, 'hold him up' and 'clear the way'.

Maggie rushed into the foyer, and her stomach lurched.

Gabe had been beaten; his face cut, bruised and swollen, his nose and face covered in dried blood.

"Bring him in here!" Maggie took command. "Put him on the couch. Serena, I need hot water and clean rags."

The two officers helped him to the sofa where he collapsed with his eyes closed.

She moved next to him, calling out, “Gabe! Gabe! Can you hear me?”

He cracked opened one swollen eye. “I can hear just fine, it’s the rest of me that’s having a little trouble.”

Maggie looked him over, and it wasn’t just his face that was covered in blood. “Where are you hurt?”

He reached over, took her hand and squeezed. “I’ll be fine Maggie, don’t worry.”

Serena arrived with the water and rags.

Maggie started cleaning up his face.

One of the men who brought him in said, “We have an army doctor on the way to see to him, ma’am.”

It was Gabe who spoke up. “That won’t be necessary. I am fine, just a few bumps and bruises.” He started to sit up, but Maggie pushed him back down, her finger in his chest.

“Sit! Stay!”

He looked at her slightly annoyed. “Will I get a bone if I am a good doggie?” he snarked.

Maggie knew at that point that he was fine.

The other officer cleared his throat. “Sir, we will need to debrief you when you are feeling up to it.”

Gabe shifted, groaning. “You can debrief me now, there isn’t much to tell. I was jumped by three men on my way to the first checkpoint. They tied me up, worked me over a bit, covered my head and rode me into a camp. I spent the night bound up in a tent, but I have no idea where. The next morning, they covered my head again, threw me over the back end of a horse and took me to another smaller encampment. When they were turned, I managed to free my hands, steal one of their horses and found my way back to town. And before you ask, they didn't get any information. I can only assume that I escaped before they had a chance to get me to their interrogator. I will write a full report tomorrow, but tonight, I would just like to eat and get some rest."

Maggie listened, not saying anything.

The other officer nodded. "Of course, sir. I will check back in the morning. Please send word if you need anything. I am glad to see you back home safely. Good night."

Gabe bobbed his head in acknowledgement, and the men left.

Maggie stood, getting a glass and the brandy decanter. She poured a healthy dose and handed it to Gabe.

He accepted it gratefully.

Maggie went back to cleaning up his face. "You had me scared to death."

He looked at her, wincing in pain as she hit a tender spot. "I'm sorry, Maggie. I did not mean to worry you. It was supposed to be a simple information exchange, and the fact that they caught me was simply good luck on their part."

"Still, whatever would I have told Mrs. Fannie Bright if you hadn't come back? She might worry if you weren't back in time for your wedding." Maggie smirked and rung out the rag.

Gabe made a face. "On second thought, maybe I should have asked the Continental army if they were accepting new recruits."

They both laughed until he grabbed his ribs and cringed.

"All right, mister, let's get you upstairs."

Maggie instructed Serena to get a bath ready for him, and the maid scurried off to do so. Once she'd managed to help him up the stairs, Maggie helped Gabe out of his clothes and into the tub. She ran her fingers over the bruises on his chest and back.

He saw the pain in her eyes, caught her hand and kissed it. "I'm fine, Maggie. This is nothing to be concerned about. I have had much worse."

She helped him bathe, washing his hair for him the way he had done for her so many years ago. After getting him fed and into bed, she lay down beside him, lightly touching his bare chest while he lay with his arm around her.

"Don't ever scare me like that again, Gabe. You are the only family that I have, and I would do anything to keep you safe."

Gabe looked down at her, wondering what she meant by that.

They fell asleep together, still holding each other the same way when they woke up the next morning.

Gabe spent the next few days at home recovering. He was in worse shape than he had let on. Word had gotten around town, and there was a constant flow of visitors, mostly British officers.

Maggie played mother hen, staying close by his side, making sure that he wasn't overdoing it. It was during a brief time when no one else was there, and Maggie was pouring a drink for Gabe, while he was relaxing on the couch when she heard a commotion in the hall. Maggie turned her head in that direction when she heard Gabe mumble, "Shite!"

And that's when Maggie saw her. She knew instantly who it was, a wide devilish grin spreading across her face as she propped herself against the buffet. Taking a sip of the drink she'd just poured for Gabe, she stood there watching, waiting for the show. She looked over at Gabe, who was looking back at her with a desperate, pleading look on his face. Maggie shrugged her shoulders at him and concealed her smile behind her glass.

He snarled at her, knowing she would be no help and that he was trapped.

The one and only Mrs. Fannie Bright stood before them, a sight to behold. She was a middle-aged woman, short, with a full, buxom hourglass figure, her waist cinched by a corset tight enough to cut off the flow of blood to the rest of her body, pushing her breasts nearly up to her chin.

Gabe seemed to still have a penchant for attracting big breasted women.

She wore a bright blue, snug-fitting dress, topping off the outfit with a bright yellow, tall, plume-feather hat, accenting her unnaturally colored red hair, that, when paired with her rather long nose, gave her the unfortunate appearance of being a brightly colored macaw parrot.

Her gaze fell upon Gabe on the couch and she spoke with the dramatic flair of an out-of-work theatre actress. "Oh, my poor, poor Colonel Asheton!"

She rushed to him, pulling him into a bear hug that planted Gabe's nose directly between her breasts, his hands gripping the couch as if he were hanging on for his very life.

Maggie angled her head to get a better view of the unfolding show.

After a couple of minutes, Fannie pushed his head back, leaving Gabe gasping for breath after being smothered by the rather obnoxious amount of lavender water that she had applied.

Mrs. Bright took Gabe's face in her hands, looking him directly in the eye. "Why, when I heard that you had been taken by those horrible men, I was absolutely beside myself. I couldn't eat, I couldn't sleep, I couldn't even shop. I was most distressed at the thought of what they must be doing to my poor darling."

"I'm quite alright Mrs. Br..."

She cut him off, raising her hand. "Now, don't you worry. I am here now, and I will nurse you right back to health." She sat down beside him, her hand on his knee and sliding ever higher by the moment. Every time her hand got too close to his manhood, he pushed it away, only for it to start its climb again.

"I shall not leave your side, my dear. This will give us more time to get to know each other better."

Gabe squirmed, pushing himself further back into the couch as her hand continued to make progress. He looked back at Maggie, still behind them, mouthing the word 'help'.

Maggie rolled her eyes; as much as she was enjoying this, Gabe really did need her assistance. "Excuse me, but I don't believe we have met." She came around the side of the couch to stand beside Gabe.

It seemed that Mrs. Bright was so focused on Gabe that she hadn't even noticed Maggie; the woman was startled by her appearance.

"I am Mistress Maggie Bishop. I am…"

Gabe finished her sentence, "My fiancé. Maggie is my fiancé." He snatched her hand, shrugging with a faint smile.

Mrs. Bright was speechless. She turned her look to Gabe, asking the question, "You are engaged?"

He looked at Maggie, silently pleading for mercy. "Yes, yes, I am. Maggie and I are very much in love."

Mrs. Bright looked at the two of them with narrowed eyes. "And when did you become engaged?"

Maggie answered for him. "Just today. He asked me this morning and I accepted."

Maggie and Gabe offered Mrs. Bright the best smiles they could muster.

Seeing that she wasn't buying the story, Gabe decided to convince her once and for all. "We are very much in love. We will be married as soon as possible," and with that, Gabe pulled her down on his lap, took her in his arms and planted a deep, passionate kiss on her lips.

When he pulled back, Maggie was flabbergasted.

WHOA! What just happened?

Mrs. Bright gave her loudest 'humph' and stormed out the front door.

Maggie was still dumbfounded when she heard Gabe say, "Oh thank God, I think it worked."

Maggie didn't understand. "Huh?"

Gabe looked at her strangely. "I said, I think it worked. Maggie are you alright?"

Maggie shook herself all over. "No, I am not! Where did you learn to kiss a WOMAN like that?"

Now, he was the stunned one.

"Well my dear, I did have to bed a few women before I decided that I preferred men."

There was another knock on the door, and Maggie wagged her finger at him, walking by. "Details! I want details! After all, I should know these things about my 'fiancé'."

Maggie called back to Serena, "I will get the door," assuming it was just more officers stopping by.

When Maggie answered it, she was surprised to see Captain Russell standing there. "Mistress Bishop."

"Captain Russell. I am glad to see you back safely. Come in, please."

He hesitated. "Before I do, there is someone who insisted upon coming, and he absolutely refused to take 'no' for an answer."

Maggie stepped further towards the door, and standing to the side, was Onyx. She squealed with glee. "Onyx! Oh, Onyx! I am so happy to see you! I have missed you so much." She hugged the horse and he wrapped his head around her back in his own hug.

"Harm said he had been having fits since you left. When I told Harm that I was headed back to get you, Onyx here, broke down the stable gate and the fence. He was beside me before I got halfway up the drive."

Maggie was thrilled beyond words to see him; Onyx was exactly whom she needed right now.

Gabe joined them outside. "Are you still riding this old fellow?"

Onyx turned his head and butted Gabe hard in the chest as if to say, "Who are you calling old?" going right back to loving on Maggie.

"My apologies, Onyx, I did not mean to insult you. I meant it as a term of endearment."

Onyx snorted at him.

Captain Russell spoke up, "Mistress Bishop, all the men are back in Williamsburg, safe and sound. I have them on the estate building new wagons. If the ship has not been accosted, we can be ready to leave tomorrow."

"I'm sorry, Captain Russell, but there has been a change in plans. You will take my ship home without me. I will be staying on in Philadelphia for an indefinite amount of time."

Captain Russell looked at her as if he knew better than to argue. "If we don't sail soon, you may have a harder time getting back with winter coming."

"I am well aware, Captain."

Walking over to her, Gabe steered clear of Onyx's head. "Maggie, you should go home. It will be safer there. Philadelphia is a powder keg that could explode at any moment."

Maggie looked at the ground, remembering her bargain. "I know, Gabe, but I won't leave you alone in this condition and, besides, now that Onyx is here, I have everything I need."

Gabe looked her up and down, thinking that this Ben fellow she had been seeing was more than likely the real reason she wanted to stay, and he *was* the one that told her to take some happiness where she could, so he didn't argue.

"Besides," she said, "I wouldn't be a good fiancé if I deserted my soon-to-be husband."

Gabe rolled his eyes. He would NEVER hear the end of this.

Maggie got Onyx settled in and bedded down. She gave Captain Russell instructions, along with a handful of letters and written instructions for the people at the estate.

Gabe wrote papers of passage so that the Captain could get through the checkpoints without any trouble.

When he left, Maggie realized she was officially here for an extended amount of time.

That night, Gabe was lying in bed when he heard a soft knock at the door. "Come in, Maggie."

Dressed in her nightgown and robe, she carried a bottle and two glasses. Hopping on the bed next to him, she sat cross-legged while pouring them both drinks.

Gabe scooched up against the headboard.

Maggie had the look on her face of a kid on Christmas morning, her eyes twinkling in anticipation. "Okay, give me all the sordid details."

Gabe cocked his head in a questioning manner.

"Oh, don't give me that, Gabe Asheton! You know damn well what I am talking about. That kiss was, well—you knew EXACTLY what you were doing, and I want to know how."

He took a sip. "You do know that male lovers kiss, don't you?" he asked, amused.

"Oh, I know that! What do you take me for?"

He lifted his eyebrows in response.

"You said that you had to bed a few women to decide that you preferred men, so cough it up, mister! I want details."

"Alright!" Gabe gave her a thoughtful look before he told his story.

"When I was sixteen, my older brother Robert took me to a certain type of establishment while we were visiting in France. He said that women were special creatures who were put in this world to make man happy. In return, they had a few needs that needed tending as well, and that if I wanted to ever hang on to a woman, I needed to know what they were. He must have needed a refresher course — he had already been married two years by then."

Maggie sat with her mouth open, hanging on his every word.

"We went inside this place that apparently was private, exclusive, and extremely expensive. It was filled with scantily clad and completely naked women— some lounging and a few 'servicing' other men in many different types of ways. As soon as we came in, we were made to feel extremely welcome and at home. My brother requested a woman that he saw every time he was in town. Her name was Monique. She was exotic and beautiful; she also seemed to rather 'enjoy' her work. Robert introduced us and whispered something in her ear. She left and returned with another young woman by the name of Mathilda, who took me by the hand and led me into a private room. She kissed me as she skillfully relieved me of my clothing, and said she knew that I was inexperienced in the ways of lovemaking. Mathilda then told me that she was going to make sure I enjoyed my first time— which she did — I found it pleasant enough for a boy who had never experienced anything like what she did to me. Afterwards, she showed me, in perfectly explicit detail, exactly how to please a woman in return. Robert had always talked so much about how wonderful making love to a woman was, but by the time I left that night, I had no idea what he meant. I mean, don't get me wrong, I enjoyed what I had done to me, but what she wanted me to do to her was not appealing. I attributed it to the fact that it had happened in a whorehouse, which I assumed would probably put any 'normal' man off, and I put the thought out of my head."

Maggie couldn't help herself. "I cannot believe you lost your virginity in a French whorehouse. Gabe, I am truly shocked. But I am telling you now, I will expect you to show me EVERYTHING you learned that night on our honeymoon." She batted her eyelashes in an exaggerated manner.

Gabe shook his head. There was no way he was EVER living this down.

"Do you want to hear the rest, or do you have a few more virgins stored away somewhere you need to seduce?"

Maggie wrinkled her nose at him. "Oh please, continue."

"When I turned twenty, my parents encouraged me to wed. I had attended law school and was making a decent living at it. The next socially acceptable thing to do was to take a wife and start a family. I eventually proposed to a young lady named Penelope — Penny. She was a sweet girl, and we got along well. We married, and on that night, I performed my 'husbandly duties'. She was a virgin like I once was, so I took my time, doing everything to make it a pleasant experience for her, and it was—for her. Again, I found myself— uninterested. It seemed to please her, so I continued to do what was expected of me, but there was never any passion, never any fire, nothing like what people have written and raved about since the beginning of time. We settled into a routine, and pretty soon, she became pregnant with our first child."

Maggie gradually lost her smile.

Gabe had never mentioned a child before, and his face had just become serious. He looked down into his glass and let out a deep sigh.

"The baby came too early. The birth was difficult; there were too many complications, and Penny was not a strong woman. She and my baby boy both died that day," he paused and swallowed hard, "I named him Samuel, and I had them buried together."

Tears came to Maggie's eyes as this lighthearted conversation took a horribly tragic turn. No wonder he had never mentioned them before.

She leaned over taking his hand and said, "Gabe, I am so sorry, I had no idea."

He looked down at her and smiled, squeezing her hand.

Clearing his throat, he continued his story, "I was beside myself, and I bore responsibility for the situation. Penny wouldn't have died if I hadn't gotten her with child, and the guilt from that ate at me more and more each day. I couldn't continue being a lawyer because there were far too many memories in that town. I went to my father and told him I wanted to join the military. He wasn't thrilled about it, but he understood. He purchased a commission, and I entered the army as a major. I found that I really liked it; the discipline, the daily routine, the camaraderie, and the falling in bed too tired to dream at night. I rose through the ranks quickly. A few years in, I met Jonathan at a state dinner party; he was the eighteen-year old son of an officer. We found ourselves inexplicably drawn to each other and became fast friends. We would go to dinner out, and have lively discussions about everything and nothing at all. It didn't matter what we talked about as long as we were together. I felt something with him that I had never felt before, but I was afraid to tell him. If I proclaimed my feelings, and he didn't reciprocate, not only would I lose him, I would very possibly hang for being immoral. Not everyone is as understanding as you are, Mags. He went away to school, and I missed him terribly, but he came back a different person— mature and very sure of himself. We renewed our friendship, much to my delight, my feelings still as deep as they ever were. I was a colonel by then, and I received word shortly after that I was being sent to the Colonies in a month, much to my chagrin and Jonathan's. The next day, he asked me to take a ride out in the country with him to a place he knew. We rode out to a hunting cabin in the middle of nowhere. We stopped, made a fire, had some dinner — and ended up making love. It was everything I ever thought it should be and more. We spent every minute together that we could before I left. Once I was here, we wrote back and forth, missing each other very much. Then, I received a letter from Jonathan saying that he had joined the military and was working on getting sent to the Colonies. Once he was here, I made arrangements to be transferred to Williamsburg and — the rest, you know."

Maggie was at a loss for words. What could she say? Gabe had so much pain and loss in his life, more than anyone should ever have to bear. She crawled up next to him and wrapped her arms around his waist.

"Gabe, I can't tell you how sorry I am that you had to go through all of that, and it breaks my heart that you have had to hide who you truly are, because you are the best person I know."

He tilted up her chin with his finger so he could look her in the eyes. "Maggie, please don't feel sorry for me. Yes, I have had a great deal to bear, but if I hadn't lost my wife and child, joined the military, and if Jonathan had never joined the army and come to the Colonies, then I never would have met YOU. You are so special to me, and my relationship with you has made everything I have had to endure easier."

Maggie broke into a crying laugh.

Gabe looked at her in horror, trying to lighten the mood. "What the bloody hell is this? You can't cry and laugh at the same time. What am I supposed to do? Am I to hold and comfort you, or laugh with you? No, ma'am, you have to pick; I cannot handle both at once, not from you of all people."

She smacked his chest.

Maggie felt the urge to share something with him, after all, he had just poured out everything to her. "Gabe, I have a confession to make. There is something about me that you don't know."

Actually, there's a whole lot you don't know.

He looked at her, waiting for her to continue. She sat back up, holding his hand. "Bishop isn't my married name," he tilted his head, curious, "because I have never actually been married."

It was now Gabe's turn to be shocked. "What do you mean — you have never been married?"

Maggie chewed on her thumbnail. "Before I came here, I was engaged, but we were separated, and now he's gone."

Gabe was thoroughly confused.

"But how did you buy land? And why would you lie?"

Maggie chose her words carefully to make sense. "We became engaged on the coast of Carolina, near New Bern. He gave me a very expensive ring as a token of his love. And then, he was gone, and it was just me with no family, no friends, no one and nothing. Not a shilling to my name, just a big black horse that found me. I took the advice of a stranger in a tavern who suggested that I sell the ring and use the money to take care of myself. I knew there would be a problem if I were an unmarried woman trying to buy anything, so I just said that I was a widow. I sold the ring for a great deal of money and got off the boat at Williamsburg. Nobody knew me, and I didn't know anyone, so there was no questioning it. I bought the house on the steps of the Raleigh Tavern the same day. Frankly, that lawyer wanted to be rid of that property so badly, I think he would have sold it to me even if I had horns, a tail, and a pitchfork. I have never told another soul what I just told you."

Gabe squeezed her hand. "You did what you had to do to survive. You didn't hurt anyone and look what you did with that money. Look how many people you have taken care of with it. Maggie, you have nothing to be ashamed of. And if you hadn't lost your fiancé, and come to Williamsburg, we never would have met, so, I for one, am alright with it."

Maggie nodded. It felt good to talk to someone, even if she couldn't tell him everything. She laid her head on his chest. "Gabe, promise me something."

"Anything sweetheart."

"If something should happen to me, promise me you will take care of the people on my estate. Make sure they are safe."

Gabe frowned. "Nothing will happen to you, Maggie. I won't let it."

"I know, but just in case, promise me."

He squeezed her tighter. "You have my word."

15

CHAPTER FIFTEEN

The next morning, Maggie answered a knock at the door to find an officer delivering an invitation addressed to both her and Gabe. He handed it to her, tipped his hat, and said, "Congratulations, ma'am," before walking away.

"Thank you?" Maggie called to him as he left, a little perplexed. She broke open the seal and quickly read the contents.

"GABE!"

He appeared at the doorway, using his napkin from breakfast to wipe his mouth. "What? What is it?"

Maggie cut him a scathing look as she held up an invitation, an annoyed look on her face. "It seems we have been invited to dinner to celebrate our engagement."

Gabe dropped his napkin to the floor, taking the paper from her. "Our what?"

"I guess word travels fast in this town."

He looked at her with a stupefied look.

"So, shall I pick out our china pattern, or do you want to surprise me?" Maggie asked sarcastically.

Gabe flipped the invitation in the air. "Oh, good God!"

The next day, Maggie and Gabe stood at the front door of Judge Edward Shippen IV, trying to decide whether to knock or make a break for it.

Maggie held out her hand. "I need a drink. Give me the flask."

"What flask?" Gabe asked.

Maggie rolled her eyes. "The flask you keep in your coat pocket every time you have to come to one of these things."

It was Gabe's turn to roll his eyes, but he reached in and pulled it out.

Maggie took a big swig and handed it back.

He did the same and as he went to put it away, Maggie grabbed it back taking another long drink.

Gabe wrestled it away, putting it back in his coat. "Ready?"

"Not even close," Maggie replied.

Gabe knocked on the door.

They were escorted in.

Gabe introduced her to Judge Shippen and his wife, Margaret, who were full of good wishes for the newly engaged couple.

Maggie plastered on a smile as she was led from one officer to another for formal introductions and more offers of 'congratulations'. Gabe was pulled away for drinks and cigars, as Maggie was grabbed by the womenfolk. He shot her an apologetic look, and she wrinkled her nose at him in return.

Maggie was hit with a full volley of questions from 'how did he propose?' to 'when's the big day?' Maggie and Gabe had agreed to go through with the charade, mainly to keep Mrs. Fannie Bright at bay.

In a few weeks, and hopefully, after Fannie had moved on to her next prospect, they would stage a breakup of some sort.

Maggie decided to have a little fun with it, merely for her own entertainment. She told them how, that after his return from captivity, they realized how much in love they really were, and that Gabe, in his weakened condition, barely being able to stand, had gone to great personal pains to get down on one knee and ask for her hand. She laid it on thick, spinning quite a romantic tale. As she spoke, she looked over at Gabe, who was listening from a few feet away.

He mouthed the word 'seriously' to her.

She shot him a sadistic smirk with a twinkle in her eye. He had gotten her into this, so there was no reason not to make him suffer.

A voice broke their silent conversation, "That sounds like something out of a fairy tale."

More like a sitcom.

Maggie turned her head to see where the voice had come from. A young, beautiful teenage girl had joined them.

Margaret Shippen laid her hand on the girl's shoulder. "Allow me to introduce our youngest daughter. This is Peggy."

It took a minute to register who it was that Maggie had just met. The young lady standing before her would go on to become the wife of Benedict Arnold and play a tremendous part in what was to come.

Maggie nodded. "It's very nice to meet you, Peggy."

Peggy offered an enthusiastic smile. "Mistress Bishop, please allow me to offer my sincerest 'congratulations' on your engagement. Colonel Asheton is a lovely man, and I expect quite a few ladies' hearts in Philadelphia are broken. I wish the two of you many happy years together."

"Thank you, Peggy."

They went on to chat about where to find the best dressmakers and the finest fabrics. The girl even offered her assistance with the planning. Peggy Shippen was a very charming creature. Maggie got the impression that she knew exactly how to get what she wanted, and that maybe the stories of her being naive about her future husband's activities were greatly exaggerated. She doubted that Peggy missed anything that was going on around her; she was too bright for that.

Gabe touched Maggie's back. "Excuse me, ladies, I hate to interrupt all the wedding talk, but my fiancé looks parched and I must admit, I cannot bear to be away from her for too long."

They all swooned over the romantic gesture, but then again, women just did that around Gabe anyway. There was something about women and forbidden fruit.

He leaned in. "You looked like you could use a drink...and an exit plan." He escorted her to where the refreshments were, pouring her a strong one.

"Thanks."

Gabe moved closer. “I promise I will make all this up to you.”

“Yes, Gabe, you WILL.”

Another officer approached the table for a drink.

“Maggie, allow me to introduce our city’s newest resident. He has just arrived this morning. This is Captain John André...Captain, this is my fiancé, Mistress Maggie Bishop.”

Maggie had to force down the drink she had been holding in her mouth. “Captain André. It is a pleasure to meet you. Welcome to Philadelphia.”

He took her hand and kissed it.

“The pleasure is all mine, Mistress Bishop. Congratulations on your engagement. Colonel Asheton is an incredibly lucky man to have found such a beautiful jewel such as you.”

It was Maggie’s turn to swoon. This man was not only handsome, but he was very charismatic and well-mannered, obviously coming from a fine background.

Before she could reply, everyone was called to dinner.

Maggie stayed mostly quiet during the meal, only speaking when answering a question directed her way. She was too busy watching the people around her. Mrs. Fannie Bright was giving Maggie some major stink eye while hanging adoringly on Gabe’s every word. Most of the women were giving Philadelphia’s newest resident a good once over, liking what they saw very much.

Captain André was quite the storyteller, enchanting everyone with his wonderful stories, having everyone on the edge of their seats, clapping and laughing. He was the latest and greatest entertainment for

Philadelphia's loyalist families, while they ignored the war that was effectively at their doorsteps.

Dessert was served, an apple dumpling with a brandy sauce.

Maggie lifted her hand to her mouth as she looked down at it and then over at Gabe, who was intently staring back at her. They each had similar flashbacks to a dinner from a few years ago and both skipped dessert that evening.

After dinner, Gabe was pulled away by some of the other officers for a private meeting.

Maggie managed to duck the other ladies long enough to find her way outside to the garden for a few quiet moments. It was a little chilly, even for November, but she was suffocating inside, the beginning of a panic attack coming on, and the cold air was most refreshing. She found a bench, sat down and closed her eyes to think.

Today, she had met two more key players. She knew the parts they would be playing in the months to come, but Maggie needed information for General Washington now. She had made a bargain with him that she intended to keep. He still needed to win this war, after all.

Gabe had been on light duty since his return, not handling the amount of paperwork that he had before, so she had no opportunity to get any information that way. She was, however, now in the unique position of being his fiancé, meaning there would be many more military functions that she would be expected at, possibly getting her something she could use.

The pressure of the deal that she made pressed in; she had to come up with something soon. If for no other reason than a chance to see Ben. She desperately needed some time alone with him, her time with him being the one thing these days that helped to calm the endless chaos in her mind.

Knowing the future was as much a curse as it was a blessing and trying to keep it on the right course was, frankly, exhausting.

Maggie was so lost in thought that she barely noticed the cloak being wrapped around her shoulders. "Managed to escape the boring officer's club, did you, Gabe?"

"Fortunately, I wasn't included tonight."

Maggie froze. That wasn't Gabe's voice. She looked up to see that Captain John André was the one who had wrapped the cloak around her.

"You looked cold, and I cannot in good conscience, let a lady catch her death."

Maggie didn't know what to say, but she needed to do some damage control. "Thank you, and I didn't mean to imply the officers were boring, just the meetings."

André smiled. "No, you were right the first time. Some of those officers are so incredibly boring, that they should be taken out back and shot."

They both laughed.

"May I sit?"

Maggie motioned. "Please."

He looked straight ahead. "You didn't touch your dessert tonight. Not a fan of dumplings?" He had noticed.

Of course, he did! Knowing who he was and his future, it would be foolish to think he wouldn't.

"Yes, well. The last time I had that particular dish, it didn't agree with me. I was sick for days."

There was a moment where they remained silent.

"I take it you are not a fan of these military dinners."

Careful Maggie.

"It's not that, Captain; it's just been a trying time."

He nodded. "I heard of Colonel Asheton's capture. I trust he is recovering well."

"He is, but the whole situation was a little unnerving, to say the least."

"War is unnerving, but don't concern yourself, Mistress, it will be over soon. On a much brighter note, have you and the Colonel set a date?"

"Uh...no."

André raised an eyebrow. "Do I detect a note of doubt?"

"No, not at all. I have no doubt that Gabe and I will be together for many years to come."

"You said together, not married."

Damn, he is good.

"Please forgive me, Captain André, if I misspoke. It has been an exceptionally long evening."

"Of course, I did not mean to imply anything about your relationship with the Colonel." He changed the subject, pointing out how lovely the garden must have been in the spring, reciting some verse of poetry to go along with it. A few moments later, he had her laughing at one of his wonderful stories.

He was an impressive man, quite the charmer, and Maggie honestly liked him. Maggie saw Gabe through the window, his meeting ended.

"I am afraid I must excuse myself, Captain André. I think Gabe is done."

She stood up, handing back his cloak, thanking him again.

"Before I go, may I ask a favor, Mistress Bishop?"

She turned. "Of course."

"Will you please call me John?"

Maggie nodded. "I will, but only if you call me Maggie."

He took her hand and kissed it. "Good night, Maggie."

She smiled and turned to leave. Inside, she and Gabe said their 'goodbyes' and were heading out the door when Maggie looked back. Captain John André was speaking with a few other officers, and Peggy Shippen was staring at him from across the room like a lovesick puppy.

Gabe was distracted the entire trip home.

"What's wrong Gabe?"

"Huh? Oh, I'm sorry Maggie."

She handed him a drink. "Something is obviously bothering you."

"Yes, well, General Howe has sent his letter of resignation to England. The word is that he is trying to blame his irrational battle plans on a lack of troop support. Trying to save face, I suppose."

That was some information.

"And will they accept it?"

"I have no idea what their response will be."

But Maggie did. Howe was replaced by Clinton right after Valley Forge. She could intertwine what she learned, and what she already knew from history, to pass along to Washington. This was good; this was a start. Maggie took a good look at Gabe. She hated seeing him so stressed out all the time. She knew how things were going to turn out. and it wasn't good for the British soldiers.

She took his hand and led him to the couch. "Gabe, I am worried about you. You have too much on your shoulders."

"You're a good one to talk."

"No, Gabe, I'm being serious. This job is too much strain on you, and it's unnecessary. You don't need the money."

Gabe smirked. "Did I become wealthy overnight?"

Maggie bobbed her head. "Well, you ARE marrying one of the wealthiest women in the Colonies."

"And I am to become a kept man?" The sass was back in his voice.

"Depends on what tricks you learned from Mathilda at the whorehouse," Maggie bantered back while giving him a wink.

He laughed.

Maggie became serious again. "Resign your commission and come back to Virginia with me. I have plenty of money and land. I can deed some acreage to you, have a house built for you, and you will never want for anything as long as I am around."

He put his arm around her. "You know I can't do that. What's brought all of this on?"

Maggie leaned into him. "I just don't want anything to happen to you. This war, it could take you away from me in an instant, but I have the means to keep you safe if you will just let me."

He could see the distress in her eyes. "Maggie, you need to stop worrying so much. Honestly, I am more worried about you. You are starting to develop crow's lines."

Maggie slapped his chest. "I am NOT."

He touched her face. "I'm afraid you are, there is one here," touching around her eyes, "and here, and here." He kissed her forehead. "Don't concern yourself so much."

He watched her head upstairs to bed, the worry lines now on HIS face.

16

CHAPTER SIXTEEN

Fortune shined bright on Maggie a few days later in the form of a visit from Captain John André; she was pleasantly surprised to see him at the front door.

"Good morning John. It's good to see you. Please come in."

André seemed taken aback to see her as well. He removed his hat and took her hand. "Good morning, Maggie. I am indeed a fortunate man to start my day off in the sight of such a lovely lady."

Maggie blushed. "Please sit down."

"Thank you, Maggie. I must admit I wasn't expecting to see you here so early."

She served him a cup of tea. "Why wouldn't I be?" and then poured one for herself.

André had a puzzled expression on his face. "Forgive me for asking, but are you living here with the Colonel before you are wed?"

It dawned on Maggie how that must look to other people. "I am. Please, allow me to explain. Gabe and I have been the closest of friends for a very long time. He was in New York for two years before he was sent here. It just so happened that I found myself in Philadelphia on some business at the exact same time. I had not secured a place to reside, so he insisted I stay with him, as he has done with me many times at my home in Virginia. I should have secured a separate residence sooner, but now, it just seems pointless."

"I see, what kind of business if I may ask?"

Careful Maggie.

"I own a shipping company; some of my employees found themselves in a little trouble after too much fun at a tavern one evening. I came to lend my assistance."

André turned his head as he lowered his cup, an awareness coming to him. "Oh, my goodness, how did I not realize sooner? You are the Mistress Bishop from Williamsburg that I have heard so much about."

Uh oh.

"All good, I hope," she fished.

"All VERY good. I have heard you are a very shrewd businesswoman who has managed to build a small fortune after being widowed."

"I am not sure that I would use the term 'shrewd', John, 'extremely fortunate' may be a better description."

He smiled.

"What can I do for you, John?"

He put his cup down. "I was having such a delightful time that I almost forgot," he reached in his coat pocket, "I have some documents for the Colonel. Is he, by chance, around?"

"No, he stepped out for a bit, but I would be happy to give them to him for you," she saw his hesitation and said, "or you are welcome to wait. I am not sure how long he will be."

André pulled out his pocket watch to check the time. "As much as I would enjoy the thought of your company for the rest of the morning, I have to be at a meeting shortly, and the Colonel wanted these plans as soon as possible."

Maggie took a shot. "I can tell him that you are looking for him when he returns, or I can place them on his desk so that he will see them first thing when he gets back. If you are worried about them being secure, I can assure you that no one else will be in that room until he returns." She batted her eyelashes.

John thought for a moment. "I have no doubt they will be safe in your very capable hands." He handed them over.

She showed him out, and rushed back to Gabe's desk, closing the door behind her. The papers were in a leather binder but were not sealed. They were drawings of troop locations and numbers of the British army. Maggie took out a piece of paper and jotted down the numbers and a crude, unrecognizable map that only made sense in her mind. She carefully folded everything back up and placed it on Gabe's desk. She then went to her room and jotted down a 'love letter' for Ben, to signal for a meeting. She had a quick dinner at the tavern, delivering her message.

Gabe arrived home just a few minutes after she returned from dinner. He found the leather journal as soon as he stepped in his office. “Maggie, do you know how these papers got on my desk?” he called over his shoulder.

She stuck her head in.

“Oh yes, I almost forgot. Captain André delivered them this morning. He said you needed them right away.”

“Yes, I do. Thank you for keeping them for me.”

She hovered in the doorway.

“Gabe, I was thinking about what you said, when you said that I was worrying too much.”

He turned to face her. “Yes?”

“I think you are right. Being cooped up in this house is beginning to wear my nerves just a little thin. I think tomorrow, I might take Onyx out for an extended ride in the country. I will be back the following day. I just want to get out long enough to clear my head.”

Gabe folded his arms, leaning against his desk. “Do you think I believe that for one minute? I know you better than anyone Maggie Bishop.”

Panic rose in Maggie as he placed his hands on her shoulders, his lips pressed firmly in a straight line. “I know what you are up to.”

Shit.

Maggie prepared herself for the worse. “Gabe, I can explain!”

“You don’t need to explain. You are going out to meet Ben.”

Maggie looked down, knowing that he knew.

“I think it will be good for you,” he said with a smile.

"You do?" she asked, confused.

Gabe gave her an understanding look. "Go, spend the night with him. Get rid of some of this nervous energy that you have pent up. Nothing like a good night of...well, you know… to make you feel like a new person."

Whew!

"I have missed him," she said softly.

Gabe started around the desk. "Let me give you this first." He wrote something down and fanned it to dry.

"What's this?"

He showed her. "Passage papers. No one will stop and question you at checkpoints with this. I can't very well have my fiancé sneaking around without my knowledge and blessing, can I?" He rolled it up and handed it to her. "Enjoy yourself."

Ben was already at the tavern with a room by the time she arrived, leaving a note downstairs to direct her. When he let her into the room, he was stripped down to the waist. He took her in his arms, kissing her tenderly, whispering how much he missed her in her ear.

He slowly undressed her, not allowing her to do anything, taking his time, savoring every inch of her body. Once all of her clothing was gone, he scooped her up and carried her to the bed. He touched every part of her body with his tongue, before suckling her to her first orgasm of the night. She watched him work while running her fingers through his hair until her body shuddered with pure delight. He then climbed up, kissing her mouth sweetly, gently as he entered her. He moved slowly, treasuring every second that he was inside of her, until the orgasm built in them both, exploding at the same time.

When he was done, he didn't move, leaving himself on top of her and inside her, kneading and nibbling her breasts, until he came back to life again, starting the slow, rhythmic dance all over, until he was done, having given her a third orgasm. Lying to the side, he pulled her to him tightly, wrapping his arms and legs around her, engulfing her entire body into his. They lay as one, nothing between them but each other until they dozed off.

Maggie was standing at the table, deep in thought, when Ben awoke. She was writing on several pieces of paper, drawing from her memory.

He came up behind her, slipping his arms around her waist, kissing her back, and whispering, "What is this? What did you bring me?"

She finished jotting everything down, leaning back against him. "A map of the area, with the location of all the British camps and the number of men." She pointed out each section.

He watched and listened while kissing her neck, stopping to ask a question every now and then.

When she was finished speaking, he pressed against her from behind. He slipped inside her, moving in a slow, deliberate groove. She soon matched him, stroke for stroke, until they peaked together, and his seed filled her.

For a newly deflowered virgin, he sure did catch on quick.

Maggie turned to face him, and he greedily claimed her mouth, tasting, exploring and savoring her until she returned the favor. He gathered her up, carried her back to bed, so they could lay holding each other and talking.

"Oh Maggie, I can't think of anything but you. Thoughts of you fill my head all day and at night, they take over my dreams."

She stroked his arm. "I feel the same way." She snuggled closer. "There are a few other things you need to know. General Howe has sent his resignation letter to England."

Ben brushed her hair with a kiss. "Well, that is certainly good information to have."

Maggie continued, starting her weave of current information and future history with a whole lot of filling in the blanks. "He will more than likely be replaced by General Clinton in the spring. Ben…" she sat up, "I need you to listen to me very carefully."

He straightened up and nodded.

"It is important that General Washington spends his time at Valley Forge training men and laying in battle plans. The British are going to dig their heels in at Philadelphia for the winter, spending it with all the creature comforts they can muster, while *your* army suffers greatly through the winter, simply trying to survive."

Ben interrupted her. "Valley Forge is well fortified. Our army will be safe there."

Maggie took in a breath, hoping she was doing the right thing. "That's not what I mean. The British intend to cut off supplies, leaving you without anything. They think if they can starve you out, the troops will revolt against General Washington, leaving you without a leader and ending the war. General Washington cannot let that happen. He needs to keep up morale, whether it be by motivation or strict discipline. He has to emerge as the leader in the spring,"

Ben agreed. "There is already talk of replacing him."

"Ben, as long as he can keep his men loyal to him, the Continental Congress will not replace him, but they have to know that Washington has a truly loyal army behind him, willing to suffer personal sacrifice for the cause. You must help the General keep them motivated and on track. One more thing about this coded message thing that we came up with —remember it, because it may come in handy later."

"I will. You have done very well, Maggie. I am sure the General will be pleased."

Maggie hesitated to tell him the rest.

"Is there something else?"

"Well, it's not army related, and you might not like it..."

"Go on," he said slowly.

Maggie blew out a breath. "I may, kind of sort of, but not really….be engaged."

Ben went pale.

"Let me explain. Gabe had become the object of affection for a middle-aged woman looking for her next husband. After his 'escape,' she showed up at his house, professing her intent to nurse him back to health. He panicked, rightly so, and told her he was unavailable because we had become engaged. We thought that was the end of it until a party invitation arrived wanting to celebrate our engagement because she had told all of Philadelphia. We are playing that part until she finds another prospect, soon hopefully, so we can stage our very public breakup."

Ben shook his head. "What happens if she doesn't move on?"

"I don't know. We will figure it out, but there is a silver lining. I now have an invitation to every officer's dinner party in town. That's how I got this information."

Ben looked alarmed. "Maggie, that is a very dangerous game to play, especially that close to the ones you are spying on."

Maggie closed her eyes, the signs of strain back on her face. "I know Ben, but I don't know what else to do."

"You could go home to Virginia while I explain to Washington that things became too dangerous for you here," he said softly. "Go back and be safe until the war is over, until I can come for you."

Maggie took his face in her hands. "Oh Ben, I wish more than anything that was possible." She kissed him and then made love to him again. She had no idea how she was going to let him go.

While they lay in the afterglow, she spoke, "Ben, if anything should happen to me, I want you to go on with your life. Get married, have tons of kids, live a long and happy life."

His reply was swift and absolute. "Maggie, if anything happens to you, I don't want to go on."

Maggie pushed up on her elbows. "But if it does, you must. Promise me."

He kissed her. "I don't make promises I can't keep."

Ben walked Maggie to the stable.

"Ben, there is someone I want you to meet. This is Onyx. Onyx, this is Ben."

Onyx looked Ben up and down carefully before whinnying at him.

"It is nice to meet you Onyx. You are a beauty, aren't you?" Ben leaned toward Onyx and winked. "Make sure you take good care of our girl."

Onyx nodded in response and appeared to wink back.

Ben looked at Maggie. "Did he just answer me?"

"Yeah, he does that. Don't ask, just go with it."

Chuckling, Ben took Maggie in his arms. "Keep yourself safe, Maggie. I'll see you soon. I love you."

He kissed her.

"I love you, too, Ben."

17

CHAPTER SEVENTEEN

Maggie spent the next few weeks going to boring dinner parties and talking about plans for a wedding she had no intention of having.

Mrs. Bright had not found a new man to latch on to; it seemed that one of her finer qualities was being loyal to a fault.

John André seemed to have become the highlight of society. He was handsome, very entertaining, and always managed to appear and rescue Maggie at the most opportune times.

Maggie enjoyed their conversations together, and he seemed to always know the perfect thing to say.

He was the toast of the town and rumors were abounding about the number of ladies that he was keeping company with. He had always been a perfect gentleman to Maggie, so she largely ignored the gossip.

At one of the dinners, Maggie and John were discussing some of the lovely silhouette work that he did, when she noticed Peggy Shippen watching. "I think you have an admirer. Miss Shippen seems to enjoy keeping an eye on you." She inclined her head towards Peggy.

John turned slightly. "Miss Shippen is a lovely girl indeed, however, she is still a girl. She is very smart and well-mannered from what I can garner from the conversations we have had, but still young on many levels."

"Just the same, I think she may be developing a crush on you."

He looked across the room towards the girl. "How interesting."

Gabe was being called away more and more on overnight trips. He never mentioned details, and Maggie didn't ask. She couldn't pass along information she didn't have.

With winter quarters beginning, there would not be much movement anyway. She still checked in at the tavern a couple of times a week. One day, close to the middle of December, Maggie did indeed have a note waiting.

'Counting the days, can't wait to see you.'

No new information, but I need to see you.

Gabe was leaving the next morning for a couple of days, so the timing was perfect. Maggie headed out the following afternoon, egg basket in hand. She hadn't used Gabe's note yet, but she carried it, nonetheless.

She arrived a little early and was enjoying a drink downstairs when Ben came in. She would recognize his cloak anywhere, having been so up close and personal with it.

He came straight to her, taking her hand. “Hello, Maggie. I just had to see you one last time before we left for Valley Forge.”

The words were barely out when the tavern owner came over. “Soldiers headed this way fast. I’ll meet you out back with your horse.”

Ben took Maggie by the hand, getting to her feet just as two soldiers came through the door. He guided her upstairs, and out the back entrance. Ben leapt on his horse, pulling Maggie up behind him before taking off in a full gallop.

The soldiers shouted orders behind them, close on their heels.

She wrapped her arms around Ben, molding her body to his.

Ben was an expert horseman, dodging back and forth, putting further distance between them and the soldiers. They were almost clear when the gunfire erupted. The soldiers fired their pistols, their shots mostly nowhere near hitting their marks— all save one.

Ben called back to Maggie. “We are almost in Germantown. I will set you down near the town stables. Take a horse and double back to the tavern, so they won’t suspect you. I will find you as soon as I can. I love you, Maggie.”

“I love you too, Ben.”

“Ready? Here we go.”

Ben rode right up to the stables, took her arm to help her down, kissed her forehead and was gone, all in less than a minute.

Maggie found a saddled horse, climbed on, waited for the soldiers to pass and started back towards the tavern. Once she reached it, she dismounted and searched for Onyx. The tavern owner had been gracious enough to saddle him for her, assuming they would be back. She climbed up and told him to get her home. Maggie folded the bottom of her cloak over, pressing it against her wound.

She didn't dare tell Ben that she had been hit. He would have given himself up just to get her medical attention. He would be safe. Maggie, on the other hand, was another story.

By the time she reached the checkpoint, she had almost passed out. She felt someone pull her down to the ground. She heard lots of shouting and a familiar voice.

"Maggie...Maggie!"

Was it Gabe? No, it wasn't Gabe's voice, but someone else's.

"Whose voice?" was her last thought before everything went black.

Captain John André was smoking a pipe, enjoying a stroll close to the edge of town when he heard shouting coming from the checkpoint. Assuming they were being attacked, he ran in that direction. He was surprised to see, not an attack, but someone on the ground next to a horse. Getting closer, he made out the shape of a woman—a woman he recognized!

He pushed his way through the men. "Maggie! Maggie!" He looked her over.

She was bleeding very badly from the back of her hip. He scooped her up and shouted for one of the men to find a doctor. His house was the closest safe place; he carried her upstairs and put her in his bed, stripping back her dress to get a better look at her wound.

It was bad —very bad.

Maggie couldn't open her eyes; something was wrong. She heard voices speaking around her and felt her sword being taken off her back.

No! Don't take that.

She felt her clothes being removed, then a sudden stabbing, digging pain in the back of her leg. She struggled to scream, but it wouldn't come out. She wanted to move, but she couldn't. The pain was unbearable. She tried to move again, but something held her down. The digging pain was finally gone, replaced with a throbbing, beating fire. Something wet was put to her lips; it tasted strange and made her fall into a welcome, blessed oblivion.

Maggie drifted in and out the entire next day, waking up to muffled voices, not understanding what they were saying. She felt something cold and wet on her forehead, and it felt good. She was hot all over.

She tried to lift her arm, but it was useless; it wouldn't obey. She tried to move her legs, but pain shot through her entire body like a lightning bolt; she felt tears drip down the side of her face. Whispers filled her ear, soothing, shushing noises, a hand on her head, one holding her hand. She stopped fighting, allowing herself to drift back off.

John André stood by the downstairs window looking out, having a drink. His thoughts drifted to the previous night when he found Maggie on the ground, unconscious, and bleeding from a bullet wound. The surgeon had removed the shot from her leg, but she had not yet woken up to tell anyone what had happened to her.

His thoughts went back to the sword he'd found strapped to her back and the two daggers in her boots. Why would a woman carry a sword or knives that way? Sure, these were dangerous times, but that seemed a little excessive.

A banging on the door broke his concentration.

His servant answered, and Colonel Asheton pushed past her.

John saw the anguish on his face.

"John, where is she?"

He pointed. "She's upstairs resting. She has not woken up yet. Come and sit down, Gabe. You look as if you are about to collapse."

Gabe made his way to a chair, as John poured him a drink and handed it to him. "Here, you look as if you could use this."

Gabe thanked him and downed it. "How bad is it?"

John took the seat opposite him, crossing his legs. "Maggie was shot in the back of her hip. The army doctor removed the fragments, but she has lost a great deal of blood. She has developed a high fever and has been restless all day. She finally settled down a little while ago, when the doctor gave her something to help her rest. He just left."

Gabe covered his face with his hands, moving them away to speak. "What happened?"

John shook his head. "I have no idea. She was already completely out of it by the time her horse got her to the checkpoint."

"I need to see her."

John got up. "Of course. Come with me."

Starting up the staircase, John stopped, looking back at Gabe as he asked, "Do you have any idea why she would have been carrying a sword on her back and knives in her boots?"

Gabe was startled by his question and the timing of it. "Why yes! Maggie always traveled with them. She was attacked many years ago and never goes anywhere without them."

John stared back. "And she knows how to use them?"

Gabe nodded. "I taught her." Which brought the question to Gabe's mind —why didn't she use them?

Maggie could take down any man she chose to, but here she was, with a bullet in her backside.

Gabe staggered a little, leaning against the doorframe when he saw Maggie. She was as white as a sheet and so still. For an instant he thought she was dead — until he saw the slight rise and fall of her chest.

John noticed his reaction. "The surgeon gave her laudanum. She was so restless from the fever; he was afraid she would tear open her wound."

Gabe went to her side, taking her hand, sitting down on the edge of the bed. His hand went to her forehead; she was burning up. He lightly stroked her hair, tucking it behind her ear as he leaned down and whispered, "Maggie, I am here. I am not leaving your side until I know you are well, so could you hurry it up a little, please. I need you...Hettie needs you...Onyx needs you. And there is no way you are leaving me here alone to take care of that blasted horse of yours. I swear he fully intended to take a bite out of my arse last week."

John looked down into his glass with a slight smile. He admired the relationship those two had —their unique bond, the witty banter they countered back and forth, and how, even in a time as serious as this, they were close enough for him to make little quips about something as serious as death to her in hopes of drawing her back from the brink. Not only did he admire it, he was jealous of it. He slipped out, leaving them to have their privacy.

Maggie woke up the next morning, feeling the extreme soreness in her backside before even opening her eyes. She sensed someone next to her; it was Gabe, his hand holding hers. He looked so peaceful, she didn't want to wake him, but the attempt to stretch out her leg, compounded by her use of the word 'fuck' woke him instantly.

"Maggie, you're awake."

She grimaced. "Unfortunately. Where are we?"

Gabe got up, getting her a glass of water. "John André's house. He found you at the checkpoint and brought you here."

Memories flooded back.

He helped her take a few sips of water. In a low voice, close to her ear, he whispered, “Maggie you need to tell me exactly what happened.”

Maggie looked at Gabe and sighed. She really didn’t want to lie to him, but everything she had done had been to protect him, and she wasn’t about to stop looking out for him now. A knock at the door broke their gaze.

“I thought I heard voices.” John was at the door. “May I come in?”

Maggie smiled. “Please. I understand I owe you a debt of gratitude.”

John stepped inside. “It was my pleasure. I am just glad that I happened by at an opportune time. You can repay me by telling me exactly what happened.”

Gabe’s back was still to John; he was giving Maggie a troubled look.

Maggie gathered her thoughts. “Of course. Gabe had left for an overnight trip, and I was feeling rather cooped up, so Onyx and I took a ride out in the country. He gets restless if he isn’t taken out regularly.”

John raised his head. “That must be the ‘demon horse.’”

Maggie cocked her head with an unspoken question that John answered, “The men at the checkpoint swore that he looked like a demon when he rode up with you. They said that his eyes glowed like fire embers and that he appeared to have smoke coming out of his nostrils.”

Gabe snarked under his breath. “Sounds like Onyx.”

Maggie cut him a side look. “Anyway, we were on our way back to town when three men came out of the woods; two of the men took Onyx by the reins, the other one pulled out a pistol demanding money. I would have given it to them, but one man stepped to the side, making remarks about dragging me in the woods, back to their camp for the night.” She gave her best-abhorred look. “So, I spurred Onyx; he reared up and took off at full gallop. The man with the pistol fired and I felt it hit me. I don’t remember much else.”

Gabe looked down, not saying anything.

John looked appalled and angry. “Continental ruffians, no doubt. I will take a group of men and we will ride out immediately. The fact that a lady cannot ride without being accosted is simply unacceptable and will not be tolerated. In the future, Maggie, perhaps it would be best if you remained in town for your rides, or with an armed escort.”

“Thank you, John. I know I shouldn’t have, but I was becoming so restless and with winter coming, I knew I wouldn’t have many more chances.”

John nodded. “I understand, but you are now the fiancé of a high-ranking British officer, and you are also a target. I would not be at all shocked if the opposing army chose to kidnap a woman to use as a pawn in their attempt at victory. But I have no doubt the Colonel will now take extra precautions to keep you safe.”

Gabe finally looked up, directly in Maggie’s eyes, and said, “You are correct, Captain. I will do whatever it takes to keep Maggie safe, even if I have to personally lock her up in her room for her own good.”

A shiver ran down Maggie's spine; the statement was meant for her and her alone.

Gabe knew she was lying, and he was furious about it.

John excused himself, detecting a note of stress, leaving Maggie and Gabe with a world of tension between them.

Maggie stayed at John's house for the next two days, until she was well enough to move back home. Gabe had mostly gone back to his usual self, but Maggie knew she was in for it when they returned home.

He stayed by her side during the day, slipping out for a few hours in the evening to handle some things for work. During those times, John would come to sit with her, keeping her company and entertaining her with some of his stories. On the night before she was to return home, he sat in a chair next to her bed after having several drinks.

"Maggie, tell me about that lovely sword that you have. I couldn't help but admire it the night we found you. May I take a closer look at it?"

Maggie looked over at it. "Of course."

He set down his glass and stood to pick it up for a closer inspection. "The workmanship on it is exquisite. I have never seen anything quite like it. Wherever did you find it?"

"Believe it or not, I purchased it from an old peddler on the side of the road years ago when I first arrived in Williamsburg."

He flipped it over. "Fascinating! What is the emblem here?"

Maggie shook her head. “No idea. It is so small that I have never been able to make it out.”

An idea popped into John’s head. “I may have just the thing for that.” He disappeared for a moment, returning with a strange contraption. “The previous resident of this home was an inventor and left a great many wondrous things behind. This one allows you to see things up close and more clearly.”

Maggie thought hard. “Who did you say was the previous owner?”

Oh... a chap by the name of Franklin, Benjamin I believe was his first name.”

No freaking way!

Maggie was in Ben Franklin’s house. Oh, if these walls could talk.

John, seeming pleased with himself, brought the sword and the instrument over to her. “Look at that. It’s a crest.”

Maggie was amazed. “What kind of crest?”

“If I had to venture a guess, I would say Scottish. It seems to be a lion with a crown. Wait, there is writing in the crest. “Hmm.... ‘S Rioghal Mo Dhream’. My Gaelic is a little rusty, but I believe it reads, ‘I am of royal descent’.

Son of a bitch! How had she missed that all these years?

John was legitimately excited by the find. “A peddler you say?” he asked, seemingly confused.

“Yes.”

“And he never mentioned where he got it?”

"No. Come to think of it, that was the first and last time I ever saw that old man. How do you suppose it ended up on his cart?"

John shrugged. "Maybe one of the Highlanders that ended up in the area needed money, but it must have been for a very good reason. This is a family sword and they would not have parted with it easily."

Strange indeed.

"Well, whatever the reason, it came along at just the right time for me and for that, I am grateful."

John laid the sword down. "Well, it is getting late and you need your rest. I must admit, I shall miss having you around, Maggie. I have grown very fond of our talks."

"I feel the same way, John, and I cannot thank you enough for all you have done for me."

He leaned down and kissed her forehead, catching Maggie a little off guard. "It has been entirely my pleasure. Good night, Maggie."

Well, that was a little awkward.

The next day, after the doctor cleared her to be moved, Gabe brought a carriage by to pick her up. He carried her to it and then, up to bed when they got home. She was still very sore and weak, so rest was the order for the foreseeable future. Maggie insisted Gabe go to work since she would be in bed resting anyway, and she didn't want him to make a fuss.

A few days later, Maggie felt well enough to venture downstairs. It was one of those evenings after the house had settled down, and Maggie found Gabe in a large leather chair, legs stretched out, drink in hand, staring into the fire.

"Everything alright, Gabe? You seem lost in thought." She sat down on the couch opposite him.

He didn't move. "I'm not sure you want to hear my thoughts, Maggie."

"Might as well, I'm already here."

He still didn't move. "I almost lost you, Maggie, to a bunch of common, filthy, disgusting highwaymen," he paused, taking a sip of his brandy, quiet anger in his voice, "only, there weren't any highwaymen, were there? We searched every inch of those woods, and there wasn't the first shred of evidence to suggest any ever existed."

Maggie sat silent, focusing on the dancing flame.

"There were no reports of any men like that in the entire area." He never broke his gaze from the fire, raising a folder with his left hand that had been resting on his lap and letting it slip from his hands onto the floor in front of Maggie. He spoke in a low, even-toned, matter-of-fact voice, "There were, however, a group of soldiers that spotted one, Major Benjamin Tallmadge of the Continental army, entering an establishment by the name of the Rising Sun Tavern. They were under the assumption he was there to receive intelligence information from a confidential informant. He was observed with a hooded, possibly female, figure on the back of his horse as he fled. The soldiers gave chase for three miles into the town of Germantown, firing pistols at the fugitives, until they lost sight of them in the town limits."

Gabe looked down in his glass.

"You were that hooded figure..." He downed his drink, resting the glass on his knee before he finished, "and Major Tallmadge is your precious Ben."

Maggie let out the breath she had been holding, watching Gabe, who only moved to raise his hand to his head, still speaking in the same, monotone voice.

"He used you, Maggie. He seduced you, convinced you that he was naive and inexperienced, he took advantage of your mind and your body and forced you to help him, all to further his own agenda. He never loved you."

Maggie shook her head slowly, speaking in a whisper. "No one ever uses me. You know that Gabe."

He turned his head to her, seeing the truth in her face as she met his gaze. "Then explain to me why you would betray England...and why you would betray me. I can only assume you gave him information that came from under my roof, so please, tell me, that he gave you no choice, that he blackmailed you, that he threatened your life...something...anything." He was pleading.

She looked back toward the fireplace, feeling the need to defend Ben. "I did what I did of my own accord. No one forced me into anything. Ben is a good and honorable man, which is why he begged me not to, but the whole thing was my idea and my decision alone."

Gabe stood up, outraged, angered, feeling completely betrayed by the only person he trusted more than anyone else. He threw his glass into the fire, fanning the flame, glass shattering everywhere.

Maggie jumped.

He turned his anger toward her, disgustedly spatting out one word. "Why?"

Maggie lifted her chin, calmly answering his question. "Why else? I did it to save you."

Gabe opened his mouth to speak and closed it again, all color draining from his face, replaced by shock, then by confusion. It took him a moment to recover. "Me? To save ME? I don't understand."

Standing, Maggie wiped a tear from her face, walking around to pour herself a drink. After a sip, she spoke. "The day your assistant came here to tell me you had been taken by Washington's army, I thought you were dead. It was the only thing I could think of when he came in to say that you wanted me to be notified if anything were to ever happen to you."

Gabe felt the sadness in her words.

"I was heartbroken, not knowing how I would ever make it in this world without the one person that meant more to me than anything. You are the only reason that I have made it this long. You are my best friend and the only person who understands me, not judging me for the person that I really am. But then he said that you weren't believed to be dead, instead taken by the Continental army. He said you would be tortured for the information that you knew, and then probably thrown into one of those horrific prisoner camps. I know how many people die in those things, and the thought of you in one of them, cold, starving, dying alone… I couldn't bear the thought of it, especially if there was something I could do about it."

Maggie paused a moment to compose herself, taking a sip to help the lump in her throat.

Gabe sat down on the edge of the chair, the anger fading away as a slow understanding crept into his conscious mind. “Oh God, Maggie! What did you do?”

She walked around to the couch and sat down, hugging herself. “The only thing I could; I made a bargain with General George Washington himself. You see, he owed me a favor. I inadvertently saved him and Ben from an encounter with some British soldiers. It was before I knew you were in Philadelphia. I had no idea who they were at the time, but when it was all said and done, General Washington was in my debt. That’s the night I met Ben. We spent the entire night just talking, getting to know each other. I told him about you and our friendship, how much you meant to me while leaving out the part about you being in the British army. I found you here because of him. He came to the tavern to warn me of a battle about to happen, and he wanted to make sure I was clear of the area. He was the reason I was in Philadelphia that day. He was protecting me. Anyway, as soon as your assistant left, I grabbed a horse from the stable and made straight for his camp, asking for an audience. They took me to a tent to wait, and it was Ben who actually came in. I explained what happened and I begged him to release you. He said that there was no way the General would let such an important source of information go. If it had been strictly up to him, I think he would have done it for me. Since he couldn’t help me, I asked to speak to Washington and when I was in front of him, I convinced him that I, as someone living in an officer’s house, could get him much more information, and I would in exchange for your release. I was, of course, lying, not having access to that kind of information, but he believed me and agreed. Ben was furious that I had put myself in danger. He begged Washington not to do it, but his mind was made up, so he ordered his men to take you to a camp north of town and give you an easy opportunity to escape so as not to arouse suspicion."

Maggie paused to look at Gabe, who had his forehead in his hand, staring at the floor.

"I was so relieved when they brought you in. You were home, alive and safe, but I knew I had made a deal, and I always keep my word. The day John dropped off that paperwork for you, I stole a look, jotted down some troop numbers and places and signaled to meet. General Washington made Ben my contact, so when I brought intelligence, I was able to spend the night with him. I only gave him information the one time. The other night, when I was shot, he had signaled me just because he wanted to see me before they left for winter quarters. He had no idea he was seen and, when he discovered he had been, he grabbed me, riding to Germantown to get me to safety. We parted ways in town, I doubled back to the tavern to get Onyx and rode for Philadelphia. Ben had no idea I had been shot. I hid it from him because I knew he would give himself up to make sure I received medical attention, and I could not let him do that. Onyx got me to the checkpoint just as I passed out."

Maggie drained her glass and looked at Gabe, who was covering the horror on his face with his hands.

"No one forced me. I did it to save you and I would do it a hundred times over again. Turn me in if you wish…" she closed her eyes, letting her tears flow before finishing, "but if I am hanged, all I ask is that you

PLEASE, honor your promise to protect the people on my estate."

Gabe was aghast by what he had just heard.

Maggie had sold herself to the devil to get him to safety. It was his job to protect her, not the other way around...and he had failed miserably. She was lost— so lost that she believed that he would hand her over as a traitor — the one woman who knew the truth about him, embracing him for it, and loving him in spite of it. He knelt in front of her as she looked away.

Taking her hands in his, he said, "Maggie, look at me."

She wouldn't.

He said it louder and more forcefully. "Maggie! Look at me!"

When she did, he saw the pain, the guilt and the burden in her eyes. She had been too strong for too long and it was taking its toll.

Gabe took her face in both his hands. "Maggie, I love you. I would never turn you in. It was not your responsibility to save me. I accepted my possible fate when I became a soldier and I am not afraid to die. But what I fear more than anything, is seeing something happen to you. You are my family. I love you more than I love my own life and I vow to you, right here and now, that I will spend the rest of my life doing whatever it takes to keep any harm from coming to you."

Maggie broke like a dam, all the pressure from the past few weeks coming out at once, her whole body shaking as she sobbed.

Gabe pulled her to him, holding her tight, comforting her like a child. Her entire body went limp against him as he picked her up and carried her to her bed. He held her, mumbling soothing words until she fell asleep. He stared at the ceiling. He was a fool to think Maggie would have done anything to betray him, and he hated himself for questioning her loyalty for even a second.

She was an amazing woman and one that he would do anything for whether she liked it or not, even if it meant he needed to make some decisions for her that were for her own good.

18

CHAPTER EIGHTEEN

Three days later, a shadow slipped through the back door of a dark house, crossing the floor to the base of the staircase. The distinctive click of a barrel hammer caused the figure to stop and raise his arms. A candle flamed to life, illuminating a man sitting in a chair, his legs crossed, aiming a gun directly at the intruder's heart as the owner of the pistol said, "Major Tallmadge, I presume."

Ben narrowed his eyes for a better look, adjusting to the minimal light. It occurred to him that he had been tricked into coming here.

Gabe looked the man over. He knew he would come. Maggie had told him all the details about how they communicated, so he'd left a message at the tavern and waited.

"You must be Colonel Asheton."

Gabe tilted his head in acknowledgment and stood up, motioning with the gun. "Major Tallmadge, you and I need to have a chat. Please join me."

Once in the drawing room, Gabe closed the door. He held up the gun as he walked past Ben. "May I have your word as a gentleman that you won't try to attack me while we speak?"

Ben lowered his arms. "You have my word."

Gabe laid the gun down on the table.

"Good!" he said and poured two drinks, handing one to Ben, indicating for him to sit.

"Where's Maggie?" Ben could no longer hold back from asking.

Gabe took a seat, crossing his legs and giving Ben a good once over. "She is upstairs, recovering from the gunshot in her backside from your little 'excursion' the other night."

The blood drained from Ben's face. "Maggie was shot?"

"Yes, she was."

Ben set the glass down, forcing himself to breathe. "Is she alright?"

Gabe took in a deep breath and let it out. "She will be."

"I didn't know."

Gabe nodded, sympathetically. "Because she didn't want you to know. She hid it from you. Maggie knew you would have given yourself up if she told you, so she covered it up, rode back to the tavern to get Onyx and made it to the town checkpoint. She nearly bled to death before one of our captains found her."

Ben was in shock, looking as if he were about to vomit.

Gabe pointed to the glass. "Drink! It will help."

Nodding, Ben took a large sip, feeling the burn as it went down.

"Major Tallmadge, you and I have a great deal in common, the biggest of these things being, that we both love a woman who will do anything for the people that she loves, even if it puts her in great personal jeopardy. I know about the deal Maggie made for my life, and I am here to tell you that deal ends TONIGHT!"

Ben nodded his head. "I pleaded with her not to make it, but she wouldn't listen. Neither would the General. I thought I could keep her safe..." he trailed off.

Gabe looked at the Major.

God, was he ever that young himself?

"Major, you and I are soldiers. We signed up for the military life, knowing full well what we were getting into. It is the life that we chose. Maggie, on the other hand, did not. I would never forgive myself if something happened to her and, if I am not mistaken, you feel the same way."

Ben nodded. "She needs to be away from all of this."

"Good, Major. I am glad to hear that we are in agreement." Gabe leaned in closer. "You need to understand something. The only thing holding Maggie in Philadelphia is— YOU. I can get her away from here and back to her home in Virginia, but I need your help to do it."

Maggie heard voices downstairs.

Who was Gabe talking to this late at night?

She put on her robe and eased down the steps. What she saw sent chills up her spine. She stood at the doorway, seeing Gabe in his favorite chair and Ben on the couch. They were leaned in close, speaking.

"Ben?"

They both turned to look at her. He rose and came straight to her, taking her in his arms.

"What are you doing here? How did you…."

Ben shushed her. "Maggie, everything is fine. Gabe and I were just having a discussion."

"About what?"

"About why you didn't tell me you had been shot for one. Maggie, you could have died. That was information that I needed to know."

The concern on his face melted her. "Ben, I didn't."

"But you could have."

Gabe stood up. "Maggie, Major Tallmadge and I are in full agreement that you need to leave Philadelphia for your own protection."

Ben kissed her forehead. "He is right. You are not safe here anymore."

Maggie looked at them, one then back to the other. "I'm sorry, but the last time I checked, I am a grown woman and I can come and go as I please. No one can FORCE me to leave."

Gabe sucked in a deep breath. "I WILL force you to leave. I am taking you back to Virginia myself."

Maggie rolled her eyes. "And I will use my personal ship to beat you back to Philadelphia."

Gabe lowered his eyes and his voice. "I am not coming back to Philadelphia. I am resigning my commission to stay in Williamsburg with you."

Maggie's mouth dropped as she moved towards Gabe. "You said you would never do that. What's changed?"

Gabe took her by the arms. "You put yourself in danger to save me. I won't let that happen again."

Ben moved next to Gabe. "Listen to him, Maggie. We both agree that this is for the best."

Maggie laughed. "So, the two of you are making decisions on how I live my life? Yeah, right... dream on." Maggie moved to the drink table.

Ben suddenly became angry. "Damn it, Maggie! That bullet in your backside made the decision for all of us. This ends tonight. No more spying for General Washington, no more clandestine meetings, none of it! I will NOT allow it!"

Maggie became angry as well. "You will not ALLOW it? The last time I checked, you were not my father or my husband, so you have no say over what I do with MY life."

Ben clenched his teeth. "Well, I sure as hell would like you to live long enough to BECOME my wife."

Silence filled the room.

Gabe looked back and forth between the two of them to see the expressions on their faces. They were both worked up and the strain showed, gazes locked on each other, the tension in the room thick enough to be cut with a knife. He folded his arms with a little anticipatory grin, anxious to see what would happen next, no one expecting those words to be said, or what was coming next. They just stood there, both breathing hard, neither one willing to flinch.

And there it was. The reality of the whole situation slammed Maggie hard in the gut. She was in love and fighting to spend time with a man she could never have any kind of life with. He wanted to marry her and she him, but that could never happen. The 'living in the moment' veil dropped, and Maggie's heart was torn in half.

She made the first move, storming out, not saying a word, stalking up the stairs to her room, and slamming the door.

Gabe's grin dropped into a worried frown watching her leave. Ben started after her, but Gabe held his arm out to stop him.

"Let me talk to her first. Have a drink and pull yourself together."

Ben acknowledged him and eased down on the couch.

Gabe knocked softly on the door. "Maggie, it's Gabe." He pushed the door open.

She was sitting on the floor against the wall, her knees pulled up to her chest, and her arms wrapped around. She didn't even look up.

Gabe quietly sat down next to her. "Mags, I'm pretty sure that man downstairs, that loves you almost as much as I do, just told you he wanted to marry you."

Maggie turned her head only slightly and whispered, "But, I can't marry him. I want to, more than anything, but I cannot."

Gabe's forehead wrinkled. "Why not?"

Maggie closed her eyes. "I have my reasons."

The answer gravely concerned Gabe. "Maggie, Ben is moving into winter quarters tomorrow, and I am taking you back to Virginia as soon as possible — that is a fact and not up for debate. You may not see each other for a very long time. If you want to spend some time alone with him, you should do it now. You need to say your 'goodbyes', be it for now... or for good."

Maggie reached over, taking his arm. "Help me up."

She looked in the mirror, wiping her eyes, and placing her hands on the dresser composing herself. "Would you send him up please?"

In only moments, Ben appeared at the door.

Maggie took his hand, pulling him in the room and closing the door.

"Maggie…"

She cut him off by kissing him. "Ben, I will go home with Gabe. I will do as you ask. I need to go home and take care of things there anyway. Let's not argue. We may not see each other for a while, and I don't want to do anything but be with you tonight."

They spent the next few hours making love, slowly, tenderly, lovingly, as if it were their last night together— because it was.

After he left that night, Maggie curled up into a ball on her bed and grieved for the life she would never have with him.

19

CHAPTER NINETEEN

The next day, true to his word, Gabe gave notice of his resignation. It would be about three weeks before they were able to leave for Virginia.

That afternoon, John, who had become a regular visitor, came by the house to pay a visit and noticed Maggie wasn't her usual self. "Maggie, you seem sad today. May I ask what has upset you?"

"Gabe is resigning his commission today and we will be going back to Virginia."

John was stunned. He put his tea saucer on the table, "Oh! I am so sorry to hear that. I mean, I am happy that you will be able to go home for your own sake, because I know how much you miss it, but I, personally, shall miss you terribly. I have grown quite fond of our time together."

Maggie felt the same way.

She and John had developed a great friendship and the knowledge that he would be dead in a few short years —being hanged with Ben present, no less — ate away at her. Having knowledge of the future really sucked. She wanted to warn him so badly, but his capture was a major turning point in the war.

"John, I will miss you too. I really don't want to leave, but Gabe is insistent."

John wanted to say something but hesitated. "Forgive me for saying so, and if I overstep, I apologize, but it seems that you and Gabe have not been as close since you were injured. And again, forgive me, but, Maggie, you have appeared very unhappy the past couple of weeks."

Weariness swept over Maggie. "I'm afraid Gabe reacted badly to what happened to me. He is terrified that I will get hurt, and he thinks taking me back to Virginia will keep me safe, so much so, that he is giving up his military career to do it."

"And will you marry before you leave?"

Maggie shook her head. "No."

John bobbed his head to the side. "I get the impression that you don't want to get married."

Maggie shrugged. "I have no need to marry. I do not need the money, nor the title for that matter, and I don't need to do it to keep Gabe in my life; he will always be there, no matter what."

"Then why did you accept his proposal?"

Crap, these lies were getting hard to keep straight.

"Well, I suppose that marrying Gabe would keep me from being asked by every single man in the world who knows who I am, to marry them. I know Gabe and I will be growing old together anyway, so he is as good a choice as any."

They really needed to stage this breakup.

"But you didn't say anything about LOVE."

Maggie sipped her tea. "Oh, I love Gabe and he loves me. We would do anything for each other."

John looked concerned. He didn't want to see Maggie in a loveless marriage, there were far too many of them out there as it was. He placed his hand on Maggie's knee. "Maggie, if you ever need anything, anything at all, I am always here for you."

She patted his hand. "I know. Thank you, John."

After word of Gabe's resignation got around, the invitations for retirement parties started to roll in; Maggie had at least three in hand.

Hearing her groan from the other room, Gabe popped his head around the corner. "What's wrong?"

Maggie held up the invitations and wrinkled her nose. "Boring military parties."

Gabe raised his head in acknowledgment. "Ah! Well, perk up, Mags. In a few short weeks, I will be free of all of them."

Maggie was grateful for that. She was happier knowing he wouldn't be part of the ones shipped out after the war; she just had to convert him to the American side beforehand, or make it look like he supported them anyway.

"Which reminds me, Gabe, of two things. First, we need to disentangle from this whole engagement thing. Honest to goodness, I wouldn't be surprised if one of these dinner parties turned out the be a walk-in wedding in disguise. All of Philadelphia seems to be clamoring for this wedding."

Gabe made a face. "Why?"

"Because my dear Gabe, the people in this town need new things to gossip about. The war has them in short supply. Really, you need to fix Mrs. Bright up with some poor unfortunate soul, so they will have something new to talk about besides us."

Gabe laughed. "I'll get right on that. And the second thing?" He leaned against the doorway.

Maggie kept forgetting what a stunning man he really was. The older he got, the better he looked.

"This!" She handed him three pieces of paper.

"What's all this?"

"Papers to be filed when we get back to Virginia. The first one is a deed to five hundred acres of land from my estate."

"What?"

"Gabe, I promised you if you would retire for me, that I would have a house built for you. You have to have land to build it on."

"Maggie, I can't take this."

"Oh yes, you can, and you will. And since you will be needing something to do with your time, I am giving you this as well. It is half of the shipping business."

Gabe's mouth dropped open. "Maggie, this is too much...I can't."

Maggie touched his lips with soft fingers. "Shush! I have more than enough, and you will need income. Those two things are buttering you up for the third one. This is my will and my power of attorney in the event I become incapacitated —temporarily or permanently."

Gabe's head popped up. "Your what?"

Maggie sighed. "My will. I need to know that if something happens to me, that you will handle things for me. I will have the detailed instructions put together and given to the attorney at home, but this will give me peace of mind that Hettie and everyone else will be provided for, and you will get the house and the rest of the estate in exchange."

He shook his head.

"Gabe, you are the one constant in my life and it only makes sense. I know I can count on you to do as I wish. Besides, no one else will be able to handle Onyx."

It was his turn to groan.

Maggie and Gabe were nearing the end of one of the dinner parties in their honor. Maggie was desperately looking for a quiet place to gather herself when she felt a hand on her back and heard John whisper in her ear, "Come with me so we can escape."

He led her to a small study hidden off to the side of another larger room, that was blissfully empty.

"Maggie, I have noticed that these parties seem to cause you a great deal of distress."

Maggie found a chair and collapsed in it. "Yes, I am afraid I am not well-suited to the party scene."

John rummaged through a few cabinets. "Aha! Success!" He held up a bottle, and two glasses, reading the label. "How do you feel about rum?"

A broad smile spread across Maggie's face. "It's my favorite."

He poured two glasses and took the chair next to her.

Maggie took a sip and sighed. “Oh, that is so good.”

John watched her intently, smiling.

“I hate these things, so what’s your excuse?”

John turned his head to the side silently questioning what she meant.

“Why are you hiding out here? You are depriving the lovely ladies of Philadelphia of your delightful company. They are all probably fanning themselves in distress as we speak.”

John laughed softly. “Yes, well, I much prefer the company in here. Everyone out there is in search of the most beneficial marriage match for themselves and their families based on prestige, honor and social standing. I am not exactly the marrying type— not for that reason anyway.” John looked a little forlorn.

“Then, for what reason?” Maggie asked.

“The only reason anyone should ever marry— for love, which is something I have yet to find.”

Maggie chided him a little, “Not from a lack of trying, from what I hear.”

He looked surprised and a little embarrassed.

“Not that I am judging, John, because believe me, I have no room to talk. You have to take the moments of happiness when and where you can find them, no matter how brief.” A tinge of longing tinted her voice. She swallowed hard. The void left by Ben’s departure was still raw. She had done her best to hide it from Gabe, but, here in this room, the agony was still very much present.

John sensed her pain, furrowing his brow, leaning over closer. “Maggie, you know you can tell me anything. I would never betray your confidence and, lately, you seem to be quite burdened with something. I can assure you that I am an exceptionally good listener."

A single tear slipped out.

John reached over and gently wiped it away. He made a gentle, understanding statement. "There is someone else that you love."

She simply nodded, afraid that her voice would crack if she uttered even one word.

"And he loves you, but for whatever reason, you cannot be together," John finished.

There was a reason this man would become the head of the British Secret Service. He saw and felt what others did not.

"You're are marrying Gabe to forget."

There was no use trying to deceive him any longer; he was a living, breathing lie detector test and, honestly, she didn't want to. He had become a good friend. "Actually, Gabe and I have no intention of getting married."

John acted as if he had heard her wrong.

Maggie explained the situation, about how Mrs. Bright's pursuit of Gabe pushed him into such a panic that he had made it up and that she had told the whole town by the next day.

John's emotions went from shock to amazement and then to laughter. So much so, that he was wiping his own tears in a few minutes, making Maggie laugh, too.

"We have been waiting for her to move on to stage the breakup, but so far no one has snatched up the lucky lady."

"I must say, Maggie, you and Gabe must be the greatest of friends to keep up such pretenses for so long."

She looked down at her glass. “Gabe and I would do anything for each other. We may not share blood, but we are family in every way that counts.”

John swirled the liquid in his glass. “And the man you are in love with?”

Maggie set her glass on the table. “He is gone and that is the end of it. Gabe has resigned his commission to take me home because he feels the need to protect me. He seems to forget that I have done pretty well taking care of myself.”

John stood up. “You are a remarkable woman, Maggie, and I am relieved to hear that you will not be settling into a marriage to a man that you are not passionately in love with, for that would be a true travesty.”

They could hear Gabe outside the room looking for her. John held out his hand to help her up. “It would please me very much if you would allow me to spend some more time with you and do some sketches of you before you leave. I would like to have them to commemorate our time here together.”

“I would like that too, John.”

He seemed pleased, kissing her hand and escorting her out to Gabe.

A few days before they were to leave, John invited her over for dinner at his house. After a wonderful meal and even better wine, they retired to the parlor. Maggie sat on the couch, while he sat in a chair, his legs crossed, sketching her.

When he was done, he came to sit beside her and show her his work. He had done several different drawings, from different angles. John was truly a wonderful artist.

Maggie was amazed at his talent and honored to be the subject of his work. “John, you made me look so beautiful in these.”

“That’s easy. You ARE a beautiful woman, Maggie.” He leaned over, tracing her face with his finger, before cupping one side of her face and planting a sweet, gentle kiss on her lips.

Maggie didn’t move, unsure of what was happening. When he pulled back, he saw the confusion on her face. “Forgive me. I forget myself when I am around you, Maggie.”

He stood quickly, walking to stand before the fireplace.

Maggie was stunned. “I should be getting home.” She stood to go.

John took her arm. “Maggie, I am very fond of you. If you would permit me, I would like to write to you in Virginia. After we make quick work of this whole war business, I hope you will allow me to come visit to renew our friendship and explore the possibility of something more between us.”

Maggie knew he would not survive the war; he was basically a dead man walking. No need to make it worse on him.

Take the happy moments while you can.

“I would like that very much, John. I will count the days.” She allowed him one more tender kiss before she left.

Seriously Maggie? Not a decent man in sight for twelve years, and now they are coming out of the woodworks.

Maggie and Gabe were preparing to depart on a British ship to Virginia. As they were boarding, a horse and rider came galloping at full charge. They turned to see that it was John.

"Forgive me! I was called out of town unexpectedly, but I did not want you to go without saying a proper goodbye."

He turned to Gabe. "Colonel, it has been my honor to serve with you. I shall miss our friendship."

Gabe shook his hand. "Be well, John."

John turned to Maggie. "I have a small gift for you, to remember me by."

"Oh, John, you shouldn't have." She opened the small box he had taken from his coat. It was a silver bracelet that had been inscribed. She looked closer, reading it aloud, "The course of true love never did run smooth."

Maggie looked up. "Shakespeare. John, how thoughtful. Thank you."

He helped her to put it on her wrist.

"Oh, John, I shall miss our time together." She pulled him into a long hug.

He wrapped his arms tightly around her, not wanting to let go, whispering in her ear, "I will miss you tremendously, Maggie. I look forward to this war being over, so we can see where our friendship may lead."

Maggie felt like a heartless wretch not warning him about the future. She opened her mouth, a warning almost escaping, but instead, she simply said, "Please take care of yourself, John."

She and Gabe watched from the deck rail as the ship pulled away from the dock.

John waved a final farewell, as Peggy Shippen walked up next to him with a look of concealed desire in her eyes for him. He turned briefly to acknowledge her, before turning back towards the ship, unmoving until the ship was completely out of sight.

Maggie had developed her own theory about those two. Women would do crazy things in the name of love, something she knew better than anyone.

Peggy was a lovestruck teenage girl, enamored by Philadelphia's newest boy toy and John, well John, was a well-known ladies' man, who preferred his women a little more experienced and worldly. There were always rumors of an affair between those two, but Maggie somehow doubted it. Nothing was more persistent or dangerous than a young woman trying to get the attention of an uninterested man— except, of course, for one that had been scorned.

Hell hath no fury…

20

CHAPTER TWENTY

A few days later, Maggie, Gabe, and Onyx were all home. Hettie was so happy to see them, that her fussing had become comical.

Things were going well on the estate.

It was winter, so there wasn't much to do.

Maggie spent the first few days taking care of the books for the business and getting everything squared away with her attorney. Gabe's land had been deeded to him, and construction on his new house would begin in the spring; he simply needed to pick the spot. For the most part, they were stuck inside because of the weather, the winter being exceptionally brutal, so far.

She was going through the stack of mail that had accumulated when she found a rather worn letter. Opening it, she saw that it was from Ben. Reading it, her heart ached. It spoke of the harsh conditions at Valley Forge, the discontent of the men, and, lastly, of his love for her. Maggie felt like the worst person in the world all over again. She was hoping that the departure in Philadelphia would have made for a clean break, but Ben was more determined than ever to be with her, and she had no idea how she was going to break his heart, and her own.

The thought of the amount of suffering Ben and all those men were enduring was too much to bear. Maggie wracked her brain trying to figure out how to help them. She couldn't buy things and send them up; she would be connected back by the money trail and that could be dangerous. Besides, supplies would be running thin in Philadelphia with the seizures by the British. She couldn't send a ship up with reserves; they would be confiscated. She needed an unusual plan and a thought occurred to her.

Maggie went up to her attic, where she had stashed the items from the previous owners. There were loads of winter clothes, socks, and boots that had been left behind. They would be especially useful to the soldiers, but she needed a way to get them there.

That plan was formed two days later when Captain Russell paid a visit to tell her that all the new wagons had been finished and how bad the men felt about her having to bail them out. He also told her how he redesigned the layout of the wagons to include several concealed compartments to hide contraband. His design was ingenious.

"Captain, how many of those men can be discreet and a little sneaky?"

He looked intrigued. "What do you have in mind?"

They hatched a plan.

Captain Russell had a son at Valley Forge, and he was more than willing to risk anything to help when he found out how bad things were there, insisting upon leading the group. He would take several trusted men and load down the newly built wagons with the clothes and shoes from the attic, along with food and ale items from the house. No one in town would question simple replenishment items for her estate.

Maggie would also give them some of the guns from the secret room to hide in the compartments for personal protection on the road. The men would take long routes around, especially when they got close to Philadelphia. She drew out maps of the camps from the information she had taken from Gabe's desk, so they could be avoided. It would take time, but they would eventually arrive. By the time they got there, anything would be better than nothing. She gave the Captain some letters she had written and money for their travel. Maggie also agreed to pay an enormous amount for their own personal endangerment.

"Captain, there is one more thing. I have given Gabe half of my interest in the shipping business. He need not know about some of our 'side pursuits', but he does need to be discreetly connected to them. If either side catches us, I can always plead that he never knew, but when the war ends, he needs to have shown allegiance to the winning side in some way, if you take my meaning."

The Captain agreed. "I understand completely, and I will handle it, Mistress."

"Thank you, Captain, and I will make sure you are duly compensated for your loyalty, as always. Good luck Captain. This is your most important mission to date."

And with that, the supplies were on their way.

One evening, a couple of weeks after they had gotten home, and after everyone else had left the house for the night, Maggie sat in front of the fireplace, staring blankly at nothing.

Gabe came into the room with a book in his hand. "I have to say, I have really enjoyed this."

It took a minute for Maggie to comprehend that he was even there. "Huh?"

Gabe came closer. "I said, I have really enjoyed this book that I found in here."

"What book?"

He laid it on the table in front of her. "The Scottish Faerie Tale book."

He poured two drinks.

Maggie lifted her chin. "The one you gave me?"

He offered her one of the glasses, but she refused. "I didn't give you that."

"You didn't? It arrived around Christmas last year. I thought it was from you."

He sat down across from her. "I didn't send it."

Maggie mumbled, "Interesting."

Gabe could see Maggie's mind was troubled by something, and it was not a minor thing. "Maggie, what is the matter? You don't seem like yourself tonight. You barely touched your supper."

Maggie matter-of-factly made the statement without even looking in his direction. "I'm pregnant."

Gabe froze, lowering the glass that had been near his lips. "I see. Are you sure?"

Maggie nodded. "I am sure."

Gabe sat quietly for a few moments before he spoke. "You have to tell him."

Maggie turned to him. "I can NEVER tell him."

Gabe narrowed his eyes, disbelieving what he just heard. "Maggie, the man has a right to know that you are carrying his child."

Maggie lowered her voice. "If he finds out, he will come for me, he will change his life for me, and that cannot happen."

Gabe strained to hold back his anger. "Maggie! Will you listen to yourself? You love this man more than anything, there is no doubt about it, and now you carry his child and you don't even think he has the right to know. What are you afraid of? That he will, God forbid, come here and marry you to keep his child from being born a bastard."

Maggie closed her eyes. Gabe rarely raised his voice and never to her. She raised her own voice in response. "That is EXACTLY what I am afraid of."

Gabe got up to pace the floor. "You keep saying that you cannot marry him, but you never say why. Cut the shite, Maggie, and tell me, why in the hell will you NOT marry him?"

Maggie looked him square in the eye, being unable to hold her secret to herself anymore. The knowledge she held was too much for one person to shoulder alone, and the words spilled out before she had time to think. "Because Major Benjamin Tallmadge will wait until the year 1784, the year after the official end of the war, to marry a woman by the name of Mary Floyd. They will go on to have seven children, all who have roles in the future of the new American government. I know this because I studied it in my HISTORY books in school. Thirteen years ago, I fell asleep in the year 2018, and the next morning, I woke up in the year 1765."

Ashen faced, Gabe fell back against the wall for support. It had finally happened. Maggie, his dear sweet, Maggie, had put so much strain on herself over the recent months, that she had suffered a psychological break, her mind being unable to handle any more pressure. He looked at her with pity and compassion. He was partially responsible for this, his capture and subsequent rescue at her hands, had contributed a great deal to this, he was sure of it. He had to take care of her. He had to get her the help that she needed.

He moved to her, knees hitting the floor, one arm on the chair she sat in, one smoothing back a strand of her hair, his own heart shattered. "Oh Maggie, I am so sorry. You are not well; your mind has betrayed you. I promise that I will get the best doctors for you to get you better. I will ensure care for the rest of your life, if necessary."

Slow understanding came over Maggie; Gabe thought she was crazy.

Of course, he did, because she sounded like a lunatic.

She took his face in her hands. "Gabe, I am not crazy. I am telling you the truth."

It was worse than Gabe thought; she had no idea that she was living in a fantasy. He laid his head in her lap. "I won't desert you, Maggie, you have my word."

Maggie rolled her eyes, picking his head up out of her lap and holding his head to look into his eyes again. "I have proof. Let me get up."

Gabe moved to the side, watching Maggie, unsure of what kind of erratic behavior to expect. He needed to keep her calm.

Maggie walked over to the fireplace and popped open the secret room.

Gabe was stunned. All the time he had spent in this house, and he had no idea there was a hidden room behind that wall. He craned around to get a better look, watching Maggie take something from a desk drawer that had a false bottom in it.

He stepped closer as she looked for something, waving his hand around. "This new?"

Maggie didn't look up. "Came with the house. Found it." She turned to show him what was in her hand.

"This, my dear Gabe, is what you call a cell phone. You can use it to call anyone in the world in the future."

Gabe looked down. She held a strange, smooth box. It was pink, with a glass piece across the front and little buttons. He flipped it over, looking closer because he had never seen anything like it. He looked up at her, puzzled.

"In the future, when you can charge it, you press this button and it lights up with numbers that you can push and use to call people. Everyone has a unique phone number that you dial to reach them."

Gabe didn't know what to think, and then Maggie pulled out something else. It was a tiny silver thing.

"This is a flashlight. When the batteries work, you push this button and it lights up like a lantern." She showed him the tiny bulb inside.

"What's a 'battery' and why does it need to 'charge'? What is charging?"

Maggie unscrewed the flashlight and popped them out. "This is a little pack that has power in it; it's how things work, but they have to be charged up by electricity and there is none in 1779."

Explaining these things to an 18th-century man—not as easy as you think.

"In the future, every house has lights that don't need to be lit, they have these little bulbs like in this flashlight all over the house. You flip a switch, and they come on. Houses don't need fireplaces; a machine produces heat and cool air in houses to make things more comfortable."

Gabe looked at the things in his hands. How can this be possible? He looked at Maggie. There was fear and shock in his eyes.

"Gabe look at me. You know me better than anyone. Look into my eyes. Am I lying? Am I crazy? You know I am not like people in this time. I don't act like them; I don't think like them... because I am not like them. When I first found out that you liked men, I didn't react badly, because being that way is not a crime in my time, it's more common. How do you think I have made such a success out of this place? It's because I knew what was to come. Which is why I had made up my mind to stay out of the war; I didn't want to inadvertently change things."

Gabe knew somewhere deep down inside that she was telling the truth. He knew she wasn't crazy.

Maggie pulled Gabe into the drawing room and sat him in a chair. He looked as if he were about to pass out. She handed him a drink.

"How? Is travel like this normal?"

Maggie sat down in front of him. "No, it's not. All that disbelief you have, well I had all of it when I first got here. It is a pretty bitter pill to swallow."

She told him everything about how she got there, from the engagement all the way up to the present, filling in all the blanks in between.

He listened without saying a word, filled with questions, but not wanting to interrupt her.

When she was done, she went back into the room and came out with something else. It was a bottle —a very strange, beautiful, colorful piece of glass— that she poured a piece of paper out of. "This is what I found on the beach."

Gabe examined it, seeing the little symbols on it — ones that looked oddly familiar. Where had he seen them? "Maggie, the book!"

He got up and brought it back, flipping through the pages, as she watched him curiously.

"The marks on this bottle are on the spine of this book. Look!"

She looked closely; he was right, they were the same. "Gabe, I never put the two things together. I haven't looked at this bottle in years. And you are sure you didn't send me this?"

"I think I would know if I sent you a book," Gabe said dryly.

Maggie examined the edition closer, turning to the first page that was blank, then the second that wasn't.

"Dear God!"

Gabe looked over. "What is it?"

Maggie couldn't believe she didn't see it before; she always went to the text, never to the front pages. She pointed. "That is the crest that is on my sword."

"What?" Gabe looked closer. "How can you tell? The one on your sword is so small."

She explained about the magnifier at John's house.

Gabe looked astonished. "That cannot be a coincidence."

Maggie didn't think it was, either, but she had no idea what to make of all of it. She went over to the couch, propped up her feet with her hands behind her head. "Okay, hit me."

Gabe was aghast. "I would NEVER strike a woman, least of all you."

Maggie laughed. "No, I mean, let me have all of your questions. I know you must have a million."

They spent all night talking, Gabe asking about what it was like in 2018, before working up the nerve to ask about the nearer future. He was flabbergasted to learn the British lost the war and of what was to come of the Colonies.

It was close to dawn when Maggie stood to put everything back in place before the house started to come to life.

They started up the stairs to get some sleep, when Gabe said softly, "I have one more question, Maggie. What are you planning to do about the baby? He still has a right to know."

Maggie didn't have an answer.

When Maggie woke up the next morning, she felt like a new person. The weight that had been on her shoulders for so long, had lifted ever so slightly. She no longer had any secrets from Gabe, and she would finally have someone to talk to about all the things rolling around in her head. Maybe, he could help her figure out some answers that eluded her.

He already had.

Maggie would have never connected the bottle to the book or the book to the sword. Whatever it was, it was not a coincidence. She still had no idea who sent the book, or where the sword came from, but she had a strange feeling that those answers would somehow come in time. She felt a roll of nausea.

"I haven't forgotten you, little one." She rubbed her stomach.

Gabe was insistent that she tell Ben, and he had a point; he did have a right to know, but Maggie couldn't help but think it would be a selfish thing to do. What was her happiness compared to the birth of the nation?

It wasn't fair, but it was the reality. If she told Ben, he might very well leave the army for her, causing the Culper Spy Ring to never get off the ground, and the Americans would never win without it.

She couldn't take that chance, no matter how much she wanted to.

This child was a gift to Maggie. She was not destined to be with Ben; she accepted that, but now at least she carried a part of him that would always be with her, and for that, she was grateful. She would have to be satisfied with that alone. All the rest would have to work itself out.

She went downstairs to find Gabe eating breakfast. He still looked a little shell-shocked.

Maggie kissed his head as she walked by. "Good morning."

"Good morning, Maggie. How are you feeling?"

She sipped some tea. "Truthfully, my stomach feels like it is turning itself inside out, and my nipples are really sore."

Gabe made a face. "Sorry I asked."

Maggie shrugged and pulled her feet up in the chair, sitting. She leaned over and whispered, "By the way, Gabe, women from the future are pretty frank about things. Prepare yourself."

He just shook his head. "You never answered my question last night."

Maggie picked at a piece of bread trying to decide if she could keep it down. "Which one? There were quite a few."

He cut her a sideways look. "You know which one. The one about the little news you shared."

Maggie gave up on the bread, pushing it away. "Nothing to decide, Gabe. I will not tell him, but I will keep this child, and I will love this child more than life itself, that way I will always have a piece of him with me. Ben will stay in the northern Colonies between now and the end of the war and beyond. There's a very good chance we will never even bump into each other again."

He didn't like that answer.

"I have no choice. He has a future country to mold, and me, I am mentioned nowhere in the history books. I will fade away into the background."

"Somehow, I doubt that Mags. What will you tell people, about the child?"

She rubbed her stomach. "I can say the father and I were married, and that he was killed before I found out I was pregnant. I have enough money that no one will question it. I can have whatever papers I need forged."

Gabe leaned over. "Or we can follow through on our engagement."

Maggie turned her head to his until their foreheads touched. "Gabe, I love you for that, but I will not commit you to a marriage where you will not be happy."

"Who says I won't be?" He brushed a crumb from her face.

"I do because it wouldn't be who you are. Besides, as soon as I marry you, the perfect man will come along and steal you right away from me." She laughed, then covered her mouth and ran for something to throw up in.

"It's going to be a long few months around here," Gabe said to himself and went to check on her.

21

CHAPTER TWENTY-ONE

One night, two weeks later, Maggie decided to retire early. She hadn't felt well all day and just wanted to sleep. She drifted off immediately, dreaming of Ben. They were together and happy, with their baby boy, watching him sleep in his cradle. Ben was kissing her neck, telling her how happy he was with their family. Maggie turned around to kiss him back and he was gone. When she looked back in the cradle, the baby was gone as well. She was devastated, frantic, searching for them. She ran back to the cradle, that now contained the book of faerie tales. When she picked it up and opened it, there was a page that had a story moving like a movie. The movie showed her on a ship sailing away from shore, and on the shore were Ben and their baby. There was a rope that connected the ship to the dock where they stood. She frantically grabbed for it since it was running out to pull them back to her, as a sword— HER sword appeared from the sky cutting the rope in half, breaking their connection. She screamed in physical pain from the separation.

Maggie woke up, feeling the sharp cramps in her belly. The pain was unbearable. She tossed her covers back to see that she and her bed were covered in blood. Maggie screamed Gabe's name.

He was there in an instant. "Oh God! Maggie!" He went back to the door and called down, "Hettie, we need help up here!"

Maggie was in pain and sobbing as he wrapped his arms around her.

Hettie appeared in the room looking upset. "It's alright, Maggie, we are gonna take care of you." She went out of the room and came back with Cecile, who had sent out for the midwife on the estate. The midwife came and checked Maggie, confirming what they already knew with the shake of her head.

Maggie leaned into Gabe's chest, screaming in physical and emotional agony.

He held her and rocked her, while whispering in her ear that she was going to be fine, but he knew that she wouldn't be. The universe had just taken the one thing that Maggie needed the most.

Maggie woke up the next morning, completely devoid of tears and physically numb. Her baby, the only piece of Ben that she had left, was gone. She had no desire for anything, including living. She was done with the universe and its damned plans for her, whatever they were; she really didn't care. Maggie stared at the ceiling, willing it to cave in on top of her and end this misery.

Gabe watched her from his chair in the corner of the room; he had been there all night.

She had been lying in bed with her eyes open, looking up, and not moving for an hour.

He knew that feeling. It was the one where all hope in the world had left your body and mind, and all you wanted to do was curl up and die. It was the same feeling he'd had when Jonathan died. Maggie had been the only thing that kept him from leaving this world, and he intended to do the same for her.

A soft knock came at the door.

Gabe opened it; Maggie didn't even move.

It was Hettie checking in.

Gabe stepped in the hall.

"How is she?"

Gabe shook his head. "She is not in a good place. Hettie, can you have hot water brought up for a bath. I will get her cleaned up while you and Cecile get the bed changed."

She nodded, turning to leave when she stopped. "Did she know... that she was carrying the baby?"

"Yes, and she really wanted that baby."

Hettie frowned. "Maggie doesn't deserve this."

"No Hettie, she doesn't."

Gabe bathed her carefully and silently.

She didn't speak a word, just stared into oblivion, at a complete loss.

When he was done, he dried her off, slipped a nightgown over her head, and carried her back to the freshly dressed bed, laying her down. He leaned over, close to her ear and whispered, "Maggie, I know right now that you feel like you would rather die, but you will survive, and it will get better. The pain will never completely go away, but it will subside into a deep, profound numbness. You didn't give up on me when I was in the exact same place you are now, and I'll be damned if I will give up on you."

He kissed her on the forehead, covered her up and tucked her in like a child. He stepped out and closed the door. Gabe took a seat on the top step, bowed his head and silently cried for Maggie and her loss.

She didn't speak the rest of the day, nor the next. She wouldn't eat, she wouldn't drink; just laid there, unmoving.

The following morning, Gabe stood by her bedside. "Maggie, you have to get up."

She turned on her side away from him.

He went around to the other side. "Maggie, you HAVE to get up."

She looked past him. "Why? Why do I have to get up?"

Gabe answered softly, "Because you need to eat, you need to drink, you need to live. Life goes on and so will you."

She ignored him.

That afternoon, Gabe sat in the chair in Maggie's room, racking his brain trying to figure out some way to get through to her, but he was at a complete loss.

Something massive hit the side of the house, shaking the entire front wall. Jumping up, Gabe rushed out into the hall upstairs, while everyone else hurried into the downstairs foyer.

"What the bloody hell was that?"

Bam! It happened again.

It was someone, or something, at the front door trying to get in.

Gabe dashed across the hall to grab his pistol. He aimed it at the door, motioning everyone to get back. The third hit splintered the massive front door wide open in an explosion of shards. Gabe steadied his hand, preparing to fire until he saw what had broken down the door. “Son of a bitch!”

Standing in the doorway, looking as if he had come straight up from the bowels of Hell itself, was... that... damned... horse—Onyx.

Harm and a few of the other men ran around behind him, trying to corral him, but he wouldn’t move.

Onyx looked back and huffed, sending half the men running away in fear of their very lives. He came right to the base of the steps, snorting, stomping and demanding to see his owner.

Gabe lowered the gun and turned his head to the side, as of looking at the sight before him sideways might somehow make sense of this ridiculous scene.

He heard Hettie mutter, “Lord have mercy, that horse has gone crazy.”

Gabe had a thought.

Maybe Onyx wasn’t so crazy after all.

He looked down at Onyx with a scolding look on his face. “Stay there!”

Onyx huffed in response.

He went into Maggie’s room, to see her at least sitting up.

“Maggie, you have a visitor, and if you like your house standing in one piece, I suggest you see him.”

She turned towards him and slipped down off the bed.

Well, that was progress. He grabbed her robe and wrapped it around her, leading her into the hall.

Maggie's facial expression went from nothingness to astonishment to pure joy.

When Onyx saw her, he whinnied and reared up on his back legs, sending the house help that had moved in for a closer look scattering like rats off a sinking ship.

Maggie blinked her eyes, and then again. She descended the steps with Gabe's help right to her oldest, and dearest, friend.

"Onyx." She reached up, rubbing his muzzle and embracing his neck.

The horse wrapped his neck around her the way he always did when he comforted her.

Leaning into him, Maggie broke into a half sob, half laugh, burying her face against him. They didn't move for the longest time, just stood there loving each other. When she finally broke away, Maggie was laughing and talking to him, wiping away her tears.

"Harm's not going to be happy with you. If you did this to the front door, I can only imagine what you did to the stable."

Gabe could have sworn that horse laughed.

"Thank you, old friend; you always seem to know just what I need."

Gabe moved to try and back him out, but Onyx didn't care for it. He stuck his neck out and tried to bite Gabe.

"Hey! Stop it, you sadistic beast!"

Maggie laughed.

Gabe was getting nowhere fast.

"Go make up with Harm, Onyx," she called out.

On that, the horse turned and trotted back out the door he had just destroyed, like the most obedient child in the world.

Gabe shook his head in complete disbelief. "There is something very strange about that horse."

Maggie walked halfway back up the stairs and sat down, wrapping her arms around her knees.

Gabe made his way across the disaster on the floor to move beside her. He put his arm around her, and she leaned into him.

He silently thanked God for that wicked beast.

22

CHAPTER TWENTY-TWO

Maggie started to come around the next few days, eating, drinking and slowly recovering. The men on the estate cleaned up the front door mess and put in a temporary fix.

Onyx had all but destroyed the stable gate... again.

Harm grumbled about the number of times they had to fix that thing, threatening to just leave it open from now on to save himself the grief.

Valley Forge

Three wagons were met by soldiers at the entrance to the camp. Ben and General Washington were outside speaking when they arrived.

One of the men by the fire called out, “Father?”

Captain Russell rushed over to embrace his son, who was far too thin and looking unwell. The Captain took off his own coat and wrapped it around him for warmth. Captain Russell noticed the General watching and approached him. “General Washington I presume?”

“I am.”

“I have a delivery for you.” He motioned back toward the wagons, pulling a note out of his pocket and handing it to him.

Washington unfolded the page, read it, and smiled as he handed it to Ben.

It simply said…

‘*A gift from a lady in Virginia.*
MB.’

Ben smiled. “Maggie.”

Maggie approached Gabe who had been working at the desk going over some books one afternoon. “Gabe, I need a favor.”

He set aside his work and looked up, interlocking his fingers, giving her his full attention. “Anything.”

She sat down in the chair opposite him with something in her hand. “I need you to write Passage Papers, so I can send a courier north.”

Gabe was retired, but his name still carried a good deal of weight. “That shouldn’t be a problem. Where does it need to go?”

Maggie breathed in. “Valley Forge.” Gabe frowned, but she continued, “You were right Gabe, Ben deserves to know about….” she stopped to clear her throat, holding back the tears, "I have written him about what happened, and to end things once and for all."

Gabe hated seeing her like this. "Maggie, are you sure you want to do that?"

She closed her eyes and whispered, "You know I have no choice."

Gabe came around to the edge of the desk. "What if you do? I have been giving this a great deal of thought. What if you were meant to come back TO change things? What if, you were brought back to BE with him for some reason?"

Maggie leaned forward, resting her elbow on the desk, her hand rubbing her forehead. "Then I would have been mentioned in the history books. Nowhere, anywhere, is the name Maggie Bishop mentioned in relation to Benjamin Tallmadge. Besides, he would give up his commission for me, he would walk away in an instant if I asked him to, I have no doubt, and General Washington NEEDS him to win this. Without the work that Ben does, the United States of America is doomed to fail, meaning I very well may never even be born. Little things can have major consequences in the grand scheme of things. I can only assume that I am here now because I was there in the future."

Crossing his arms, a confused look grew on Gabe's face, as if his mind were about to explode.

Maggie looked up. "Headache coming on? Welcome to my world."

Gabe felt sorry for her. "Maggie, how have you managed to stay sane with all of this? The insurmountable weight that you have been carrying around alone, for so long, it's…. unimaginable."

Maggie felt she had aged fifty years. "I have had no choice in the matter."

Gabe leaned down and kissed her head. "I will make the arrangements."

Valley Forge

A messenger made his way through the camp to the tent he had been directed to, its only occupant a man sitting alone writing correspondence.

"Begging your pardon, sir, but I have an important message for you. I was instructed to have you read it as soon as possible."

General Washington held out his hand. "Thank you, sir."

The messenger lingered.

"Is there something else?"

"Yes, sir. I need to locate a Major Benjamin Tallmadge."

Washington responded without raising his head. "He should be with the men in the barn across the way."

He nodded and went to take his leave when the General spoke, "Who is this message from?"

The courier only said four words.

"A lady in Virginia."

That got his attention. Washington immediately tore open the letter and read the contents. He sat back to ponder its contents.

Ben felt his body go numb, his face completely drained of blood, shock settling in worse than anything he had ever experienced in battle. He read his letter again, in utter disbelief.

Maggie had been carrying his child, and the baby had died. He was overcome with grief for the child he would never hold, but the pain he felt was nothing compared to the misery that Maggie was obviously in. It was woefully apparent in her words that she was suffering a tremendous heartbreak from the devastating loss, so much so that she believed it to be a sign from God that He did not wish them to be together, no matter how much they loved each other, and that Ben needed to let her go.

He had to get to her, because he needed to make her understand that this was not divine intervention, just a horribly tragic thing that sometimes happens. Maggie's grief was clouding her judgment and losing her would be unbearable for him. He just needed to talk to her.

Ben rushed into General Washington's tent, Maggie's letter still in hand. "Sir, I need to take some leave. Something has happened, and I am needed elsewhere."

Washington gave the Major a deep, thoughtful look. The man who stood before him was white as a sheet, noticeably upset and in a great deal of pain. The news he had received must have been very bad, which made what he was about to do that much harder. He liked Major Tallmadge very much, even thought of him as a son, and to see him in so much distress, tore him to the very core.

"Request denied Major. I AM sorry."

Ben protested as if his very life depended on it. "But sir, we are in winter quarters, there are no campaigns going on, and truthfully one less mouth to feed around here would be to our advantage. I am begging you — PLEASE, it is an emergency."

Washington started to have second thoughts—this man was desperate—but he hardened his stance.

"Major, I cannot grant your request. I have an important job for you. I have a plan and you are the only person who can handle it. I want to set up a spy ring in the New York area, an area I understand you know better than anyone. I am promoting you to the position of Spymaster and I need your undivided focus for this. I NEED you to help me win this war and we need to start this very day."

Washington could see the distress on the young man's face. He was torn between his love of country and his love of a woman and she was a very special woman indeed. The romantic side of Washington hoped he would storm out, tell him and the army to go to Hell, to ride at breakneck speed straight for Virginia and the woman he loved, but the soldier side of Washington knew that he would not.

"Yes sir, I'll be in my tent when you are ready."

Damn.

After he left, Washington took a seat, feeling like a heel. He pulled out the letter, reading the most important part again.

I find myself in need of your assistance. Very shortly, Major Tallmadge will come to you pleading for a leave to come to Virginia. I must ask you to DENY that request. I ask instead that you give him orders, that will force him to dedicate all his time and energy to, leaving him no time to consider anything else, especially those things that may cause him a great deal of pain. To win this war, you will need intelligence information from the north, most especially the New York area where the Major grew up in and is vastly familiar with. This information will play a vital role in your victory and make no mistake, you will be victorious. You just must remember to stay the course. I have put aside the greatest happiness in my life so that you may have HIM there to achieve this end. HE is the KEY to this; you only need to put him in charge of intelligence for that area and he will do the rest. He will not fail you. He is the most loyal person in your camp, believe that above all else. I pray you will grant this small favor I ask of you. It is the best for all concerned.

Be well and God's blessings upon you all.
Yours truly,
A Lady in Virginia
MB

PS. Be wary of traitors in your camp, for they do exist where you least expect.

After reading the letter again, he looked closer. He was fairly certain some of the ink had been smudged by drops of tears. God help him, he hoped he was doing the right thing.

23

CHAPTER TWENTY-THREE

Maggie took things day by day, feeling stronger all the time. She still missed Ben and their baby, but Gabe had been right, the pain was starting to dull, never leaving, but easier to bear.

Ben had written to her, telling her of his love for her and his sorrow over the loss of their child. He begged her to reconsider and to not take that as a sign from God that they were not to be together. He wanted to be there, but he would respect her wishes because he did not wish to be a source of additional pain to her. He hoped that, after some time, if she would allow it, that they would be able to see each other again.

Construction had begun on Gabe's new house, as spring had sprung, though Maggie hated the thought of his leaving, even if it were only to move next door. Maggie received regular letters from John, telling her all about the social parties and the gossip of Philadelphia. His latest letter came speaking of General Howe's departure. Maggie relayed the information to Gabe.

"It seems that John is planning a grand affair for Howe's departure, a Mischianza... whatever that is? It looks like it will be a huge party complete with a parade, a regatta, jousting, fireworks... wow! Sounds like quite the shindig. He has invited us up if we wish to come. And he says to tell Gabe, that the 'coast is clear' because it seems Mrs. Bright has procured a new husband."

Gabe chuckled. "Well, I am relieved, I must say. I have been expecting her to show up any day now."

Maggie read a little further. She burst out in laughter. "The lucky groom's name is Mr. Richard Manny."

Gabe looked at Maggie with a twinkle in his eye. "You mean…."

She finished his sentence, "She is now Mrs. Fannie Manny."

They both broke into a boisterous laughter.

Gabe was pleased to see Maggie laughing again; it had been entirely too long. She was still far thinner than he liked, but she was eating and getting back to the business of life, though she seemed a little restless lately. Maybe….

"Say, Mags, what do you say we go?"

"Go where?"

"To this grand affair that John is planning. It may be fun. We wouldn't have to stay long, and a change of scenery might be good."

Benjamin Tallmadge would still be in Valley Forge, so she wouldn't run into him, and Maggie was always very fond of John André. She thought for a few moments, then seemed a little sad. "And it may be the last time we ever get to see John."

Gabe gave her a guarded look. “What do you mean?”

She explained what was to happen to John.

He sank into the nearest chair. “Dear God. Can’t we warn him?”

Maggie gave him a sorrowful look as she shook her head. “Timeline.”

Gabe finally, at that exact moment, understood precisely why Maggie would become so drawn inside herself sometimes. There was a reason people didn’t need to know the future; it was too much of a burden to bear, especially to know the exact day and time of a friend’s demise and not be able to lift a finger to stop it.

Maggie said softly, “We should go to say ‘goodbye’, even if he doesn’t know it.”

He agreed.

They spent the next week preparing to leave.

Maggie left instructions for the house and the shipping company. She had hired additional people at the business to allow Captain Russell to have some help and to have contingency plans for extended absences. She did the same for the house.

Both could run for an indefinite amount of time in case Maggie was unable to get back in a timely manner. The whole Philadelphia scene had shown her that life happens, and unexpected occurrences required a backup plan.

She updated her will and the Freedom Papers along with the deeds for all the tenants on the estate, having them placed with her attorney for safe keeping.

David Percy had become invaluable to her and the estate, so much so that several years ago, she deeded him a few acres and surprised him by having a house built for him. His expression had been priceless, and so was his loyalty. She even went so far as to have a secret room added into his house for storage of her paperwork for the people on the estate, as much for his protection as hers.

A week before the festivities, Maggie and Gabe arrived, unannounced, in Philadelphia on her personal ship. The entire city was abuzz in anticipation of the grand party. They went straight to John's house where he was busy planning. The servant let them in, and Maggie peeked around the door of the drawing room.

"Have room for two more party goers?"

John turned, his surprise turning to delight when he saw Maggie's face. "Always!"

He went to her, and wrapped her in a warm, full body embrace, pulling back to gaze into her eyes. "Maggie, I am so very happy to see you."

Gabe coughed. "Why do I never get a greeting like that?"

"Because you are not as pretty as our dear Maggie. Gabe, it's good to see you, my friend." They shook hands and 'man hugged'.

"Please, please, come in." John excused everyone there and instructed the servant to bring refreshments.

"I am over the moon to see the two of you here. I never dreamed you would accept my invitation, but I am ecstatic that you have. When did you arrive?"

"Just now," replied Gabe.

John looked back and forth between them. "Where are you staying? The town is bursting at the seams for the celebration."

Maggie was the one to answer. "We aren't sure yet. We really didn't make plans, just came on a whim."

"Well, allow me to handle that small detail for you. You shall stay here."

Gabe smiled. "If it is not an imposition?"

"Nonsense, I will not be satisfied if you stay anywhere else. I have plenty of room and I could not ask for better company."

Gabe laughed. "Thank you, John, although I hope your stable door is solid. We brought that devil horse with us."

Maggie cut him a displeased look. "Onyx is NOT that bad."

"Not to you!" Gabe muttered dryly. "But try telling that to the front door."

Maggie rolled her eyes.

John looked to Gabe for an explanation.

"That damned horse completely destroyed the five-foot-wide front door, smashed it into little pieces, and walked away without a scratch on him."

John grinned. "Impressive!"

Maggie sighed. "Yes, yes! He's a strange horse, or so I have been told."

They chatted for a while before John had to excuse himself because duty called, but he assured them he would be back in time for supper.

After enjoying a pleasant meal together that evening, Maggie announced she was turning in early because she was completely exhausted. That gave Gabe and John time to catch up.

The two men were enjoying drinks and smoking pipes downstairs, when John brought up something that concerned him. “Gabe, is Maggie unwell? She seems to have lost a great deal of weight, and her coloring is a little off.”

Gabe looked toward the staircase. “She is slowly recovering.”

John suddenly looked extremely worried. “Recovering?”

Gabe nodded. “When we returned from Philadelphia, she found out she was with child. Not long after, she lost the baby.”

John was stunned. “I had no idea. And the father? I know she was in love with someone, but she never shared any details.”

“He did not know, and she would not let me send word to him. Maggie wrote to him afterward, telling him what happened and asking him to stay away. The pain was too much for her. Her body has healed, but her heart, I’m afraid, is another story. It was awful, I couldn’t reach her. I thought she was going to die, but thankfully that Beelzebub horse of hers was able to get through to her. That’s when he shattered the door. She and that beast share a connection I shall never understand. They need each other unlike anything I have ever seen.”

John chuckled. “Well, here’s to the ‘devil horse’.” He raised his glass in a toast.

John was busy the next couple of days, so Maggie and Gabe entertained themselves during the day, shopping and visiting some of their friends. They even ran into the newlyweds, Mr. and Mrs. Manny.

He was short, lean, bald, and madly in love with his new bride. They seemed very happy together.

In the evenings, Maggie and Gabe had supper with John, spending hours each night enjoying each other's company.

The night before the festivities were to begin, Maggie could not sleep, so she slipped downstairs to find the brandy. She was surprised to find John sitting there reading a book.

"You are up very late."

"As are you," he replied.

"Yes, I could not sleep, and I thought an extra nightcap might help."

He closed his book and stood. "Allow me to join you." He handed her a poured glass and sat down on the sofa next to her. They had not had a chance to spend any time alone.

"I have missed our time together, Maggie."

"So have I, John," she said sweetly, "but, I am sure you have had plenty of company since I left."

He looked down with a grin. "Yes, well, while I have had plenty of company, I have yet to meet anyone here that I adore nearly as much as you."

Maggie blushed. "Flatterer!"

He almost spat out his drink.

He took her hand when he noticed she was wearing the bracelet he gave her, tracing over the words.

"I never take it off. That, and my mother's necklace, are two of my most treasured possessions."

He wrapped his fingers around hers and squeezed. "That makes me very happy," he bowed his head, "Gabe told me what happened with the baby. Maggie, I cannot tell you how sorry I am."

Maggie didn't say anything, just stared down at their intertwined hands.

"Is this man truly out of the picture?"

Maggie swallowed hard. "Yes. It is the way things must be. I cannot bear the pain of ever seeing him again, so I have asked him to stay away."

He could feel her torment; he knew how it felt and he wanted more than anything to ease her ache. When he noticed a few tears sliding down her face, he turned sideways on the couch, facing her, kissing her hand. He used his fingers to wipe her tears away. "Don't cry Maggie. If he is not here with you now, he is a fool, and he is not meant to be."

Cupping her face, he lightly brushed his lips against hers, then pressed his forehead to hers, softly whispering, "I would do anything to take away your pain."

Maggie became fully conscious of something she had not been aware of — just how lonely she truly had been. It dawned on her at that very instant, that feeling had not been just since Ben, but since she had come to the 18th century. She had not allowed herself the luxury of physical love until him and depriving herself had left a wide gaping hole in her soul, that her time with him had sated for just a little while. It was a missing part that would need to be fulfilled, one way or the other, to keep her sane. And while she was sure she loved and cared for Ben, the perception of exactly how much just may have been jaded by the emptiness she had been feeling before he came along.

Maggie slowly raised her free hand to touch his face. He kissed her lips gingerly to see if she would back away.

She did not.

John cared a great deal for Maggie. She had consumed his thoughts often since she left and finding out that she and Gabe were not actually engaged, pleased him very much. She was a beautiful soul that did not deserve to feel pain because a man was not there to take care of her needs. He may not be the man she was in love with, but he could be the man who was there in that very moment to console her and fulfill her emptiness.

"Maggie, let me comfort you tonight," he whispered.

She nodded, stood, while still holding his hand and led him upstairs to his bedroom. He closed the door and spent the rest of the night making her forget, and for that, she was grateful.

John left early the next morning since he had so much to do. He kissed her forehead lightly as not to wake her.

At breakfast, Gabe noticed Maggie in a rather cheerful mood — more like her old self — relaxed and slightly carefree. He wondered what had changed.

They spent the day enjoying themselves and the merriment that came along with the celebration.

That night as they were watching the fireworks, John came up beside Maggie and discreetly slipped his hand in hers, leaning over to whisper in her ear, going unnoticed by anyone, save one— and the look on Peggy Shippen's face was one of a girl who had just had her favorite play toy taken away.

Maggie and Gabe had each already retired for the evening when John got home from an extremely late night with the officers. He grabbed his sketchbook and slipped silently as a church mouse into Maggie's room. It was a full moon and the beams came through the window, hitting her in the perfect light. He took a seat and made several sketches of her in his book.

When she stirred, he went to her, sitting on the side of the bed and tenderly stroking her hair as she opened her eyes. They didn't speak a word as he undressed, climbed into bed, and 'comforted' her again. He didn't want to waste a single moment of being with her; the next day was their last day before heading home.

The following morning, John asked her to go on a walk with him.

"I hope you have enjoyed your time here, Maggie. I do wish you and Gabe would stay on longer."

"I have very much, John. Thank you for everything, but with the new administration coming in, I am sure your plate will be more than full."

"I am afraid you are correct. I don't think I will be here much longer though. Since winter is practically over, I am sure we will be moving on soon."

Maggie knew they would, and where he specifically would end up—at the end of a rope—the thought broke her heart.

"If I find myself in Virginia, may I come to visit you?" he asked.

"You had better. I shall be terribly upset with you if you do not."

He laughed. "I would very much like to come for an extended visit when this war is finished."

Knowing it would never happen, Maggie forced a smile. "I will count the days until your arrival."

He stopped, taking her hand and lifting it to his lips. "I hope our time together has been enjoyable and beneficial to you in some small way."

"John, you have done more for me than you will ever know."

He was delighted.

"I actually have something for you," Maggie held up the necklace she had been clutching in her hand, "It is a Saint Michael, the Archangel. He is the protector of soldiers. I hope you will wear it to keep you safe."

She slipped it over his head.

"Maggie, I don't know what to say to such a thoughtful gift. I will cherish it and never take it off."

"Just say you will be safe, that's all I want," she replied.

He bowed. "You have my word. Thank you, my dear, sweet Maggie."

That evening, he came to her bed for the final time; the two created a special bond that night.

The next morning, at the dock when the ship was about to disembark, Gabe's former assistant ran up waving something. "This came for you here this morning, Colonel. It looks important."

"Thank you." Gabe stepped to the side to read it.

John turned to Maggie and handed her something. "I completely forgot until this morning. I found this book a while back, and I have been meaning to send it to you, but since you are here. It is a book of Scottish crests and the information on the names. YOUR crest, from your sword, is in here; I have marked it for you. I thought you might like to have it."

Maggie was excited to find more information. "Thank you so much, John!"

She embraced him so tightly that she thought she may have cracked his ribs, tears dripping from her eyes. "I shall miss you immensely."

"What's all this? Don't cry, Maggie; it's not like we will never see each other again."

She nodded, but she knew it would probably be the last time, because, in a few short years, he would be dead, hanged by the Americans because of another strange little twist of fate. He leaned over, giving her a final farewell kiss.

"Be well Maggie."

Just then Gabe walked up, looking very pale.

"Gabe, what's wrong?"

Gabe looked up from the letter. "My brother has just written to me; my mother is extremely ill. He wrote that I should come as soon as possible if I wanted to say 'goodbye'." He was in a state of shock.

Maggie took his hand. "Then we should go."

She called out, "Captain Russell, steer the ship for home port to take on supplies and after that, we are bound for England."

To Be Continued…

Epilogue

(Before his scheduled execution on October 2, 1780, Major John André would be visited by Major Benjamin Tallmadge. They would speak of their admiration for each other and the details of some of their missions. The talk eventually turned to the sketchbook that Major André always had with him.)

"Are those your sketches?"

John looked down. "Yes, a collection of my favorites."

Ben motioned. "May I?"

John handed him the book. "Please."

Ben turned the page carefully, admiring his work. It was unfortunate that such a creative soul had ended up in the army and was now facing such a death. Ben liked the man, there wasn't anything NOT to like about him. He could even see them being great, life-long friends if dwindling time were not the issue. Ben turned the page and, upon seeing a familiar face, he softly whispered, "Maggie."

John looked back from the window he was looking out of, seeing the stunned look on the other man's face and asked, "You know Maggie?"

Ben nodded. "Yes. I met her a few years ago in Philadelphia. We were…." The pain in his eyes helped John to make the connection, and John finished his sentence for him.

"You were in love."

Ben looked at him, the truth in his face.

"YOU were the one she was in love with, the one who fathered the child that she lost."

Ben swallowed hard. "I didn't know until the baby was gone, and she asked me not to come. I had caused her so much pain and put her in so much danger, she had already almost died once for me."

Another awareness came to John. "SHE was the woman on the back of the horse in Germantown, the night she came back with a bullet in her."

Ben nodded. There was no harm in telling a man about to be hanged the truth, and, truthfully, he needed to unburden his soul. "She had brought us information before, I guess you could say she was our very first female agent, but that night, I just wanted to see her, to be with her before we left for Valley Forge for the winter. It was my fault that she was shot. That's why I insisted she go back to Virginia. If I had known she carried my child, I never would have sent her away. I would have quit the army, on the spot, just to be with her."

John saw the same degree of pain on his face that he had seen on Maggie's all those years before.

Ben looked at the images again. "How do you know her?"

John took in a deep breath. “I was the one that found her at the checkpoint that night. She recovered under my roof and we became close friends.”

He left out the rest, no need to cause this man any more grief; he had already lost so much in losing Maggie.

“She spoke of her great love for a man that she could not be with. She was very much in love with you.”

Ben whispered, “Not nearly as much as I was with her, and, truthfully, still am. After she wrote me and told me not to come, I was out of my mind with grief. Thankfully, General Washington, at that very same time, put me in charge of his spy ring. The work was long and tedious, but in the end, focusing on that was the only thing that got me through.”

John leaned forward. “If I may ask a favor, Major Tallmadge? If, and when, you reveal your contacts after the war, please protect Maggie’s name. She has a great deal to lose if the Crown finds out about what she did, even in the years to come, they may send someone after her in retribution.”

Ben replied, “I would do anything to protect her, still to this day.”

John patted him on the back, his small way of comforting the poor man, a man he had grown very fond of. John knew that the loss of a woman like Maggie was a hard thing to accept, he himself feeling the same way about her.

A knock came at the door.

John sighed. “It seems my date with destiny has arrived.” He remembered something.

He slipped the Saint Michael from around his neck and motioned for Ben to lean forward. Slipping it over his head, he said, "Maggie gave this to me, and I have never taken it off. It is a Saint Michael, the protector of soldiers. I am sure she would be happy to know that I passed it on to you. Treasure it as I have... and keep the sketches, as well. I hope they bring back the good memories of the love that the two of you shared, and if you do ever see her again, please give her my love. Tell her I thought of her until the very end."

Ben stood. "I will. Thank you."

He reached out to shake his hand. "Major André, it has been a pleasure. You have been a formidable foe, and it has been my deepest honor to have known you."

John gripped Ben's arm firmly, smiling, resolved to his fate. "Major Tallmadge, the pleasure has been all mine."

ABOUT THE AUTHOR

Tempie W. Wade is an author of historical fiction that incorporates elements of fantasy and the supernatural. She uses real-life events and timelines to make her stories more real, while encouraging the audience to take a step back into history, and to research the lives of those who played such an important part in the founding of America for themselves.

She is a long-term resident of Williamsburg, Virginia.

www.TempieWade.com

More

Book Two in The Timely Revolution Series

is coming soon.

Made in the USA
Middletown, DE
09 June 2020